DARK ANGEL'S OBSESSION

THE CHILDREN OF THE GODS BOOK 14

I. T. LUCAS

FOLLOW I. T. LUCAS ON AMAZON

Also by I. T. Lucas

PERFECT MATCH

Perfect Match 1: Vampire's Consort
Perfect Match 2: King's Chosen
Perfect Match 3: Captain's Conquest

SETS

The Children of the Gods books 1-3: Dark Stranger trilogy—Includes a bonus short story: The Fates take a Vacation

The Children of the Gods: Books 1-6—includes character lists

The Children of the Gods: Books 6.5-10—includes character lists

---

TRY THE CHILDREN OF THE GODS SERIES ON
AUDIBLE
2 FREE audiobooks with your new Audible subscription!

CHAPTER 1: CALLIE

Twenty-two months ago.

"What's wrong? You look green." Iris's worried eyes met Callie's in the mirror.

Ugh. The nausea should have passed by now. Morning sickness at two in the afternoon was unacceptable. But then her queasy stomach might have had less to do with her pregnancy and more to do with her upcoming nuptials.

"I think I'm going to be sick again." The train of her wedding dress clutched in her hand, Callie bolted for the bathroom.

Locking the door behind her, she eyed the toilet and contemplated kneeling on the floor, but doing so in a white, voluminous dress was asking for trouble. It could get dirty or wrinkled, and she didn't need the extra stress.

Instead, she put a protective hand over the plunging neckline and leaned over the sink, trying to purge the swirling sensation from her gut. Nothing came up, only painful dry heaves.

1

"Are you okay in there?" Iris knocked on the door. "Can I help? Do you want me to call Donald?"

"No. Just give me a minute," Callie called out. The last thing she needed was for her father to freak out. The man couldn't deal with anything female related. She still remembered his reaction to her first period. It was good that the supermarket had been walking distance from their house. There was no way her father would have survived buying her tampons.

It was a freaking miracle that man had managed to raise a daughter on his own since she was a tiny toddler.

Another knock. "Callie, let me in. I can at least hold your hair back while you puke," Iris pleaded.

"I'm fine. I'll be out in a minute." *Gah.* The woman was so irritating.

Iris meant well, but she was too young to play mother of the bride. A big sister, maybe, but not really. Less than a year ago, when her father had finally remarried, Callie had been genuinely happy and excited to welcome Iris into their lives, even though the woman was only eleven years older than Callie and thirteen years younger than Donald.

Iris was chatty and smiley and filled their quiet home with life.

Callie had hoped for a sisterly relationship with her new stepmother, but things hadn't worked out that way. Though not for lack of trying on both sides. They were just two very different people. The only thing they had in common was their love for her father.

Iris made Donald happy.

Before she'd tumbled into his life, he had rarely smiled, which made Callie wonder whether he'd been a happier man when her mother was still alive.

Getting him to talk about her was impossible. It made him too sad. But the many pictures and few home movies told a story of a perfectly normal little family, with two doting parents and a chubby baby girl whom they'd seemed to adore.

Callie sighed and leaned her forehead against the cool mirror.

One tragic moment had shattered their family forever, taking away her mother from them and leaving Donald a broken, sad man to raise a daughter on his own.

"Callie, are you okay?" Her father's voice.

Damn it, Iris. She'd told her not to bother him.

"I'm fine. I'll be out in a moment." If she could work magic, she would've gotten rid of them both, sent them to mingle with the guests and let her breathe for a few moments, but the best she could do was get rid of at least one. Temporarily. "Can either of you bring me a coke?"

"Sure thing." Her father jumped at the opportunity to be useful doing something other than dealing with his daughter's prenuptial jitters. Or worse, her pregnancy nausea.

Callie waited another moment before opening the door.

"Feeling better?" Iris asked.

She forced a smile. "Much. Can you do me a favor and bring me some saltines from the kitchen?"

Iris patted her arm. "That's a splendid idea. Saltines work miracles on nausea." She rushed to the kitchen, or rather attempted to. Hindered by her spiky heels and long tight dress, it was more of a waddle than a fast walk.

Alone at last, Callie sat down in front of her vanity and picked up the pink lipstick, hoping the bright color would help offset the green hue of her skin.

Pregnancy should have made her glow with health, not look pale and sickly. Except, that was likely true for those overjoyed by the prospect of motherhood, not those tricked into it at nineteen.

Too young.

She hadn't done anything with her life yet.

No regrets, Callie. It was the mantra she'd adopted after the shock of discovering she was pregnant had worn off.

It was all happening a little sooner than she would've preferred, but she was going to make it work. Her life was going to be great. She was going to build a cozy home for her sweet, adorable baby and loving husband.

Except, Callie wasn't so sure about that last one.

Did Shawn really love her?

Did loving people trick their partners into marriage?

Relationships were supposed to be built on trust.

Theirs wasn't.

Callie had no proof that he'd gotten her pregnant on purpose. After all, condom failure was not unheard of. But from what she'd read online, it was mostly due to mishandling. At twenty-seven, Shawn should've had plenty of experience in handling one properly.

As the door to her bedroom opened, Callie took a deep breath, bracing for more of Iris's prattle, but it wasn't her stepmother.

"Dawn!" Callie jumped and turned, almost tripping on the gown's long train. "You made it!"

"Of course, I made it. You think I would miss my best friend's wedding?" Dawn handed her a Coke can and a pack of saltines. "I told your dad and Iris that I'm taking over and that they should stop neglecting their guests."

"Thank you." The tears prickling the back of Callie's eyes were threatening to ruin Iris's carefully applied makeup. "Aren't you missing finals?"

"All done. I took the last one yesterday."

"How did it go?"

Dawn waved a hand. "Easy peasy lemon squeezy."

Callie laughed. "You are probably the only one that can say that about MIT's electrical engineering department finals."

"Not really. To my utter horror, I discovered I wasn't the

4

smartest thing to ever grace the lecture halls of that prestigious institution."

Callie pretended to gasp. "Get out of here. Really? It can't be."

Dawn shook her head. "Sadly, it is. But enough about me. How are you holding up?"

"I want to throw up."

"That's to be expected from one who is expecting."

Callie sat back on her vanity stool. "I don't want to marry Shawn."

"I don't blame you." Dawn knelt in front of her and clasped her hands. "You can still call it off. I'll go out there and tell everyone to go home including Shawn, who, by the way, is strutting around like a peacock, happy as can be."

"I bet. He got his way, the bastard. He's been pestering me to marry him since the day he popped my cherry, obsessed by the idea of marrying a girl who's never been touched by another."

Dawn's eyes narrowed. "Do you think he did it on purpose?"

"I can't be sure, but I have my suspicions."

"So why the hell do you refuse to get an abortion?"

Cradling her middle protectively, Callie shook her head. "I can't. It's not this little one's fault that his or her father is an underhanded jerk. Besides, you know I love children. I'm going to be a great mother."

"I know, sweetie, but is Shawn going to be a great father? Or husband?"

"I don't know," Callie whispered.

He'd been so charming and attentive when they'd first met three months ago. Still was. But Callie couldn't shake the feeling that Shawn was putting on a very convincing act, hiding a darker, more sinister side underneath all that smooth talk.

The thing was, when he turned it on full force, it was hard

to hang on to that suspicion. It was much easier to believe that she was worried for no good reason, scared by nonexistent shadows.

Shawn was older, bossy and dominant. It was what had attracted her to him in the first place. Except, that bossy attitude was getting annoying. Especially when his dishonesty and manipulative behavior brought about disillusion and disappointment.

The thing was, blinded by her attraction to him, she hadn't noticed any of it until it was too late and she was carrying his child.

Callie had never been drawn to guys her age. Ever since she had become sexually aware, she'd craved something that for the longest time she couldn't define or name. Naturally, she'd assumed it was what every woman craved and hadn't been overly bothered by it. But the sweet romances she'd sneaked under the blanket at night had painted a different picture.

Much later, she'd found a series of books that had opened her eyes. As a high fantasy it was mostly about adventure, not about romance, and the few intimate scenes were by no means descriptive, but the tapestry it had woven contained many more shades than Callie had been aware of.

"Love as thy wilt." That imagined society's main motto was that nothing was taboo as long as it was consensual.

Easier said than done.

It had been difficult to accept that she wasn't like everyone else, and that the things she craved were somewhat outside the norm.

Why the hell did she crave sexual dominance?

Callie wasn't combative, but she wasn't timorous either. She didn't accept authority without question, and had her own opinions about pretty much everything, which she never shied away from expressing.

She was a strong, capable, and independent woman.

She had no other choice.

With no mother and a father who worked long days, she had been basically left to her own devices since she was a very young girl. No one had ever supervised her schoolwork, and yet she had always been a straight A student. No one had ever moderated her behavior, and yet she had always been polite. No one had told her how to dress, and yet she had always dressed modestly.

Perhaps the reason for her good-girl model behavior was that she had never had a reason to rebel. Why would she? And against whom or what?

With no one to tell her otherwise, Callie could do whatever she wanted whenever she wanted.

Her father had trusted her with running the household from a very young age, giving her a bank card and a checkbook filled with signed checks. Callie had done all the grocery shopping and paid the bills. It was a lot of responsibility, but she'd never shied away from it. Her father needed her help, and she'd given it freely, glad she was able to do it.

So why the hell did she crave sexual domination?

Why did nothing else turn her on as much? Or at all?

Those were questions she'd grown tired of asking.

It just was.

CHAPTER 2: CALLIE

One year ago.

Shawn parked the car behind the club, cut the engine, and turned to regard Callie with a deep scowl. All during the drive she'd watched his simmering irritation intensify. She knew how to manage his anger tantrums and violent outbursts, but they still made her anxious.

"Are you sure you want to go through with this?" he grated.

No, she wasn't, but she needed an answer to a question that had been bothering her for months, and the club was the only place she could think of that could provide it. A lot of self-talk and nerve had gone into suggesting the visit. "We are not going to do anything in there. We're just checking it out, and if it's gross, we'll leave."

"How do you even know about a place like that?"

"I told you, Dawn's ex-boyfriend took her there."

Dawn had been her best friend since middle school, though Callie hadn't confided in her about her unorthodox preferences. It was too embarrassing. But after Dawn had told her about the club, Callie jumped at the opportunity in the name of adventurous experimentation. It had been so good to finally talk to someone about it without fear of being judged or humiliated.

It shouldn't have taken her so long. Dawn had no qualms about sharing her most intimate experiences with Callie. It wasn't that her friend was promiscuous, so far Dawn had had only two serious boyfriends, but she liked to live dangerously and experiment—perhaps as a way to dispel her dorky reputation.

"She is a bad influence on you."

Yeah, Shawn thought everyone was a bad influence, doing his best to isolate Callie.

"Don't be silly. Dawn just has an open mind and likes to get a taste of different things. Anyway, she said it is pretty tame, with a clientele of mostly committed couples and nothing overly kinky going on in the open." Supposedly, the club held nightly lectures and presentations on different techniques. The demonstrations were being done on fully dressed volunteers. Shawn should have no problem with that.

"She said it was very educational and that we were going to like it." In fact, her words were more along the lines of Callie getting turned on as hell watching whatever subject was taught that night and wanting to jump the next available male, which unfortunately was going to be Shawn.

There was no love lost between those two.

"Fine." He gritted his teeth and opened his door. "I don't understand why we need this crap. Am I not enough for you?" His voice had risen in volume.

Damn it, just as she'd managed to calm him down, Shawn was working himself up again. The only way to defuse the upcoming storm was to stroke his ego. She patted his arm. "You're my stud muffin. I'm doing it for us. We might learn something new to spice things up. Aren't you curious?"

The ruddy color leaving his cheeks, Shawn's chest inflated

with self-importance as he pointed a finger at her. "I'm only going because you want to. There is nothing these people can show me that I haven't seen already. But you'd better not forget who you're with and who you belong to."

Callie stifled the urge to roll her eyes. For a guy who believed he was the big bad wolf, Shawn was ridiculously predictable and easy to manipulate.

Flattery worked on him like a charm.

"Never." She shook her head dramatically. "How could I?" He was so full of himself that there was no chance he'd detect her mocking tone. "You're the best."

Out of necessity, Callie had gotten very good at acting over the past year.

Shawn was a big guy, and with his volatile mood swings and aggression, he could turn really scary really quick. Defusing and deflecting his rage was an exercise in survival.

So far, she'd been lucky.

During his temper tantrums, Shawn had taken out his rage on the walls, the furniture, the appliances, the dishes, and other inanimate objects, but not on her.

Not yet.

It hadn't taken her long to realize that her husband was a bully who thrived on belittling her, manipulating her into bending to his will, and generally pushing her around. The funny thing was that he didn't see it that way. Shawn was convinced that he was a great husband and that she should be grateful for him.

It was easier to just let him believe that.

Instead of fighting an outward war, which she was sure to lose, Callie learned to roll with the punches and get what she wanted in a roundabout way.

Shawn believed he had a subdued, agreeable wife, when in fact she was only letting him win the small things while going after what was really important to her.

When he'd said she couldn't go to college because she needed to help pay the mortgage, she'd taken a waitressing job at the Aussie Steak House where Dawn's sister was a manager, and the tips were more than generous. Working only four evenings a week, including weekends, she made decent money, and could still take college classes with enough free time left over for homework and housework. As a car salesman, Shawn also worked evenings and weekends. As long as she brought the money home and deposited everything into their joint account, he had no problem with her schedule. As with everything else, he wanted complete control over their finances.

Whatever. It wasn't all that important.

She made their marriage work, but the effort that went into it was becoming more and more exhausting.

Were all marriages like that?

One big compromise?

Other than books and movies, which romanticized the reality of everyday life, Callie had nothing to compare her marriage to. Growing up in a single-parent household, she could only imagine what a loving partnership was like.

Perhaps what she and Shawn had was as good as it got?

Still, she couldn't help thinking that it shouldn't be so difficult, and that power games, lies, and manipulations shouldn't be part of a good marriage.

Then again, it was possible that in her youth and naïveté she was imagining an ideal that was unattainable, and she should be thankful for what she had.

Shawn wrapped his arm around her shoulders. "Instead of watching perverts in a kink club, we should go home and work on putting another baby in here." He rubbed a hand over her flat belly.

As devastating as losing the baby had been, Callie was grateful for her apparent difficulty in conceiving. Given that they weren't using contraceptives, though, it was only a matter of time. Ever since her miscarriage, Shawn had been obsessed with getting her pregnant again.

She rested her head on his chest. "There is no reason to rush, Shawn. It will happen when it happens."

He tightened his hold. "God willing."

She hated when he talked like that. Shawn wasn't a religious man, and those kinds of sayings just rolled off his tongue without any real meaning behind them. Growing up in a devout home, he hated anything and everything to do with religion.

He wasn't a believer, and neither was Callie.

When he'd knocked her up, her refusal to consider abortion was not because of the dictums of some scriptures; she'd followed what was in her heart. Even though she was now smarter and somewhat disillusioned, if faced with the same decision today, she wouldn't act differently.

At the time, she'd believed that if they nurtured their attraction and infatuation with each other, they would grow and mature into love. A year later, she was less hopeful but not ready to give up yet.

Not everything was lost.

In his own convoluted way, Shawn loved her. She didn't love him back, but she didn't hate him either. Their marriage was salvageable. In Callie's opinion, people were giving up on their marriages too easily and for the most trivial of reasons.

Besides, giving up was not an option.

The truth was that Shawn would never let her go voluntarily. Aside from his temper, which was worrisome enough on its own, she could sense that something was off with him. She couldn't put her finger on it, but there was a darkness lurking inside him—just waiting for the right catalyst to manifest.

Leaving him would unleash it with a vengeance.

She would have to run—flee to either South Carolina,

where her father had been transferred, or Massachusetts, where Dawn was still attending MIT.

The situation with Shawn was far from desperate enough to make her do either.

She would make it work.

Somehow.

The problem was that she had no clue how to tame Shawn. Instead of getting better, he was getting worse. His newest control freak-out was demanding to know where she was and what she was doing every minute of the day. He didn't even try to hide the fact that he was tracking her by her phone's GPS.

Whatever. The tracking had at least ended the baseless accusations.

Before that ingenious solution, he used to put her through a merciless interrogation every time she'd left the house, and then not believe anything she'd said.

Some battles were just not worth fighting.

Compromise was the name of the game.

CHAPTER 3: BRUNDAR

One year ago.

"*B*oss, can you come up front? I have a situation." The receptionist sounded annoyed and just a little scared.

"On my way," Brundar spoke into the microphone attached to his T-shirt.

One of the biggest hassles of being a part owner of a nightclub was throwing out undesirables. After the last idiot who'd harassed the girl, Brundar had bought a taser gun and instructed her and her weekend counterpart on how to use it in case he and Franco were both occupied elsewhere.

Buying half of Franco's club hadn't been a financial or business decision. Brundar had done it to help the guy out of a tight spot in exchange for a share of the profits—if there were any—and had had no intentions of getting involved in the day to day management of the place. His Guardian job wasn't the kind that allowed time for a side business.

As the saying went, no good deed went unpunished.

Whether he liked it or not, time and again Brundar found himself stepping in.

The financial rescue hadn't been a favor to a friend. Brundar didn't have any. He liked Franco, but the guy was little more than an acquaintance.

Brundar's reasons had been entirely selfish. Finally finding a place where he was comfortable, he refused to let it go bust. When Franco needed an infusion of cash to keep it running, Brundar came up with the dough in exchange for fifty percent ownership just so he wouldn't have to search for a new club.

What made the place different than others was Franco himself. He started it as a regular nightclub, adding the private basement level much later to provide a safe space for himself and a group of like-minded friends to socialize and play. Over time, his friends brought along other friends and membership had expanded, but Franco still treated it as his private playground and was very picky about who he allowed in there.

The upstairs clubgoers didn't even know about the lower level.

Making most of his money from charging entry to the nightclub, selling drinks, and renting the place out for private parties, Franco kept the membership fees to a bare minimum. The guy was more concerned with the quality of his clientele than with their ability to pay.

The upstairs club subsidized the maintenance of the lower level.

Unfortunately, Franco's business acumen left a lot to be desired, and Brundar was slowly getting sucked into getting more and more involved, implementing changes that would make the member portion of the club if not profitable, then at least self-sustainable.

Most of the time Brundar didn't mind helping, but occasionally he had to get involved in inconsequential crap. Drunks and the like were handled by a bouncer, but sober paying customers were usually not turned away unless a private party was going on. He wondered what it could possibly be that required his intervention.

Hopefully, it wasn't another nosy journalist like the one he'd kicked out a week before.

As he neared the anteroom, the waves of aggression wafting from the receptionist station had Brundar's fangs throbbing and lengthening even before he pushed the door open. "What seems to be the problem, Belinda?" he asked in his usual icy tone.

The troublemaker turned around, his face red with anger. "This bitch you have sitting here refuses my wife entrance," he spat.

That was unusual. Women were never turned away from the nightclub. On the contrary, twice a week they got in free. There were always more guys than girls.

The lady in question was hiding behind her husband's broad shoulders, but Brundar could smell her embarrassment. It wasn't an unpleasant scent like the stink coming from the husband; in fact, it was quite alluring despite her discomfort. A mix of soft femininity and strength of character. The last was not a scent most immortals could detect, but it was one Brundar was especially attuned to.

"I tried to explain that no one under twenty-one is allowed in the nightclub or in Franco's basement," Belinda said. "And that it doesn't matter that they have a member's recommendation."

Sidestepping the angry jerk, he peeked at the slender woman standing behind him.

To call her a woman was an exaggeration, and yet she took his breath away—a beautiful, delicate flower that had no business in the club above let alone the one below.

She was still a child. No wonder Belinda refused her entry. The girl looked eighteen at the most.

Why the hell was she married at such a young age and to that asshole?

"This is ridiculous. She is a married woman, for fuck's sake," the jerk fumed.

Yeah, and you should get flogged for robbing her of her childhood. The thing was, Brundar had the sense that the girl wasn't scared of the big bully, only embarrassed by his behavior.

"That's okay, Shawn, let's go." She tried to thread her arm through his.

He shook her arm off. "Stay out of it, Callie." He turned to Brundar. "So what is it going to be? Huh? If you don't let us in, I'm going to trash your club on every review site and every newspaper I can get to." The guy inflated his chest, thinking to intimidate Brundar.

So that was why Belinda had asked him to intervene. The jerk had probably threatened her with the same crap. Bad reviews were bad for business, and one jerk with a vendetta could do a lot of damage.

Behind the desk, Belinda groaned in frustration.

Brundar affected a tight-lipped smile. "I don't think that will be necessary. We can resolve this misunderstanding in a mutually beneficial way." He imbued his tone with influence.

Trying to resist the command, the guy pinched his forehead between his thumb and forefinger. A few seconds later, he faltered. "Yes, that would be better." His chest deflated.

"Come. I'll escort you to your car." Brundar opened the front door.

The girl named Callie cast him a perplexed glance. To resist the influence, her brain must've been stronger than her husband's.

What was a smart girl like her doing with a moron like that?

"Sometimes a calm tone is all that's needed," Brundar whispered in her ear.

Staring at him, she shook her head, once, and then again.

Perhaps she was wondering about her husband's uncharacteristic response, or still feeling the influence and fighting it.

As they reached the couple's Honda Civic, the husband unlocked the doors with the remote and got behind the wheel, leaving his young wife standing on the sidewalk.

Brundar walked around to the passenger side and opened the door for her. "My lady." Without thinking, he offered Callie his hand, a rare gesture for him. He hardly ever shook hands with a woman and never with a man.

"Thank you," she whispered, her eyes trained on his face, his offered hand outside her peripheral vision. "Can I have your name, sir?"

"Brad." He gave her the name he was known by in the club. "A pleasure to make your acquaintance, Callie."

She smiled shyly. "It's Calypso, but I go by Callie." She shook her head. "I don't know why I'm telling you this. I never use my real name." Pink flooding her cheeks, she looked down.

Unable to resist, he hooked a finger under her chin and lifted her head. "Calypso. It suits you better. A unique name for a unique girl. One of a kind and beautiful."

She chuckled, blushing again. "Funny that you would say that about me. Talk about unique." She waved a hand at him. For a moment, it seemed like she wanted to say more, but then she decided against it.

"Look at me, Calypso," Brundar commanded softly.

She did, her green eyes losing focus as he delved into her mind. "You're beautiful, and I'm just a guy who is way too old for you. Forget about me."

"I'm not a kid. I'm twenty," she protested.

A little older than he'd thought, but still a child. One with a strong mind, though.

Curious, Brundar delved a little deeper.

He didn't like what that little glimpse he'd allowed himself revealed. The girl wasn't safe with the man she called her

18

husband. Brundar knew the type well. For now, Shawn was just a controlling bastard and a verbally abusive jerk, but his behavior was going to escalate. It always did with bullies.

"Get in the car, Calypso." He waited for her to buckle up before closing her door and going around to the driver's side.

The guy was still in a trance-like compliance.

Weak mind.

"Look at me, Shawn," Brundar commanded.

The guy raised a pair of unfocused eyes.

"You're going to pay attention to the road and drive home safely. You're going to take care of Callie and treat her well. Do you understand?"

"Yes, sir."

Brundar closed the door, then waited for Shawn to turn on the engine, put the transmission in drive, and ease out of the parking lot.

As he watched the car disappear from view, he committed the license plate number to memory. The thrall he'd put on Shawn was going to hold for a while, but not indefinitely.

Once it wore off, Calypso would be in danger.

CHAPTER 4: LOSHAM

The present.

$\mathcal{L}$osham poured himself a shot of whiskey and walked out the French doors to the presidential suite's balcony. Nothing but the best for him and Rami. The twelve men Navuh had grudgingly allotted for his use were comfortable enough in a nearby extended-stay hotel.

Leaning over the railing, he took a sip and held it in his mouth to savor the flavor. It wasn't the best there was, just the best the hotel had. Decent, but not what he was used to drinking at home. And to think the place promoted itself as the fanciest in town.

Rami followed him outside. "What are we going to do with the new men?"

Losham knew what he meant. Navuh had authorized less than one fifth of the personnel Losham had asked for. "That's not nearly enough for all the clubs, but it is for one. I'm going to keep them here. We know that at least part of the clan is residing somewhere in this area. It makes sense for them to hide in a big city. San Francisco with its tech hub is also a good bet. But I have a hunch their leadership's base is in Los Angeles. If it were me, I'd have chosen the larger city as my command center too."

"As always, you are right, sir." Rami glanced at his watch. "We should head out. The men are waiting."

"Yes." Losham finished his drink and handed Rami the empty glass. "Call the valet and have the car ready."

"Yes, sir."

After much deliberation, Losham had decided that the best place for holding meetings with his men was in a rented warehouse in an nondescript industrial park, one of the hundreds scattered throughout the large city. Keeping his operation low key was prudent on top of saving him money.

The place was the size of a classroom, with a kickboxing class as a neighbor on one side, and a spinning class on the other, where sweaty humans exerted themselves on stationary bikes to the screeching sounds of loud music.

Perfect for his needs.

With various fitness trainers renting spaces in the park, there were plenty of people coming and going. His men wouldn't stand out.

Rami parked next to the two minivans he'd rented for the men. Through the windows, Losham could see them sitting inside.

"Rami, transparency doesn't lend itself to covert activities."

His assistant followed his gaze. "The rented vans are a temporary solution. I'll make sure that the cars they get have tinted windows."

"Indeed."

As Rami unlocked the door, Losham motioned for them to come out of the vehicles. "Welcome," he greeted each one, offering a handshake.

Following instructions, the men didn't salute.

When everyone was inside, Rami locked the door behind

them and lowered the shades, then walked over to the stack of folding chairs leaning against the wall. "Make yourselves comfortable," he said, pointing for the men to make use of them.

Forming a semi-circle, they sat facing Losham and Rami.

"Welcome," Losham greeted them. "Let's get straight to the purpose of your deployment. As you were all briefed, the Brotherhood now owns a chain of luxury sex clubs. The original goal was to lure rich clan members, with the intent of capturing and torturing them for information about the location of their leaders. Unfortunately, it seems that the civilians have no idea where the clan's command center is located. Therefore, we need to catch a Guardian."

Twelve apprehensive sets of eyes met his gaze.

Losham raised his palm to forestall questions. "I know these warriors are fearsome, but even the best fighter can't overpower twelve well-trained men. All we need is to catch one. That's why I'm keeping all of you here in one location instead of distributing you as reinforcements between the clubs."

The team's commander raised his hand.

"Yes, Gommed." Losham gave him permission to speak.

"Are we going to wait around until a Guardian shows up? It might never happen, sir."

"Good point. That's why we need to make sure one of them comes to investigate. I don't know their procedures, or if they usually send one or two. I'm betting on one. With such a small force, they can't afford to send more."

"Investigate what, sir?"

"Either another civilian that we catch and kill, or several of their human pets."

Gommed frowned. "I don't understand, sir. You want us to start killing random humans? Why would the Guardians care?"

Losham smiled indulgently. Simple soldiers needed to be fed information like baby birds. Their deductive skills were nonexistent. "They would care if the humans bled to death from two puncture wounds to the neck." He put two fingers on his carotid artery to demonstrate.

"Are we to instigate fights? Seek out gang members and other violent human scum to kill?"

The question was so naive it bordered on embarrassing.

His men were not going to like his idea, but they were soldiers, and they were going to obey orders. Nevertheless, Losham would pretend the course of action he was about to set was as unpalatable for him as it would be for the men.

"I wish it was that simple. But the clan leaders are not going to care about us eliminating random human scum. They might even think we've been reformed and come to care for the humans."

He smirked, making quotation marks with his fingers. "Your victims will have to be female. When several are found dead in a pool of their own blood, obvious bite marks on their necks, it will make the news. Naturally, the Guardians will know who's responsible. When they send one to snoop around, he will follow a trail of false clues that will lead him into a trap."

"What kind of a trap, sir?"

"I'm working on it. I'll let you know as soon as the plan is finalized."

"Yes, sir."

Gommed was a good soldier who didn't ask unnecessary questions like why and if there was another way. Except, it was written all over his face, as well as those of the others.

Although Mortdh's teachings held females in low esteem, they were considered a crucial resource. Since the soldiers' early years in the training camp, it had been drilled into their heads that human females were fragile and were to be used with care so as to not harm their breeding capabilities.

"Killing young fertile females is wasteful, but that's the

23

nature of war. Sacrificing resources is unavoidable. If there were another way, I would've gladly taken it."

He got some approving nods but also some involuntary grimaces.

They would adjust.

"What are our orders, sir?" Gommed asked.

"First order of things is to get you settled. You need to buy cars, used ones from private owners. Rami will give you the cash needed, explain how to go about it, and take care of registration and insurance. When it's time for you to go to work, I want you to spread out and cover a wide area."

After several more questions had been answered and instructions clarified, the men left.

"Should I find us a nice restaurant, sir, or do you prefer to dine at the hotel?" Rami opened the sedan's door for Losham.

"Let's go back to the hotel. I find their culinary offerings acceptable."

"As you wish, sir." Rami closed the passenger's door and walked around to take his place at the driver's seat.

"Have you made any progress with your cult idea?"

Rami turned on the ignition and eased out of the parking spot. "I've spent some time thinking it through, and I think I have a solid plan."

"Please proceed."

"The men we want to recruit into the cult should be true women haters. I'm not talking about men like you, sir, who consider women inferior but still enjoy their company, or womanizers who use them, or men like me who are just not into them. I'm talking about those who've gotten rejected, thrown out, emasculated. Western society and the freedom of choice it affords women ensures that there is no shortage of those."

Very astute observation for a man who'd never had a relationship with a woman in a sexual, romantic, professional, or any other capacity. Doomers interacted with females only on a sexual basis, and Rami wasn't interested in that.

"I agree. How do you propose we find those angry rejects?"

Rami's lips turned up in a lopsided smirk. "You know how Americans have all those silly support groups? We make one for recently divorced men, men who were kicked out by their girlfriends, or simply all those who got rejected over and over again. There will be an avalanche of applicants."

"A brilliant idea, my friend. But how are we going to promote it?"

"Facebook. Paid advertisements can be targeted to a certain age group, gender, and other factors. We can employ an expert to help us narrow the selection."

"And who will lead that fake support group?"

Rami shrugged. "We either hire an actor or a quack therapist with women issues himself."

"What about the cult leader?"

"I thought you would want to do that yourself, sir."

Losham shook his head. "I'm a thinker, not a motivator. We need someone charismatic, someone who can incite men to violence. We either hire another actor, one with charisma and no scruples, or we choose one of the participants. We can observe a few of the initial meetings and look for someone who fits the role."

CHAPTER 5: CALLIE

*H*ands trembling with equal part excitement and anxiety, Callie opened the letter from UCLA.

Dear Ms. Davidson,

I am pleased to congratulate you on behalf of University of California – Los Angeles upon our acceptance of your application. As you know, UCLA has a long tradition of academic excellence and reviews the many applications it receives with the highest standards.

Callie skipped over to the next part.

You will find all the necessary forms for your enrollment included with this letter. We request that you fill them out and return them to us no later than October 1, 2018. This will help us to ensure that your spot remains open and facilitate the enrollment process. Please contact us if you have any questions or problems regarding this letter.

Oh boy, did she have problems, but none that a call to the university's admissions office could solve. Tuition was tenfold what she'd paid at the community college, and there was no way Shawn would agree to the expense. Not because they couldn't afford it, after all she could apply for a student loan, but because he would use it as an excuse and throw a tantrum if she insisted.

It had crossed her mind to ask her father for a loan, but she'd rejected it out of hand.

Donald would gladly give her the tuition money if he had it, but after buying the house in South Carolina, she knew he was short on cash. Besides, with Iris ready to pop at any moment, they would need whatever was left over from his paycheck to buy things for the baby.

As of late, the little half-brother she was expecting was the only bright spot in Callie's life. Hopefully, Shawn wouldn't object to her going to see the baby. Not that it would stop her. There was only so much jerkiness she was willing to put up with.

No way was she missing out on holding her newborn brother and cuddling with him as much as Iris allowed.

"What do you have there?" Shawn looked over her shoulder at the letter in her hands.

She would rather have waited to tell him after having some time to think of the best way to spin it in her favor. On the other hand it was better to get it done and not obsess over it for days. "I got in. This is from the UCLA admissions office."

"Did it come with a scholarship?"

Callie sighed and folded the letter. "We don't qualify for financial aid, Shawn. Between your paycheck and mine, we make too much."

He snorted. "Right, as if there is that much left over after the mortgage and the car payments and all the other bills."

She wanted to tell him that leasing a car for close to a thousand dollars a month was not considered a life necessity, and that the difference between the payments on his luxury BMW and her basic Honda Civic would've paid for half of her tuition, but she knew it was no use. He would go into a whole tirade as to why he needed to drive the BMW because he was selling them and how would it look if he drove something else.

As if any of his customers cared what car he was driving.

Shawn was a selfish prick, that's all.

"I could take out a student loan," she said softly. "I got the credits from the community college transferred, which means I only have two or three years of tuition left."

"With the interest those fuckers are charging on student loans, even that is a lot. We will never get out of debt. And for what? So you can become a teacher and make even less money than you make waiting tables? I don't think so."

It was hard to argue with that logic. Except, waiting tables was not her life goal. Teaching was. Callie loved kids, and working in an elementary school, preferably with kindergarteners, was her dream job.

"Yeah, I guess you're right," she said, to get him to leave her alone.

He looked disappointed. She'd robbed him of the opportunity to argue and work himself up so he could wreak havoc on the house and terrorize her.

Over the past year, Shawn had gotten worse. The anger tantrums were becoming more frequent and more violent. Most everything in their house was either broken or scratched, the walls covered with discount store framed art to hide the many holes he'd made in them.

Sadly, Callie was reaching the end of her rope. She couldn't save their marriage no matter how hard she tried, and frankly, she was tired of trying. Changing Shawn for the better was not going to happen.

Quite the opposite. The harder she tried, the worse he got.

If she wanted any kind of life for herself, she had to leave.

Grabbing a can of soda from the fridge, Callie walked over to the living room window and pulled the curtain back. There was something oddly calming about doing that, as if by gazing out on their quiet suburban street she could pretend that their home was as peaceful as the grassy lawns and young trees lining the sidewalk, their skinny, pliable trunks swaying in the light breeze.

It was a sorry state of affairs when the outside of her home felt safer than the inside.

Away from the suffocating confinement of those hole-ridden walls, she could breathe. Out there she felt whole, capable, free. Working, grocery shopping, or just taking a walk, it didn't matter where she was or what she was doing as long as she was out.

That good feeling would gradually evaporate the closer she got back to her house. Returning from work, her heart would skip a beat as she pressed the remote and waited for the garage door to lift.

Whether Shawn's car was there or not determined if her pulse sped up or slowed down. The times he was gone, the adrenaline drop that came on the heels of the relief would often make her dizzy.

It was no way to live.

Callie hated the thought of being alone, but staying with Shawn was like living inside a horror film. She knew the boogieman, she knew he was coming for her, she just didn't know when.

Except, until she figured out her route to freedom, Callie had to pretend that everything was all right. In order for her to escape unharmed, Shawn couldn't suspect that she was unhappy and planning to leave.

CHAPTER 6: JACKSON

*J*ackson parked in the keep's guest parking garage and took the public elevator to the lobby, wondering what would it take to get in. But when he stopped at the guard station, the guy buzzed him in without question.

"Go ahead. We have you on file."

"Thanks." Jackson gave the guy a two finger salute and proceeded to the concealed side door marked as maintenance. It clicked open as soon as he pressed his thumb to the scanner.

Right. He'd almost forgotten about the mandatory sex-ed class he and his buddies had participated in so long ago. They had been granted a security clearance to enter the underground facilities, and apparently it was still good.

At the time, he'd been pissed at Kian for forcing him to endure Bhathian's lectures, but that class had ended up changing his life in unexpected ways.

Jackson must've left an impression on Bhathian because the guy introduced him to his daughter Nathalie, which turned out to be a great business opportunity for Jackson. More than that. While managing Nathalie's café, he'd met Tessa.

If not for that sex-ed class, he might have missed his one chance at a true-love match. It might have come and gone without him knowing it had been so close.

Must've been fated.

A nasty prank that had gotten him in shitloads of trouble ended up bringing him the love of his life.

Taking the clan's private elevator down to the basement, Jackson stepped out on the clinic's level.

Hopefully, Dr. Bridget wasn't busy and would agree to see him. He would've made an appointment, but he didn't have her private phone number, only the keep's emergency hotline, and there was no way he was explaining to whoever was answering the phone why he needed to see the doctor.

In fact, he was hoping no one other than Bridget was there to see him come in. He could count on the doctor to keep their conversation confidential, but not anyone else. The last thing he needed was for the gossip machine to start spinning.

Knocking on the door, he pushed it open a crack. "Dr. Bridget, do you have a moment?"

She waved him in. "Of course. Come in, Jackson."

"Thank you." He closed the door behind him.

"Please, take a seat and tell me what brings you here."

"My mate," he started, and stopped at Bridget's surprised expression. "I mean my girlfriend, but she is so much more than that."

Bridget smiled. "Tessa, right?"

"Yeah. So I guess the rumor machine is already working."

"I don't know about that. Per my request, or rather demand, I get informed about all possible Dormants. Actually, I would appreciate it if Tessa would come in and give a few blood samples before her transition starts. Have you bitten her already? And if yes, how many times?"

Jackson pinched his forehead between his thumb and forefinger. "Enough to induce her transition. But it's not happening."

Bridget's eyes filled with pity. "I'm so sorry, Jackson. Maybe she is not a Dormant. We are so eager to find new ones that we are grasping at straws. I was told that she doesn't have any special abilities, so it was a long shot from the start."

"No, she doesn't. But I'm sure she is my fated mate. I don't want to sound like a sap and tell you all the reasons why I believe that. But I think I know why she isn't transitioning, and I need to run it by you."

"Of course."

By her compassionate doctor's tone, it was obvious that Bridget was just humoring him. She'd already removed Tessa from her potentials list.

He pinched his forehead again. "Tessa has issues. I don't want to get into details without her being here or giving me her consent to talk about it with you." He sighed. "We haven't had sex yet."

Bridget looked puzzled. "What about the biting? How did you get so close to orgasm without having sex?"

Jackson tilted his head sideways and narrowed his eyes. Did the doctor need him to explain about the birds and the bees?

Her eyes widened, and she slapped her forehead. "Duh. I just didn't expect you to pull a Clinton. Oral sex is sex, you know."

He chuckled. "We are not even there yet, but we've done some heavy necking. When that's all there is, it's enough stimulation to get my venom glands primed."

"And you think that's the reason?"

"Yeah. Maybe the bite works together with intercourse or something. Some hormonal interaction. I'm not a doctor or a scientist, but it makes sense to me."

"Hmm…" Bridget tapped her keyboard with one finger without typing anything. "According to Annani's stories, the

Dormant girls of her time transitioned from just the bite. But it was done at the peak of puberty. Perhaps that's why it was enough. The adult Dormant females that transitioned under my care were all sexually active with their mates. The biting was congruent with not only intercourse, but also insemination. You might be on to something."

Jackson slumped in his chair, his arms dropping to his sides. "Thank you. You've just given me hope."

Bridget smiled. "You're welcome. It's only a hypothesis though. Time will tell. By the way, is Tessa getting professional help with those issues you mentioned?"

"No. She refuses."

"You should encourage her to at least talk to your mom. Whatever trauma Tessa has been through, it should be treated by a professional."

"I suggested seeing either my mother or one of her colleagues, but Tessa vetoed it. I'm not pressuring her because she is making progress without any outside help. In the beginning, she couldn't tolerate any intimacy at all, not even a kiss. Things are much better now. I learned the trick is to go slow, holding back even when she wants to push forward, and not scare her or overwhelm her. Patience is the key."

Bridget put a hand over her heart. "You're such a sweet guy, and so mature for your age."

The tips of his ears tingled in embarrassment. Jackson didn't like compliments like that. He wasn't doing anything special. If he wanted a future with Tessa, there was no other way. He didn't volunteer for the task out of the goodness of his heart. He was doing it for selfish reasons. Helping the woman he loved to heal was like helping himself, and no one would've called him sweet for that.

"Did I embarrass you?" Bridget asked. "I'm sorry. It's just that I envy you a little."

"Envy me? Why?"

"I envy your youth. Only the very young can love with such passion. Your heart is still wide open, and you gaze with hope upon the future. I'm jaded. Even if I found my true-love match, I don't think I could fall so deeply in love."

"What about Bhathian and Eva? Syssi and Kian?"

She nodded. "Yeah. I guess it's a lot like having a first baby. No matter how much everyone around you gushes about their love for their children, you can't imagine the intensity and the power of that love until you hold your own child in your arms."

Jackson lifted both hands in the air. "One thing at a time, doctor. I'm only eighteen. All this talk about babies is freaking me out."

Bridget laughed as she rose to her feet. "Let me escort you out. I'm going to the café." She waited for him to join her then threaded her arm through his.

The mighty doctor was petite, the top of her head reaching a few inches below his shoulder. Jackson smiled down at her. "You would like Tessa. She is tiny, like you."

Bridget wasn't as skinny, though, and had flaming red hair. But he was smart enough to know it wasn't something a guy should remark on. Women took offense to the silliest of things.

Jackson liked females of all shapes and sizes, and in his eyes beauty didn't equate with skinny or tall, or the other way around.

Her lips pursed in mock affront. The doctor managed to look down her nose at him even though she had to crank her head way up. "The correct term, young man, is vertically challenged."

He snorted. "Good to know. I'll keep it in mind."

CHAPTER 7: BRUNDAR

*P*arked on the street across from Calypso's house, Brundar heard her husband's irate voice. "What do you think you're doing?"

"I'm filling in paperwork."

"What for? I thought we agreed that you're not going to waste your time studying a worthless profession like teaching." His voice got louder.

"I know. But what if I can get several scholarships that together will cover the tuition? I can still work my shifts at Aussie and make the same money I'm making now."

"And what about the house? Who is going to clean and cook, huh?"

"I've been managing that just fine with work and classes at the community college."

"No one is going to give you money so you can play at being a student. But by all means, go ahead and play pretend. Maybe you should buy a lottery ticket too. Who knows? Maybe you'll win?" he mocked her.

Asshole. Brundar didn't need to delve into the guy's sick mind to know what this was all about. It wasn't about money, or Calypso earning less as a teacher than as a waitress. It was about control. A moment later Brundar heard the door slam, then the garage door lifted and Shawn backed his fancy car into the street.

It was so tempting to arrange an accident. All Brundar had to do was project an illusion, something that would cause the jerk to hit the brakes, put the car into a spin, and hit a tree. The problem was that the neighborhood was new, and the trees were mere saplings.

The lamppost wasn't sturdy enough either.

Besides, Brundar couldn't do it. He was a Guardian, a law enforcer, and arranging an accident was the same as murder. Regrettably, Shawn's behavior and nasty intentions didn't justify an execution.

Not yet.

The problem was that when they did, it would be too late.

Calypso's husband was a sick fuck. She needed to leave him as soon as possible and run as far away as she could.

If he could only talk to her and convince her of that. But knocking on her door and getting invited inside wasn't happening. She wouldn't remember him. Calypso had seen Brundar only once, almost a year ago, and he'd made sure to muddle her memory of the entire incident before sending her on her way.

The garage door opened again, this time to let Calypso out.

Brundar frowned. Why was she wearing the steak house's red T-shirt on her day off?

The girl must have switched shifts with another waiter again. She'd been doing it a lot lately. Probably to get out of the house and away from the abusive jerk.

Verbally abusive. Brundar ordered his fangs to retract. Shawn hadn't abused her physically yet, that was why he was still alive. Nevertheless, he was systematically squashing her spirit. But one of these days, he was going to snap and hit her.

With men like him, once that mental barrier was breached it never went down again.

Brundar couldn't let it happen.

It was time to take action.

He would follow Calypso to work, walk in as a customer, order a steak, and strike up a conversation while gently returning her memory of their first and only meeting.

But what if the reminder embarrassed her, and she refused to talk to him?

Trying to get into a kink club and getting thrown out because she was underage at the time probably wasn't her proudest memory.

What if she wanted to forget about it?

He could always take a peek at her mind and gauge her reaction, but it was a dishonorable thing to do. An invasion of privacy. The clan had very strict rules about what, when, how and why it was allowed.

The rules of conduct Brundar lived by were even stricter.

Protecting the clan and the secret of its existence was basically the only reason thralling a human was allowed. Not that everyone adhered to the letter of the law. But as long as the thrall was minimal and not done to gain an unfair advantage, it was considered more of a misdemeanor than a criminal offense.

He'd done it himself before, but it was to protect her, not for his own benefit. Brundar couldn't claim that defense in this case.

Driving slow, he got to the Aussie Steak House a few minutes behind Calypso and parked his car at the other end of the restaurant's parking lot, as far away from her Honda as he could.

There was a small chance Calypso might recognize his car from the many times he'd been parked across the street from her house. Continuous shrouding took a mental toll, and sometimes he'd been too tired to bother. Besides, even if Calypso had noticed the same car coming around and parking next to one of her neighbors' houses once or twice a week, she probably assumed he was their guest.

Pulling a leather string from his pocket, Brundar gathered his hair back in a tight ponytail and tied it. He liked eating steaks, but not smelling them on his hair.

Aussie was a trendy steak house. Even at seven in the evening on a weekday, there was a twenty-minute wait. Brundar slipped the hostess a twenty, asking to be seated in Calypso's section, took the pager she'd given him, and went back to sit in his car. There were class schedules to check, updates to read, and once it was all done he even had time to catch up on the headline news before the pager went off.

The hostess escorted him to his table. "You look so familiar. Are you an actor?" she asked as she handed him the menu.

He got it a lot. It was the hair. He reminded people of a character in that *Lord of the Rings* saga—the elf guy with the pointed ears.

"No." He opened the menu, making it clear that the conversation was over. It was pointless to humor people with lies or idle chitchat. A simple no didn't waste anyone's time.

"Well, enjoy your dinner." The hostess sounded cheerful despite what she must've perceived as rudeness. The girl probably assumed he was an actor who didn't want to be bothered.

From behind the large menu, Brundar observed Calypso interacting with the other customers. The bright smile she offered everyone wasn't faked even though she had no reason for smiling today, or the day before, or the one before that.

Her husband was a mean and angry jerk, and between her classes, work, homework, and keeping the house the way the asshole liked it, she had no time for friends.

Or maybe she was just reluctant to have anyone she knew meet Shawn and witness how he was treating her.

As she got nearer, Brundar's breath caught in anticipation, but then she stopped by the couple sitting one table over, and he had to wait a moment longer.

Damnation, the girl was making him nervous. He couldn't remember being so anxious in centuries.

Bloody battles? Bring them on.

Outnumbered and surrounded by enemies? No problem.

Before Calypso had entered his life over a year ago, Brundar hadn't needed to slip into the zone to be at his best. He'd lived in it. A well-oiled, efficient, killing machine who experienced no fear, no hatred, no emotion at all.

It had been his shield, staving off mistakes, keeping him alive, and making him invincible.

But one young woman had managed to ruin all that. She was stirring a storm of emotions within him that he had no idea what to do with. Between one spying visit and the next, he had to work hard on blocking thoughts of her and getting back into the zone.

Being here, talking to her would only make it worse. He should just get up and go.

Too late.

She was coming over, that bright smile of hers searing him like a beam of sunshine on a vampire.

"Good evening, sir. What can I offer you to drink?"

"Whiskey."

"Sure thing. Which one would you like? We have Johnnie Walker, Chattanooga, Jameson, Crown Royal, Jim Beam, Chivas Regal, and Jack Daniel's."

"Chivas."

"Neat?"

"Is there any other way?" Ice cubes had no place in a whiskey. It wasn't a bloody soda.

She smiled. "You've got it. Some bread to munch on while you wait for your steak?"

"How did you know I was going to order a steak?"

She tapped her temple. "I'm a mind reader."

Strange, she was teasing, not intimidated by him at all. That didn't happen often.

Calypso laughed, the sound going straight to his balls. "Just joking. It's not like there is anything else on the menu, and you don't look like the type who orders an appetizer salad."

"No, I'm not." He debated whether he should release her memory of him now or later. "You look familiar. I think we've met before."

She put a hand on her hip. "Yeah, you look familiar too. But that's probably because you look a lot like Legolas."

Brundar frowned. "Who?"

She rolled her eyes. "The elf prince from *Lord of the Rings*."

He nodded. "I've been told that before. Though the only thing we have in common is the hair."

She looked a little closer, examining his features. "You're right. You're much better looking than Orlando."

"Who?" He was starting to sound like a broken record.

"Didn't you see the movie? That's the name of the actor who played Legolas. I used to have a huge crush on him."

It was good she'd used the past tense. Otherwise...

What? Why was it even bothering him that Calypso liked that Orlando guy? "I don't watch movies," he grumbled.

"Well, you should watch that one and see why everyone thinks you look like him."

"Do we have the same eyes?"

As Callie bent down to take a closer look, he trapped her gaze and went in.

Sifting through a year's worth of memories took time, but he was good, speeding through them as if it was a fast forward movie and taking care not to peek at the many scenes flashing by. Not only to protect her privacy, but also to save himself from seeing things that would incite him into a murderous rage. No amount of self-talk and restraint would save Shawn then.

He held her captive for a good two minutes before finding the one buried memory he needed to flush out.

When Brundar released Calypso, she swayed on her feet, her hand going to her head. "Wow, where did this headache come from?"

He got up, ready to catch her if she fell. "Do you need to sit down?"

She shook her head. "No, I'm fine. It was just a weird moment. It's already getting better." She lifted her eyes to him. "Now I remember where I've seen you before. You were the guy at that club..."

He pretended surprise. "That's why you look so familiar."

CHAPTER 8: CALLIE

The guy from the club.
         She should've remembered him. Not only was he the best-looking man she'd ever seen, but the circumstances of meeting him were quite memorable.

Except, for some reason, everything from that night had been hazy.

Shawn hadn't remembered much either.

Maybe they had both suppressed the details of the episode because it was an uncomfortable memory. Getting thrown out like a couple of trespassing teenagers had been embarrassing, and they hadn't even made it into the kinky area. The receptionist had refused them admission into the nightclub that everyone else over twenty-one could get into.

After that night, things had been good between Shawn and her for a while, so maybe that was the reason she'd pushed that memory into some dark corner of her mind where it had joined other unpleasant moments she wasn't keen on remembering.

At the time, Callie had hoped that they were on the right track, that they had reached a turning point and that their marriage was going to survive. But the good times hadn't lasted long. Shawn's anger tantrums had returned and then worsened. It had taken her a while, but eventually she realized that more than an expression of his inner turmoil and fury, the tantrums were a tool meant to intimidate her and control her.

"Did you ever try again?" the guy asked.

She knew he didn't mean going to a nightclub. Callie shook her head. "No." She was spending way too long talking to this customer, Brad, if she remembered his name right. A quick, friendly chitchat was part of her job description, but this conversation was going places she'd rather not talk about in the middle of the restaurant. "Did you decide on a steak?"

Brad didn't look at the menu. "The largest you have. Medium well."

"Fries or mash potatoes?"

"What do you recommend?"

"We are famous for our mash potatoes."

"Then that's what I'll have."

"Anything else I can get you?"

"Food wise, no. But I would like to talk to you after your shift ends. If you're so inclined," he tacked on at the end as if remembering to mind his manners.

Callie wasn't sure about that. He was a stranger she'd only met once before and under peculiar circumstances.

Was he safe?

Logically, no, he wasn't. Take away his good looks, and his demeanor was straight up creepy.

And yet, her gut told her differently.

Or was that her hormones?

He was incredibly attractive.

"My shift ends at midnight. I'm sure you have better things to do than waiting around for me." She collected his menu.

He caught her hand. "I only want to talk. We can sit out on

the patio and have a drink. I checked, and the bar stays open until two in the morning. We will not be alone out there."

She shrugged as if it didn't matter to her one way or another, but the truth was that his offer was more than enticing. She wanted to sit out on the patio with him and talk, find out more about this mysterious man. "If you're there when I'm done, I'll stay for a few minutes."

"That's all I'm asking for, Calypso."

Callie smiled a fake little smile and walked away on shaky legs.

He remembered more about her than he'd let her believe. Her name tag said Callie, the name everyone knew her by. She'd told this stranger her real one a year ago, and he remembered. Which meant he'd been faking the whole 'you look familiar' thing. He knew exactly who she was.

She should stay away from him.

What if he was a crazy stalker?

Yeah, right. And he waited almost a year to approach me.

Not likely.

Why would a movie-star-gorgeous guy stalk a Plain Jane like her?

He wouldn't.

Maybe his strangeness was the result of a personality disorder?

Who talked like that?

Clipped answers spoken in a flat computer-like voice. Heck, the text-to-speech on her phone sounded more human than Brad.

Maybe he had a speech impediment?

She shouldn't be afraid of him because of a disability. As someone who had dreams of teaching kids with learning difficulties, she should be more open-minded than that.

When she brought him his drink, Callie made sure to serve it with a smile. "Here you go, Brad. It's Brad, right?"

For a split second, he looked uncomfortable. "That's the name I use in the club."

Okay?

And?

At that point, any normal person would have offered the name he wanted her to know him by.

The guy was definitely on the spectrum.

She should encourage him. "What's your real name?"

"Brundar."

For some reason, she thought it fitted him better. A warrior's name. Not that she knew what it meant, but it sounded like it. "Is it Nordic?"

"Scottish." He said it with an accent.

She was a sucker for foreign accents, especially Scottish. "It's a good name. It suits you."

He nodded in agreement.

"I'll go check on your steak."

He nodded again.

Not a man of many words.

When he was done with his meal, Brundar rose to his feet, put cash into the padded folder she'd handed him, and walked outside without saying a word to her.

Spectrum or not, the guy definitely needed help with his social skills.

Unfortunately, she was in no position to offer him or anyone else help. Not until she resolved the situation with Shawn.

———

As her shift drew to an end, Callie got nervous.

Was he going to be there?

Waiting for her?

God, she hoped he was.

Brundar was such a mystery. The man she'd remembered from the club was self-assured and dominant in a way that had resonated with her on a primitive wavelength of sexual attraction.

Maybe that was why she'd suppressed the memory of him? At the time she'd still thought of herself as a married woman who shouldn't have naughty thoughts about another man.

Nothing had changed about his looks, he was still sinfully attractive, but he wasn't projecting as much dominance as he had that night. In fact, she sensed vulnerability in him, and that resonated with another facet of her—the caretaker.

In short, she was confused as heck.

"Callie, are you just going to stand there? Go home!" Katharine slapped her arm.

Right. She'd zoned out in the middle of the employee break room, standing like a zombie with her purse in her hand and her jacket draped over her arm.

She smiled at her friend. "Goodnight, Kati."

"You too. Are you okay to drive? If you're not, I can take you home after my shift ends in an hour."

"Thanks, but I'm fine. I just have a lot on my mind."

"Yeah, just make sure you pay attention to the road and don't zone out while driving."

"I will."

But not right away.

First, she would indulge in a rendezvous with the mysterious guy waiting for her on the patio.

CHAPTER 9: BRUNDAR

*O*ut on the patio, Brundar sat with his back to the other diners, thinking about Callie, or Calypso as he preferred to call her.

The two names represented two different aspects of her personality.

Not personas. She wasn't pretending to be one thing and then another. They were more like modes she was switching between depending on the situation. Most people did it to some degree.

There was that saying about a perfect wife human males liked. A lady in the living room, a cook in the kitchen, and a harlot in bed, or something crass like that.

Maybe that was what he was observing.

But he had a feeling that Calypso's demarcation lines were clearer and deeper. The partitions she erected between the different roles she assumed were thick and solid.

Not that he was such an expert on human emotions, but she was so different here from how she was at home. Yet another reason to free her of the asshole she'd married. Hopefully,

Brundar could persuade her to leave the jerk. Otherwise he would have to kill him—and the clan's penalty for murder was entombment.

Nevertheless, one way or another he was going to make sure Calypso was free.

Her time was running out.

He felt her the moment she stepped out on the patio and turned around to look at her.

"Hi, you waited," she said.

Brundar cast her a puzzled glance. "I said I would."

"You did."

He stood up and pulled out a chair for her.

"Thank you." Calypso draped her jacket over the back of the chair and sat down. "But often enough people don't mean what they say or change their minds."

"Not me."

She smiled. "No, I guess you don't. With how little you say, I bet you mean every single word."

"I do."

Damnation. He was so used to talking in monosyllables that it was difficult for him to articulate his thoughts in complete sentences. He needed to do better than that if he wanted a sliver of a chance convincing Calypso to listen to him.

Looking at him expectantly, she was waiting for him to say something.

"Are you twenty-one yet?" He knew she was, but that was the first conversation starter that popped into his head.

"Yes. I turned twenty-one a couple of months after the incident."

"Why didn't you try again? Did I scare you away?"

Not that he would've allowed her inside the lower level even after she'd turned twenty-one. At Brundar's prompting, Franco had changed the minimum age to twenty-eight for anyone seeking admission to the lower level. Another club in town had been involved in a case of minors using fake identification, and Brundar used it as an excuse to raise the age to one that would be more difficult to fake.

She shook her head. "No. It's just that things came up and experimenting was the furthest thing from my mind."

"So you didn't go to other clubs either?"

"No. I dropped the whole thing. It was a silly idea to begin with." She blushed and looked away.

"How about your husband? Didn't he want to try again?" The last thing Brundar wanted was to hear about that jerk, but he needed her to start talking about her marriage.

Her cringe spoke louder than words. "Believe it or not, it was my idea, not his. He didn't want to go that first time, and after what happened, I never mentioned it again."

As with everything else in her life, Callie had shelved her needs and wants in the pursuit of marital peace. She must've been so frustrated, and not only sexually.

He leaned forward and clasped her hand, surprised again by the urge to do so. It had been the same the first time they'd met. When Calypso didn't pull away, allowing him the small touch, it encouraged him to say something that was too personal for people who'd just met. "You can't ignore your needs forever. It's like letting a part of you wither away and die."

Sucking in a breath, she leaned away from him. "It's a choice, not a life necessity or a compulsion. I don't have to have it."

Her naïveté was endearing.

"Would you say homosexuality was a choice?"

Taken aback, Callie's eyes widened. "Of course not. But it's not the same."

"That's where you're wrong. Denying yourself because you

think you should, or because others don't understand it, is not going to make the need go away. As long as it is not harmful, emotionally or otherwise, there is nothing wrong with wanting something different with another consenting adult."

Calypso crossed her arms over her chest. "Wow. I was under the impression that you have a problem expressing yourself, but evidently I was wrong. Did you have that speech memorized? Do you recite it to new club members?" She kept her voice low, casting worried glances at the people sitting next to them.

Her outburst didn't offend him. Clearly, the subject was making her uncomfortable, and she was getting defensive.

Brundar leaned forward, making sure no one other than Calypso heard him. For her sake. Not his. "That's not part of my job. Do I look like someone who makes people comfortable?"

Her smile was back. "No, you don't. So what is your job? Are you the bouncer? The scary dude who throws undesirables out?"

"Sometimes, when those whose job it is are not available, or when the situation demands it. I'm not an employee of the club. I'm a member turned silent partner. It was an investment, a way to help out the owner and keep the business afloat. Except, I find myself doing things I didn't sign up for."

Why was he telling her all that?

Her eyes were full of understanding. "Of course you do. I'm surprised you expected it to go differently."

That was news to him. "What makes you say that?"

Uncrossing her arms, she leaned forward. "You're the kind of guy that takes charge," she said. "You can't just let things go and wait for others to fix them. You either tell someone to do it and then verify it's done or do it yourself."

He chuckled. "You're right. I should have known I'd get

involved. Instead of buying half of Franco's business, I should've offered him a loan."

"But you didn't. Which means that subconsciously you wanted to change how he was doing things."

"You're a very smart young lady, Calypso. You figured me out."

CHAPTER 10: CALLIE

*C*allie snorted. "Right."

As if. She might have peeled away one layer out of a hundred. And the way he'd called her *young lady*, as if he was an old man and not a twenty- or thirty-something-year-old guy, was odd, but she liked it anyway.

Still, she knew her insight and his acknowledgment of it was no small achievement. Brundar wasn't the type who let people get close to him.

"It's true. I didn't realize it until you spelled it out for me."

She shrugged. "Glad I could help. Talking with others about things clarifies bothersome issues. While you're too bogged down by the minutiae, you can't see the big picture."

"Smart girl. Do you know how smart you are?"

She wasn't sure how she felt about him calling her a girl, but she liked the other part.

Well, she'd always gotten good grades, but book smart wasn't life smart, as evidenced by her ill-fated marriage. "I don't know about that. I did my share of dumb things. If I were so smart, I wouldn't be in the mess I am in now."

"Perhaps I can help. What is your minutiae, Calypso?"

A chuckle escaped her throat. "Mine is not a minutiae, it's a bigutiae. Here, I invented a new word. Does that make me smart?"

Brundar didn't laugh at her joke. Not even a tiny smile. What would it take for this guy to loosen up?

"Talk to me, Calypso."

She was tempted. Yeah, he was a stranger, but in a way that was easier. She probably wouldn't see him after tonight, and getting things off her chest might ease the vice constricting her lungs.

Taking a napkin, she wiped the table clean of a few drops of condensation. "I don't want to burden you with my problems. I'm sure you have enough of your own."

"No."

Again with the one-word responses. "No what? You need to talk in complete sentences to me. I know you can." Contrary to what she'd thought before, Brundar had proven that he had no speech impediment and no personality disorder. He was just a tight-lipped guy who was stingy with words.

"I don't have any problems."

"You see? That was a clear answer."

One corner of his lips twitched in a smile. "Yes, teacher."

Callie sighed. "I want to be."

"What's stopping you?"

"Not what, who. My husband."

"You want me to beat him up?"

Lifting her eyes, she was prepared to answer with a joke, but Brundar looked dead serious.

Was he acting?

She tilted her head, narrowing her eyes at him. "If I said yes, you would. Wouldn't you?"

"I always do as I say."

"Good to know." For some reason, his answer and the tone

he'd used evoked a few erotic scenarios that had no place in this conversation.

Brundar's nostrils flared and he shifted in his chair.

Callie sniffed but detected nothing unusual. Not surprisingly, the steak house always smelled like steaks.

"What is it? What do you smell? Is it smoke? A few days ago, there was a brushfire nearby, and the wind carried the smell of smoke for miles."

He shook his head. "Not that kind of fire. Do you want a drink?"

"Sure. Another whiskey for you? I'll go get it." She started to lift off the chair.

Brundar caught her hand and pulled her down. "You're not working now, Calypso. Let others do their job."

"They are my friends. I'd feel weird ordering drinks from them. And besides, they all know I'm married. There will be a few raised brows."

"I'll order the drinks, and you can introduce me as your cousin."

Not a bad idea. That would kill two birds with one stone. Brundar would order them drinks, and she'd stop the rumors before they started.

"Where should I say you came from?"

Brundar spread his arms. "Scotland, of course," he said with a lilt.

"God, I love your accent," she husked.

Ignoring her comment, Brundar turned around and waved Kati over.

"Hello…" Kati looked from Brundar to Callie and back.

"Kati, meet my cousin Brundar."

Kati smiled and offered her hand. "Nice to meet you, Brundar, cousin of Callie who she never told me about and should have."

Callie rolled her eyes. Kati knew she wasn't supposed to

flirt with customers. Especially not this one.

"Nice to meet you." Brundar didn't take her hand.

Some people didn't do handshakes—germophobes and the like.

Kati frowned and retracted her offered hand. "What can I get you, guys?"

"I'll have an apple ginger, and Brundar will have Chivas, no ice. Right?" Her cheeks warmed as she realized her faux pas.

He nodded.

"I apologize for ordering for you," she said after Kati had left. "I shouldn't have done it. It's a waitressing reflex."

"You knew what I wanted, so why not?"

Why not? Because if she'd done something like that to Shawn, he would have thrown an anger tantrum.

"As long as it's okay with you."

"It is. Back to my offer. It still stands."

"Thank you, but no. It won't solve my problems. I need to get a divorce, that's all."

"What's stopping you?"

Where to begin? And did she want to pour her heart out to this sexy stranger? Not really. He would think her weak. He would ask why she hadn't left Shawn a long time ago.

Brundar wouldn't understand.

Callie didn't consider herself weak for staying, she considered herself strong. Quitters ran at the first sign of trouble, and Callie was no quitter.

But she wasn't blind either.

All the effort in the world wasn't going to fix what was wrong in her marriage because nothing and no one could change another person. Shawn was who he was and she couldn't see herself enduring him for the rest of her life, or worse, having children with him.

Someone kill me now.

"Calypso?" Brundar snapped her out of her head.

"I'm sorry. I zoned out a little. I was thinking of how to answer that in a way that wouldn't portray me as the victim." She looked away. "I'm not weak, you know."

He took her hand. "I know you aren't."

The sound of truth in his words was like a benediction, his hand offering comfort and support she hadn't had in forever. Regrettably, a moment later he dropped her hand.

Fast.

Kati came back with the drinks.

"Apple ginger for Callie, and a Chivas no ice for Brundar." She put down the drinks. "Anything else I can get you?"

"No." Brundar's one-word answer was delivered in such a commanding tone that Kati dropped her flirtatious smile and beat feet back inside.

"You don't have to be so rude to people," Callie blurted.

"I'm not rude. I'm efficient."

"It's not what you think that matters, it's how your communication is perceived."

"Don't try to fix me, Calypso."

Oh shit. Now she'd made him mad. Instinctively, Callie shrank back in her chair. She saw a flash of anger in his blue eyes, but it was gone in a split second.

"I hate to see you scared like that. Does that jerk you're married to get violent with you? Does he hit you?"

She shook her head and grabbed a napkin. "No. But if I tell him I want a divorce he will."

In the moment of strained silence that followed, Brundar took the napkin out of her hands and clasped them. "Trust your instincts, Calypso. You need to leave. The sooner the better. Don't tell him your intentions. Go out the door and hide somewhere safe until the divorce is final."

"There is nowhere safe," she whispered. "Shawn knows that there are only two people I can turn to. My father and my friend Dawn. He'll find me. But that's not the worst part. If I go

56

to either of them, I'd be putting them in danger. I'm afraid of what he'd do." She looked into Brundar's pale eyes. "I don't know why I fear him so. Other than destroying our house he never hit me. And yet I expect the worst."

"As I said before, trust your instincts. You need to run. I'll help you. I'll hide you and protect you until you're free of him. Youll be safe with me."

She narrowed her eyes at him. "Why? Why would you do that for me? You don't know me." People didn't just offer help out of the goodness of their heart. There was always a hidden agenda, an ulterior motive.

Brundar closed his eyes as if she was tormenting him. "I don't know why, Calypso. But I know I'd protect you and shield you with all I have. And trust me when I say that there is no one in the world who can do a better job of it than me. That's what I do best."

"You're a bodyguard?"

"Yes, that's exactly who I am. The best there is."

From anyone else, it would have sounded like boasting, but she knew that Brundar was just stating facts as he saw them.

"I need to think about it. I need to get an appointment with a lawyer, so I know what to expect. The problem is that Shawn monitors every penny I spend and tracks my every movement." She lifted her phone from her pocket. "He has this tracked. And you know what? I don't mind because when he knows where I am at all times, he has fewer reasons for exploding. Like now. He thinks I'm still working because the signal is coming from the steak house. That's how I can sit here and talk to you without worrying."

"You'll have to leave your phone here while I take you to a friend of mine. Edna is a great attorney. She can answer all your questions. But if you want my opinion, you need to run first and do everything else later. The longer you stay, the more dangerous it is for you. Go to the bank, take all the cash you can, leave your credit cards and your phone at home and drive off. I'll meet you somewhere where you can leave your car, and I'll take you to a safe place. Edna will take care of the divorce papers. Clean exit."

No one went to so much effort to help another unless they were family, or they wanted something. But that didn't make sense. Brundar could've snapped his fingers at Kati, and she would've gone home with him. Heck, if Callie weren't still married she would've gladly accepted an invitation too.

Brundar was sexy as sin. But she was done letting her hormones lead her astray. That was what had gotten her in trouble in the first place. She'd thought Shawn was sexy too, and that didn't end well.

Not at all.

Once she got free, she should find herself a nice guy, an accountant or an engineer or a teacher. Someone mellow and agreeable with whom she could have a nice, peaceful life.

Contrary to what Brundar believed, sex wasn't all that important.

"What are you thinking, Calypso? What's going through your head?"

She looked up and gazed upon his perfect face. Sincere blue eyes the color of a clear sky were tracking her every movement, every expression. He probably knew what she was thinking just from observing her so intently.

"What do you want, Brundar? For real. Because for the life of me I can't understand why you would go to all that trouble to help me." She had the passing thought that he might be after her money, telling her to empty her bank account and take all the cash she could before meeting him. Without a phone or money, he could leave her somewhere stranded.

"I want to set you free."

"Why?"

"Because I have to."

"That's not an answer."

"That's the only answer I have. If you're asking whether I'm attracted to you, the answer is yes. You're a beautiful, smart, and kind woman. Do I expect anything in return for my help? The answer is no. Even if offered freely, I would turn you down, or at least try to. Is that a full and satisfactory answer?"

"Yes." Not really, but she wasn't about to tell him she suspected him of staging a heist.

"When is your next shift?" Brundar asked.

She found herself answering him even though she was still suspicious. "Thursday. Same time. Five in the evening until eight, an hour break, and then until midnight when the kitchen closes."

"I'll be here for your break. Have an answer ready for me."

"I can't decide so quickly."

"You can, and you will. It's not complicated. If you want to leave him, that's the only way to do it safely. Don't procrastinate, Calypso. The first rule of survival is to strike fast and strike hard." He punched his fist into his other palm. "No hesitation, and no mercy."

"No mercy," she repeated.

CHAPTER 11: RONI

*E*ntwining the fingers of his hands behind his head, Roni leaned back in his throne-like chair.

The backdoor he'd programmed was working beautifully. He'd been testing it over the past week with no alarms going off.

As long as the current security protocol was used, he had nothing to worry about—at least for a couple of years. The guys upstairs hated making changes. A new system cost millions and wreaked havoc until every last issue got debugged.

The question was what he would do once it was eventually changed, because it would be changed. The race between the hackers and the protectors made it an unavoidable necessity. Every time the hackers gained an upper hand, the protectors had to come up with new solutions, and the race began anew, keeping everyone in business.

Through the glass enclosure, Roni glanced at his handler. The guy wasn't so bad. Most of the time he was just bored. Not that Roni could blame him. Babysitting him was a job an agent got as a punishment for a major screw-up, or in Barty's case failing the physical exams.

On purpose.

Barty was tired and wanted more time at home while still earning an agent's salary, not the reduced retirement pay.

As unbelievable as he found it, Roni realized that he was going to miss Barty. He'd gotten used to the sarcastic old goon.

But no more excuses.

It was time to leave this prison that had become his home and give Andrew the green light.

Roni was going to relinquish his seat of power for an unknown future.

He was scared shitless.

Scared of getting out into the real world he'd never been equipped to handle, scared of having to interact with people other than agents, most of whom were old enough to be his parents.

Would he have to shop for groceries? Take care of his own laundry? Roni had no idea how to do all those basic things that came naturally to other people. He understood code. Real life baffled him.

Most of all, though, he was terrified of Anandur. The guy was a giant, and not the gentle type. Sure, he was friendly, even funny sometimes, but he had muscles on top of muscles and knew how to use them. There would be pain even if the guy did his best to hold back and treat Roni like a fragile little girl.

Roni didn't like pain.

So what if he was a wuss. He had no problem admitting it. Brains were worth more than brawn, especially one like his. There were plenty of goons on the planet, but only a handful of geniuses.

The only problem he had with that was Sylvia.

No woman wanted her guy to be a weakling. Even Einstein's wife had divorced him. Not necessarily for that reason, but who knew. Maybe.

With a sigh, he pushed out of his chair and walked out of the glass enclosure that was his war room. It was dojo time.

"You're ready, Barty?" Roni asked his handler.

"Yep." Barty put his feet down. "Let's go, boyo."

"Where is your karate-gi, Barty? Didn't we agree that you would join the class today? You can't participate unless you wear the uniform." Roni loved teasing the guy.

"Up yours," Barty returned the favor. "While you are sweating, I'll be watching the girls. It's the highlight of my week. Just so we're clear." Barty pointed a finger at him. "I'm counting on you to stick with this class. If you dare quit on me, I'm going to pull you there by your overlarge ears."

"My ears are not big." They weren't. He had normal ears. Didn't he? Maybe they stuck out a little... Roni couldn't help himself, touching them to make sure.

"Just kidding. Don't take everything so seriously."

"You're not funny. What happened, did you run out of jokes?" He was counting on Barty's lame jokes to distract him from thinking about what was waiting for him in the dojo.

Think about lots of sex with Sylvia.

That was his main impetus for going ahead with the crazy plan. Immortality was not Roni's top priority. Sex with Sylvia was.

Especially since she claimed his stamina would quadruple. Roni smirked. They would be going at each other like rabbits.

"What kind of bagel can fly?" Barty started as soon as he eased the car into traffic.

Roni rolled his eyes. "A plane bagel. Ha, ha."

"You heard that one before?"

"No. It's so stupid a four-year-old can guess the answer."

"Okay. How about this one. What does one plate say to the other?"

"I don't know."

"Come on, boy genius. Dinner is on me." Barty laughed at

his own stupid joke. "Get it? Dinner is on me." He demonstrated with a palm up as if Roni needed visuals to understand it.

"Not funny."

"I have a smart one for you. What do you get if you divide the circumference of a pumpkin by its diameter?"

"Pi."

"Yeah, but what kind?"

"There is only one kind of pi. It's a number."

"Wrong. You get pumpkin pie." Barty's huge belly heaved along with his snorts.

That was a little funny.

The best part about Barty's jokes was that they filled the time until they arrived at the dojo, and for a few minutes Roni had forgotten about the giant redhead with huge muscles and scary fangs.

"Hey, guys," Sylvia said. "How are you doing, Barty?" She gave him a hug and kissed his cheek, as always, and her friends lined up to do the same.

Barty was in heaven. Roni felt a pang of guilt. The dude was going to miss all the attention he was getting from the young hotties—as he liked to call them.

If he only knew...

"Roni! Over here!" Anandur called.

Oh, boy. Were his knees shaking?

"Are you ready?" Andrew asked.

Reluctantly, Roni nodded.

"Okay!" Anandur clapped his hands. "Let's do it. It's actual sparring time."

Barty tilted his head, looking at Anandur and Roni with interest. The jerk probably wanted to see Roni getting annihilated by the red giant.

Any traces of guilt for the agent went *poof*.

Roni imagined a boxing ring with the announcer going, "*In*

this corner, we have the Red Giant, and over there is the Scrawny Chicken! Which one is going to win?"

"Barty, I have a funny story for you." Sylvia plopped on a chair next to the handler. "So, yesterday…" In less than a minute, she got him enthralled in her story.

Anandur got in position and motioned for Roni to do the same. They circled each other for a few moments, with Roni bracing for the pain and Anandur waiting for God knew what.

Finally, Anandur stopped and put his hands on his hips. "I can't do it." He waved a hand at Roni. "How am I supposed to get aggressive with that?"

Andrew shook his head. "Wait until he opens his mouth. Show him what you got, Roni."

Roni flipped him the bird. If Andrew thought he was going to goad Anandur he was dead wrong.

"You'll have to do it, Andrew," Anandur said.

"I've never done it before."

Anandur chuckled. "Oh yeah? Should I give your wife a call?"

"You're such an asshole. I mean with another guy."

Anandur feigned shock, his fingers splayed over his gaping mouth. "You don't say. You don't know what you're missing." Anandur batted his eyelashes.

Roni chuckled, enjoying the show. Now, that was funny.

Andrew looked like he was about to punch Anandur, but then thought better of it. Smart man.

Waving a finger at the big guy, he said, "I've heard about you and your antics. I'm not going to get tricked into issuing a challenge to spar with you."

Anandur pointed a finger back. "That's a shame. Because you could've gotten me worked up, tough guy."

"Oh."

"Yeah, oh. You either man up and do it, or I'm calling Brundar."

Andrew looked horrified. Who was this Brundar guy that his name made the formidable Andrew cringe?

"Not Brundar. Are you nuts? The kid will shit his pants."

"He's the only one on duty right now. It's either you or him."

With a deflated sigh, Andrew hung his head. "I'll do it." He then turned to Roni. "Make me mad, kid. You don't want the alternative."

They assumed positions and started circling each other. Andrew wasn't as scary as Anandur, but he was a big guy too with at least eighty pounds over Roni's one hundred and thirty.

The easiest way to annoy the guy was to say nasty things about his wife. "How is the old ball and chain, Andrew? Still finds you attractive? I bet she is sick of waking up to the sight of your ugly puss every morning..."

Andrew was on him in a blur of movement, and before he knew it, Roni found himself face down on the mat, one of Andrew's hands pinning his arm painfully behind his back, the other on his neck, holding his head down.

If he could, Roni would have rolled over and offered his vulnerable belly, but in lieu of that he stopped struggling and closed his eyes.

Andrew hit fast like a cobra, which was a mercy because the anticipation was worse than the bite...

On second thought, no. The bite hurt and burned like a son-of-a-bitch, for about two seconds.

And then there was bliss.

CHAPTER 12: BRUNDAR

*P*arked across the street from Calypso's home, Brundar kept a solid shroud around his car. Not so much to camouflage the vehicle as the driver. She remembered him now, and seeing him there would understandably scare her.

As it was, she was rightfully suspicious of his motives. He was sincere and meant every word he'd told her, but she wasn't a mind reader or an empath who could check the veracity of his words. Suspecting an ulterior motive was natural, and proceeding with caution was smart.

Offering her his help had seemed so natural, the right thing to do, but her questions made him realize that he might have not acted out of pure altruism. He wasn't in the habit of helping random people.

What was in it for him?

Brundar wasn't sure. Emotional entanglement wasn't something he was familiar with. As was the case for all his clansmen, his interactions with women were purely sexual. Before he'd found a solution to his particular needs in the clubs, he'd never had the same one twice, and more often than not he'd paid for the services. For a price, most hookers agreed to get tied up and blindfolded, which wasn't the case with the vast majority of nonprofessionals. Relinquishing control to a stranger was stupid, and most women had more sense than that.

The clubs, at least the good ones, provided a safe environment. What Brundar disliked about them were the labels attached to the different sexual roles people played. As an immortal male, dominance came naturally to him, but it didn't define him. It wasn't who he was.

It just happened that his specific needs fit the role.

He didn't need his partner's obedience, and he didn't need her to be subservient to him. All he needed was to tie her up so she couldn't touch him and blindfold her so she wouldn't see his glowing eyes and protruding fangs.

But contrary to popular belief, it wasn't all about his needs.

The women he partnered with in the club had needs of their own, and it was his responsibility to meet them. Brundar was fine with delivering pain when needed, but it didn't turn him on. Or off.

What did it for him was the immense pleasure his partners derived from it, and the heights they reached with his help. According to some, subspace was better than any drug-induced trip, and a lot healthier.

That state was unattainable for the vanilla crowd or those holding the flogger or the paddle. The rewards were only for those on the receiving end. The exchange of power was well worth it.

For him, though, there was another fringe benefit that was even more important than the satisfaction he derived from pleasuring women into soaring up into subspace. When tied up and blindfolded, soaring on a cloud of post-orgasmic euphoria, his partner was oblivious to his bite, which he usually delivered to her inner thigh. Later, when she came down, there was no sign of it. She either didn't remember it at all or thought that the small pain was part of the scene.

No thralling required.

A big advantage since most of the women he partnered with were regulars. Still, he tried to keep the frequency to a minimum. Brain damage from thralling wasn't the only risk. Emotional entanglement was an even greater one. The intensity of the acts, the highs and the lows, played tricks on the participants' minds. As cold and as detached as he was, Brundar wasn't made from stone.

The most he'd scened with the same partner was once a month. For their sake and his. In case his stoic attitude wasn't enough of a deterrent, playing with a variety of partners sent a clear message that he wasn't interested in a relationship.

It wasn't that he didn't care; on the contrary, he was doing his best to protect their feelings. His partners trusted him to see to their pleasure and their well-being, and he was very serious about ensuring both. But that was the extent of his obligations. Nothing more.

With Calypso, the emotional entanglement was already there, at least on his part. Not to mention that she was a green-as-grass newbie who needed a slow and gentle introduction that should be spread over several consecutive sessions with someone who knew what the fuck he was doing. She had no idea what she liked or didn't like, what scared her and what excited her. The only way to find out was to experiment. But only with someone who was patient and completely focused on her and her experience.

It was an intimate and emotionally intense journey, necessitating a prolonged relationship. Trust, which was a crucial component, wasn't built in a day, or a week. Under these circumstances, preventing a bond from forming was difficult for the initiator as well as the initiated.

He could do none of that. Even if a relationship between an

immortal and a human was possible, Brundar didn't have what it took.

The problem was, he couldn't conceive of anyone else introducing Calypso to that unique brand of pleasure either.

It would drive him insane.

He had to distance himself from her. After her divorce was final and she was free, he would sever contact with her and let her make the journey of discovery on her own. Not in his club, though. He'd provide her with a list of others that were just as good—small, tame, and with long-term members who'd been properly vetted.

"What's that?" Brundar heard Shawn asking.

Up until that moment, the only sounds coming from Calypso's house belonged to the football game Shawn was watching, and the intermittent bursts of commercials.

"Oh, it's nothing. I'm filling in applications for scholarships. Who knows? Maybe I'll get lucky and collect enough to cover the tuition? I heard that it's good practice to apply to as many as I can. A few small scholarships can add up. I probably won't get anything, but I thought it was worth a try."

Brundar approved. She was pretending a dismissive attitude toward her wish to attend the university, which should make the scumbag happy.

Shawn snorted. "You're wasting your time. No one is going to give you money. I don't know why you even bother. College education is worthless these days. I'm doing perfectly fine without it."

Aha. That was the crux of it. Shawn didn't want his "little wife" gaining a college degree because he didn't have one.

Asshole. Just for that Brundar should slit his throat. Hell, slicing his head clean off would be even more satisfying.

Why in damnation had Calypso married someone like that?

She seemed like a sensible woman, insightful, a good judge of character. Tomorrow he would ask her what prompted her to say yes when she should've said hell no and run as fast and as far as she could.

Had she ever loved him?

Had Shawn charmed her into believing that he was worthy of her love?

Her youth and innocence must've blinded her.

How old was she then?

Eighteen?

Nineteen?

Truth be told, at that age Brundar was already a hardened warrior, but then his innocence and naïveté had been shattered years before. He was only twelve when he'd learned his lesson the hard way. Sometimes evil was so well masked by a charming face that even the most guarded and suspicious couldn't detect it until it was too late.

To this day, the betrayal hurt more than the violation that had followed.

Closing his eyes, Brundar brought up the memory that had been forever playing on a loop in his head. It was what had kept him training when every muscle burned with fatigue and he could barely move his legs. When anyone else would have collapsed from exhaustion, the anger had given him the extra fuel needed to push himself harder.

That memory had helped shape him into the lethal weapon he was.

He had to become invincible.

Fates, he'd been such a soft boy. A gentle soul that wouldn't have harmed a butterfly. No wonder the human village boys had called him a girl.

His looks hadn't helped either.

He was too pretty for a boy, they'd said. He should've been born a girl, they'd teased. He was a mistake. A freak.

Lachlann had been the only one who befriended him, probably because he'd been as much of an outcast as Brundar, though for different reasons that Brundar had been too young to understand at the time.

His mother had told him to stay away from the human boys. She'd told him they were up to no good. But like every other teenager throughout history, Brundar hadn't listened.

As the only boy in their small community of immortals, he was lonely. Besides, at the time he was still a human. At twelve, he'd had an entire year ahead of him before he could transition.

Anandur was a grown man, a warrior, who'd considered Brundar a nuisance—a kid too scrawny and weak to bother even with sword practice.

"You should think of becoming a scholar," Anandur said. *"You don't have the heart of a warrior."*

Brundar chuckled. He'd proven his brother wrong and then some. Not only was he a warrior, he was the best. And as for his heart? It beat steady in his chest during the most vicious of fights.

Calm, cold, calculated, and lethal.

But he hadn't been born this way. He'd been made. A living proof that even the lowliest of beginnings can produce a champion.

There was a price to pay, but Brundar hadn't minded giving up his so-called humanity. It was a good thing. He had done so gladly. Humans were traitorous, deceitful, and cruel.

Not all of them, but enough.

"Let's go fishing," Lachlann offered.

Brundar would've loved nothing better than to join his best friend at the lake. "I cannae. My mam forbids it."

"Do ye always do what your mam tells ye?"

"I dinnae." Brundar puffed out his chest. "Wait for me by the lake," he told Lachlann. "I'm going to sneak out."

He'd lied. Brundar had usually listened to his mother, and

71

to Anandur. But to admit it would've made him look even more of a wuss than everyone had accused him of being.

He'd waited until his mother went out, grabbed his fishing pole, and sprinted for the lake.

Sitting side by side on a big rock protruding from the shallow water, Lachlann and Brundar waited patiently for a fish to get hooked like they had done many times before.

Lachlann had moved a little closer, draping his arm over Brundar's slim shoulders.

"You know you are my best friend? Right?"

"I know. And you are mine."

"You have such pretty hair." Lachlann grabbed a fistful of Brundar's chin-length hair and brought it to his nose. "You smell nice too."

Brundar shrugged. "I wash myself."

"I know. I saw you."

"So?" That summer, they had swum naked in the lake almost every day. All the boys were doing it with nothing on.

"Nothing." Lachlann dropped Brundar's hair.

He should've seen the signs, but he hadn't known about things like that yet. Brundar had had a good idea about what went on between a man and a woman. Living with animals, most everyone had those days, but not that the same could happen between two men.

CHAPTER 13: CALLIE

*J*ust as he'd promised, Brundar walked into Aussie exactly at eight, turning everyone's heads, men and women alike.

It wasn't every day that a gorgeous man with waist-long, pale-blond hair walked into the restaurant. He looked more like a movie star or a rocker than a bodyguard. But that was only upon casual observation. Those who dared to look at him for a little longer noticed his hard expression and cold as ice gaze, quickly averting their eyes.

There was a deadly aura around him that should've terrified her, but instead it made her feel safer. Brundar was putting all that lethal power at Callie's disposal. He was going to hold her within the bounds of that aura, where no one and nothing could hurt her.

There was no safer place for her than at his side. Or behind his back. Whatever spot worked.

The question was what price he'd demand for his protection services. Frankly, she would be more than happy to pay up. Whatever he wanted was his.

In fact, she was hoping he would make the demand and was afraid he wouldn't.

"Are you ready?" Brundar asked, not bothering with a hello.

Efficient, not rude, Callie reminded herself.

She'd already transferred the care of her customers to another waiter and was ready to go on her break.

"Hi, and yes, I'm ready."

He nodded.

"Do you want to sit out on the patio again?"

He nodded again.

Today Brundar was communicating with even less than the monosyllables from the day before yesterday. Was it a sign of stress? Was he more talkative when relaxed?

Callie hoped she would get to know him well enough to figure that out.

"Come on." She threaded her arm through his.

For a moment, he looked surprised, glancing at her hand on his arm, but then pulled her a little closer so their sides touched, but not as close as a lover would.

Out on the patio, she found them a table in a semi-secluded corner, signaling Suzan, whose shift had just started, that she was claiming it.

With a wink, Suzan gave her the thumbs up.

Her astute coworkers weren't buying the cousin from Scotland story.

"Are you hungry?" she asked Brundar.

"Always."

Callie waved her friend over. "My cousin would like to order dinner."

Suzan pulled out her best smile for him. "What would you like?"

"Your largest steak, medium well, mash potatoes, and a Chivas."

"Excellent choices, sir. And for you, Callie?"

"A mojito, but tell Tony to make it light. I still have a shift to finish."

"Anything to eat?"

"No, thank you."

"Perfect. I'll get your drinks."

"Have you decided?" Brundar asked the moment Suzan was out of earshot.

The guy didn't beat around the bush and neither would she. He'd probably get annoyed if she did. "Yes. I'm going to take you up on your offer."

His stoic mask slipped for a moment, showing relief. "Good."

"I have a few concerns, though, that I would like to run by you."

"Naturally."

"My father and my best friend. How do I ensure their safety? The first place Shawn will look for me is at my father's and then at Dawn's. What if he threatens them? Or worse, harms them?"

"It's a valid concern. Where do they reside?"

"My father is in South Carolina, and Dawn in Massachusetts."

"Good. It means that Shawn would have to buy a plane ticket to get to either of them. I have a friend who can put an alert on him."

Brundar sure had useful friends, but it wasn't surprising given what he did for a living. He probably had the whole protection thing figured out.

"Just out of curiosity, how is your friend going to do that? Don't you have to work for the government?"

A smile tugged at the corner of Brundar's lips, which in his case meant that he was very amused. "Who said my friend is not working for the government?" He leaned closer and whispered, "He'll flag your soon to be ex-husband as a suspected terrorist."

Callie chuckled. "I love it. It's perfect."

Suzan arrived with their drinks and a bread basket. "I'll have your dinner ready in a few minutes." She winked. "I put a rush on it."

"You're the best, Suzan."

"I know." She sauntered over to the next table. "What can I get you, folks?"

"Any other concerns?" Brundar asked.

She sighed. "Where do I start?"

"The order doesn't matter."

Sheesh, the guy was so literal. "Where do I stay? What about my car? What if Shawn goes to the police and files a missing persons report? Where will I work? How will I get to work if I don't have a car? And if I find work in another restaurant, will he be able to find me there?"

"I'll find you a place to stay."

"Where?"

"Leave it to me. I know a lot of people. I'll ask around if anyone needs a house sitter."

"What if no one does?"

"Then I'll give you a room at the club."

The kinky portion?

Not something she was comfortable with, but as the saying went—beggars can't be choosers.

"I don't want to dump all of my problems on you, but I really don't know what else I'm going to do. It would've been so much simpler if I didn't need to hide. But I know I do. I'm going to take half of what's in our savings account, but it's not much. I need to work."

"You can work at the nightclub. Serve drinks. I'll have Franco pay you cash. The car is not a problem either, the same person who needs a house sitter will probably have a car idling in the garage. You can borrow it until the divorce is final."

If it all sounded too good to be true, it probably was.

But what choice did she have?

It was either accept the help or stay with Shawn and be miserable and scared for the rest of her life.

The deciding factor was that she felt safer with this stranger than with her husband.

Brundar was dangerous, even lethal, but not to her and not to any other decent person. His enemies, however, or any who earned his wrath should be terrified.

The problem was that she was basing it all on a gut feeling, and it was difficult to read a man who displayed no emotions. Brundar's usual expression was an impassive mask, and when he spoke, it was in a flat tone with no inflection. In a movie, he could've played the part of a robot. She was betting her safety on the little glimpses of humanity she'd caught, and a sixth sense that was telling her Brundar wasn't evil.

Shawn, on the other hand, reeked of it, metaphorically speaking. Not from the very start, though. When she'd first met him, he was just a bully who pushed and manipulated to get his way.

He'd changed. Was he on something? Was he doing drugs?

She knew for a fact that on occasion he'd lied about going to work and had gone someplace else. He wasn't making as much in commissions as he used to either. Lately, his pay had dwindled down.

Was that the reason for his nasty moods? Men associated their self-worth with success at work. Maybe he was feeling insecure and taking it out on her?

Except, the decline in earnings had started about the time she'd given up, and Callie no longer cared. Besides, confronting him about it would have resulted in another temper tantrum.

"Calypso? Are you with me?"

She shook her head. "Yes, I'm sorry. Where were we?"

"The last item on your list of concerns. Shawn reporting

you missing. You call your father and your friend and tell them you left and that you fear for your life. He'll call them, looking for you. They'll tell him that you left."

And incur his wrath.

But Brundar had this covered too. They would have plenty of advance warning if Shawn made travel plans.

Callie let out a breath. "Okay."

"When?"

"A week from now. Will you meet me here?"

"What time?"

"Five. When my shift is supposed to start. I'll stop by the bank on my way and take out half the money. I'll leave my phone here. Shawn will think I'm at work. It will give me a few hours' head start."

"Why take only half? You're leaving everything else behind. Shouldn't you take more?"

Callie shook her head. "If I could afford to, I would have left that behind as well. The fewer reasons he has to come after me the better. I'm not going to ask for anything in the divorce settlement either. I just want my freedom."

CHAPTER 14: BRUNDAR

On his way back to the keep, Brundar went over the list of things he needed to prepare for Calypso by next Thursday.

First, he needed to rent her an apartment or a house, furnished if possible and if not, do it post haste, and plant fake personal items to make it look as if it belonged to someone who was coming back, giving it a lived in look.

As it was, she had a hard time accepting his help. He needed to keep up the façade of a Good Samaritan who wanted nothing in return.

A lie, because he wanted her like he'd never wanted a woman before, but that was beside the point. He wasn't going to act on it. Not even if he were human or she an immortal. He wasn't what she needed and would never be.

The thing was, it would be impossible to convince Calypso of that if she ever found out that he'd lied to her about the friend who needed a house sitter, and rented an apartment for her instead.

The car was a problem. He could buy her one, but his name

would appear on the registration. Unless he asked Kian for another set of fake papers, or Anandur to buy it for him.

Brundar didn't want his brother or anyone else from the clan involved.

Another possible solution was to find her a place to live within walking distance of the club so she wouldn't need a car.

Or maybe he could give Franco the money and ask him to buy it as part of her compensation package.

Yeah, like that wouldn't start a thousand questions.

As it was, they didn't need another waitress in the nightclub, and he was not letting Calypso anywhere near the basement level, even if she weren't way under the new age limit they insisted on.

What he'd said about giving her a room in the club was another lie. If by next week he still didn't have a place for her, he'd put her in a hotel.

It wasn't that Brundar felt the club was inappropriate for Calypso; she could probably benefit from hanging around there. Franco didn't allow public scenes, and everything happened in private rooms. The public area was a place to hang out and talk with others, with the benefit of being able to discuss openly experiences, preferences, and lifestyles. Different classes were held almost nightly.

Members could learn bondage techniques, and get introduced to the latest toys and their use. Classes were held on everything from proper etiquette and safety measures all the way to lectures on the psychology and physiology involved. Most were taught either by Franco or other experienced club members, but on occasion Franco brought in guest speakers.

Brundar himself had learned a thing or two over the four years he'd been a member.

The real reason he didn't want Calypso there was that she wasn't ready. It would be a long time before she felt safe enough to trust a man again. Her bad experience with Shawn had to fade first.

Except, it might not.

Time didn't do a thing for Brundar. He still didn't trust anyone aside from Anandur, and he didn't trust his brother with everything either.

Brundar's experience, however, had been much more traumatic, which might explain why he needed complete control in sexual situations. Hell, who was he kidding? There was no situation he could think of where he could let go, but it was most apparent with sex.

Brundar liked his partners tied up, blindfolded, and facing away from him.

Everything else was negotiable. But not that.

If a woman refused his demands, he walked out.

Needs and wants didn't always align, and that was fine. He respected the hell out of those who were clear on what they wanted and didn't want and weren't afraid of saying no.

It still left many who liked what he had to give, as evidenced by his popularity. Brundar never had a shortage of willing partners or repeat requests. Within the limitations of what he would and wouldn't do, he left his partners fully satisfied and craving the next time.

He, on the other hand, was always left with a sense that something was missing. Brundar suspected the culprit was his muted ability to feel. Even casual sex required some sort of connection, which he was incapable of.

He was hollow, empty, untouchable, and it went deeper than the physical level.

Brundar lifted the bundle of five fish strung together with a length of twine. "'Tis enough," he said. "I should be getting back before my mam notices I'm gone."

Lachlann cast him a sidelong glance, a strangely unsettling expression making him look older than his thirteen years. He was smiling, but it was not a friendly smile. "Not yet. A few more."

The small hairs on the back of Brundar's neck prickled. Something was not right about Lachlann. His friend was not himself today. He seemed twitchy.

"I cannae. I need to go." Brundar rose to his feet, balancing on the smooth rock by gripping it with his toes. "You keep the fish." He dropped the bundle next to Lachlann.

His friend looked up at the sky, his eyes following the sun's position. "Aye, you are right. 'Tis time to go." He grabbed the fish in one hand and his pole in the other, and stuffed the jar of bait into his pocket.

The uneasy feeling didn't abate as they traipsed through the forest heading toward the safety of Brundar's home. Instead, it intensified. Lachlann's eyes kept darting left and right as if he was afraid of a bear or a wild boar coming at them.

Lachlann hadn't been expecting wild animals. He'd been expecting something much worse.

Several older boys emerged from behind the trees, the evil smiles on their faces portending trouble.

Brundar's instincts kicked in. "Run, Lachlann!" he shouted at his friend as he broke into a sprint. If he made it back home to Anandur and his two uncles, he would be safe.

"Run, little girl, run as fast as ye can, but we are gonna catch ye!"

Brundar ran faster, ignoring the tree branches slapping at him and tearing into his skin, but the boys were gaining on him. He could hear them getting closer. His only hope was that Lachlann had gone the other way.

Lachlann was a fast runner. Mayhap he would bring help...

But the first hand grabbing at him and shoving him face down onto the ground, the heavy body landing on top of him, and the strong hands pinning his arms behind his back, shattered that hope.

Brundar froze in shock as a familiar voice whispered in his ear, "I know you want it, bonnie lass. Ye've been asking for it for a very long time and I'm gonna give it to ye real good."

"Lachlann? What are ye doing?"

Brundar started thrashing anew, trying to buck off the body on top of him. Lachlann was only a year older. He could take him...

"Grab his hands!" Lachlann called out.

Someone did.

Brundar fought, but there were too many of them.

He was helpless.

At first, Brundar had thought they were going to kill him, or beat him up, but he couldn't understand why. He hadn't done anything to any of them.

His first inkling of what was coming had been Lachlann pulling Brundar's pants down.

"Dinnae do it, Lachlann, I am yer friend, please!" He wasn't above begging, even though he knew it wouldn't help.

"My bitch, ye mean. And 'tis time ye put out."

Brundar felt something thick press against his rear hole.

"Nae!!!" he screamed as his body got violated, the pain unimaginable. He hadn't known such pain existed.

And then it had gotten worse.

*E*very muscle in her body aching, her light exercise shirt soaked through with sweat, Tessa felt amazing.

"Okay, girls!" Karen clapped her hands. "Listen up! Your homework is lifting weights. You are all pitifully weak."

Several of the women dared to snort and giggle.

"Pitiful, I tell you!" Karen repeated with more oomph. "Here is a printed page with all the exercises I want you to do between classes, and I don't want to hear any excuses like, 'I didn't know how.'" She imitated a valley-girl whiny tone. "It has pictures." She lifted the flyer and tapped it with a finger, then stared each of them down. "Understood?"

"Yes, Karen," they all replied in unison.

Tessa rolled her eyes. Karen had told them all about her military background, but it would've been obvious even if she hadn't.

The 'Yes, Karen' was a lot like 'Yes, commander,', and Karen insisted they say it after each instruction. Serving three years in the Israeli army as a fitness trainer of an elite commando unit, she'd developed the attitude of a drill sergeant.

She treated the women in her Krav Maga class as if they

were warriors and not a bunch of out-of-shape suburbanites. Karen was dead serious about teaching them real self-defense, the kind that might actually work against rapists and other abusers. It wasn't fancy, it wasn't pretty, and it wasn't sportsmanlike.

The merciless fighting style went against every feminine and compassionate instinct they had.

It was crude but effective.

A set of skills that could save lives.

"Eva was smart to wiggle out of it." Sharon wiped her face with a towel. "The pregnancy is just an excuse. Pregnant women can exercise."

Tessa knew the real reason for Eva's refusal to join the class was her unnatural strength, but she couldn't share it with Sharon. The same way she couldn't share Eva and Bhathian's romantic love story, or that it was not going to be their first baby, and that their older daughter was already a mother herself. It was hard to be the keeper of secrets. Especially when she had to keep things from people she cared about.

Hopefully, Nick and Sharon would be paired with nice immortal partners soon, and be told about their potential dormancy.

"How are you doing, girls?" Karen slapped Tessa's back.

"Great. Everything hurts, but in a good way."

Karen beamed with satisfaction. "You'll see. By the time I'm done with you, you'll be able to take down guys twice your size. Krav Maga teaches real fighting skills. It's not an elegant dance like martial arts, but it gets the job done."

"That's why I'm here. I want to kick ass."

Karen smiled like a proud mother. "Good for you." She clapped Tessa's shoulder, then repeated, "Good for you."

She did it a lot, repeating words and whole phrases in her guttural and harsh accent, often more than twice.

"How about you, Sharon?"

"Oy vey." Sharon groaned.

Karen laughed, slapping Sharon's back much harder than she had Tessa's. "Hang in there. My mission is to turn women into fighters, so they are victims no more. Understand?" She looked into Sharon's eyes.

"I do, I really do." Sharon was too smart to get into an argument with Karen.

Their neighbor didn't hold back punches—the verbal kind. Tessa suspected the woman could knock any of them unconscious with one jab.

Karen nodded. "It's not easy, and not only because women are not as strong as men. Women are softhearted. They don't want to hurt anyone. And what do they get for it? They get hurt instead. So be strong, be merciless, and protect yourself. Understand?"

"Yes, Karen." They both answered as one.

"As you were, ladies." Karen turned on her heel and walked up to another group.

"Sheesh, bossy woman," Sharon whispered in Tessa's ear.

"I like her. Heck, I want to be her. Imagine going through life with that much confidence and attitude. I bet no one ever dreams of messing with Karen."

Sharon pulled her shoes out of the cubby and slipped them on. "Not me. I don't want to look like her. She has more muscles than most of the guys I date, which is disturbing. Besides, imagine the endless hours of training that went into that body. Karen is a natural athlete. Neither one of us is."

"I know. And that's a shame." Tessa would not have minded a strong body like Karen's, even if it made her look more masculine. The confidence and absence of fear would've more than compensated for a little loss of femininity.

As she put on her shoes and followed Sharon out of the studio, Tessa filled her lungs with the cool evening air. It was dark outside, but for once she didn't feel a tightness in her chest when stepping into a darkened street. "You know what's weird?"

"What?" Sharon clicked the locks open.

"It's only my second class, and I already feel different. Not as fearful." She chuckled. "I'm no longer a shaking Chihuahua. I graduated to a fluffy poodle."

"Woof, woof. Congrats." Sharon turned the engine on.

"Thank you."

"Are you going to Jackson's tonight?"

"Yeah, why?"

Sharon shrugged. "It's late, that's all. Why don't you invite him over to our place? He can spend the night. You guys can sleep together, as in actual sleep. Should be nice."

"Yeah, much better than trying to squeeze onto Jackson's couch. But my room is sandwiched between yours and Nick's, and the walls are thin." Tessa felt her cheeks get warm.

"That's how you wanted it."

"I know. But things are different now. I'm not as scared anymore. Especially with Bhathian in the house."

Sharon chuckled. "How much of a badass you think he really is? All those incredible muscles could be just for show."

"Trust me, they are not for show."

"Well, he does work for some law enforcement agency, right?"

"Yes."

Sharon huffed out a breath. "Fine. I know you're all keeping secrets from me, and I'm kind of sick of it. But whatever."

Guilt churning in her gut, Tessa didn't respond.

"Can you at least tell me what the deal with you and Jackson is? Do you love him? Does he love you back?"

A week ago she would have been afraid to admit it, but after two of Karen's classes in which woman power was infused in every move and every sentence, Tessa felt a little bit like a badass herself.

"Yes and yes."

"How about, you know…" Sharon waggled her brows.

Tessa blushed and shook her head.

Sharon cast her a sidelong glance. "What are you waiting for?"

What indeed?

Sharon didn't know the whole story. She might have suspected what Tessa had been through but not the extent of it. Nevertheless, she was right.

Tessa forced a smile and fibbed a little. "I'm waiting for the perfect moment."

"If you ask me, the Nike commercial got it right: just do it." She winked at Tessa. "Just do it, girl. Just do it," she repeated, parroting Karen's harsh accent.

Good advice.

Tessa pulled out her phone and texted Jackson. *How about you come over to my place and we spend the night together in my comfortable BIG BED.*

A moment later he texted back. No words, just three emoticons: a thumbs up, a heart, and a smiling face.

CHAPTER 16: JACKSON

*J*ackson put down the phone, wondering what had prompted Tessa's invitation. They had talked about him coming over to her place before but had decided against it.

His place offered more privacy. But on the other hand, Tessa had a larger room and, what was more important, a larger bed. Up until now, the only night she'd stayed over at his place had been that one time she'd fallen asleep on his couch. He'd ended up sleeping on the floor because there was no way they could both squeeze in there. Tessa was tiny and didn't take up much space, but he did.

Jackson had thought about buying a mattress to replace the couch, but that was before the option of having a brand new house at the new development had come up. There was no point in buying new furniture when the houses came furnished with much better things than he could afford.

Besides, he didn't want to put pressure on Tessa, and a new bed might have done just that.

Should he bring a change of clothes and a toothbrush?

It wasn't as if he was moving in.

In the end, he packed a bag, deciding that he was going to leave it in the car. In the morning, while everyone was still asleep, he would retrieve the bag, take a shower, put on a fresh change of clothes, and put it back in his trunk before anyone woke up. Or, he would just drive back to his place and shower there. But then he would miss a chance to have breakfast with Tessa.

As he turned into her street, Jackson saw Tessa sitting outside on the steps. He parked and got out.

"What are you doing out here?" Sitting next to her, he wrapped his arm around her. "Did you change your mind?"

"Not at all. But I didn't want you to knock or ring the bell. Sharon and Nick are out, and Eva and Bhathian are in their room. You can sneak in with no one any the wiser."

Jackson frowned. "Why do I need to sneak in? Are you embarrassed about me staying over?"

She shook her head. "No. But I don't want to answer questions or endure the smirking looks. I'm sure you don't either."

Jackson shrugged. "I don't mind. They are going to know eventually. Unless you want me to sneak out in the early hours of the morning." He cocked a brow.

"I don't. When they see you at breakfast, it's going to be like stating a fact. You slept over. End of story. Somehow it's different."

"I'll probably be gone by the time anyone wakes up. I need to be at the coffee shop before seven."

"I'll just tell them that you stayed the night after the fact."

"Eva and Bhathian would know. Did you forget? Immortal hearing."

"It's not as if I want to hide it. I just want to avoid the looks."

"In that case, I'll go get my overnight bag from the car. I was planning on sneaking out in the morning for it."

Tessa snuggled closer. "You see? We were both thinking along the same lines. Way to make me feel guilty for nothing."

He kissed the top of her head. "I'm sorry. I'm looking forward to spending the night with you. Even if it's just to hold you close."

Tessa lifted her head with the sexiest come hither smile he'd ever seen on her. "I have plans for much more than cuddling."

Jackson was hard in an instant. "Oh, yeah? What plans?"

She humphed. "I'm not going to tell you. What's the fun in that?"

Was she talking about going all the way?

Damn, curiosity was eating at him. "Let me get my bag."

Tessa waited as he retrieved it from his car, holding the door open while he climbed the three steps.

"Let's keep it down," she whispered, taking his hand and pulling him behind her up the stairs.

With a slight hitch in her breath, she opened the door to her room and motioned for him to go ahead.

Oh, wow. Tessa had been busy.

Soft music was playing, and several lit candles cast their gentle glow on the room. On one nightstand, a bottle of wine and two glasses sat on a tray, and on the other a platter of cut fruit.

She'd gone all out preparing for tonight.

"Come here." He dropped his bag on the floor and pulled her into his arms, lifting her up for a kiss. He did it a lot. With their height difference and how little Tessa weighed, it was more comfortable for both of them. Besides, he liked to kiss her while holding her up.

Especially since it seemed to turn her on. But this was the first time she had lifted her legs and wrapped them around his torso, returning his kiss with abandon.

Sexy as hell.

Carrying her to the bed, he sat down with her still wrapped around him. Except, now that he didn't need to hold her up, his hands were free to explore. Reaching under her loose T-shirt,

Jackson cupped her perky little breasts over her flimsy bra and kissed her again.

Tessa moaned into his mouth, her hips moving restlessly and rubbing against his groin. A moment later she grabbed the bottom of her T-shirt, pulled it over her head, and tossed it to the floor.

Jackson buried his nose in the valley between her breasts, inhaling her sweet feminine aroma mingled with the strong scent of her arousal.

Her small hands cupping his cheeks, Tessa lifted his head and kissed him again, her tongue sliding inside his mouth.

Jackson's eyes felt like rolling back in his head. Never before had Tessa been so assertive, so demanding, and it was hot as hell. But was she pushing too hard? Going too fast?

"Slow down, kitten. There is no rush," he murmured into her mouth.

"Says who?"

With her lips red and swollen from their kisses, and her eyes glazed with desire, she'd never looked more ready. And yet, Jackson hesitated. He'd read her wrong before.

It was so easy to get swept away in her desire and enthusiasm, but he knew better now. Tessa's limits were in flux, and if they weren't careful, she'd overreach only to get snapped back to the starting point.

"Says I." He took her shoulders and steadied her. "I love your passion, and I would like nothing more than to get you naked and under me, but I'd rather take it slow and steady, so you can have all the time you need to process every little step and decide if you're ready for the next one."

With a sigh, she leaned her forehead on his. "You're right. But I feel stronger now, and I want to get a little further. I want you to see all of me. Touch all of me. And I want to do the same to you. Can we do that?"

"Of course, baby, but slowly."

She shook her head. "I don't want slow."

"What if I show you how amazing slow can be?"

Lifting her head, she nodded. "Show me."

The yearning and hope in her eyes as she said that made Jackson anxious. He wanted to give her every pleasure imaginable, but he'd just set the bar up high. What if she expected more than he could deliver? What if he disappointed her?

Closing his eyes, he shook the momentary insecurity off. He wasn't an inexperienced virgin. He knew what he was doing and had a well-earned reputation as an extraordinary lover. Quite an achievement for a guy his age. But then it always felt as if he was born to provide pleasure. The knowledge was almost instinctive.

With deft fingers, Jackson unclasped Tessa's bra and slid the straps down her arms, removing the last barrier between him and her bare breasts. His fangs elongated at the sight of her sweet little nipples, pebbled with need and aching for his touch.

Slowly, he extended his tongue and licked around one, then the other, then went back to the first one and sucked it carefully into his mouth, making sure not to nick it with his fangs.

On a moan, Tessa arched her back, stretched her arms behind her and put her hands on his knees to brace herself. There was nothing timid or unsure about the blatant invitation, and it made Jackson's heart swell with gratitude.

His Tessa was healing.

With a hand between her shoulder blades, he held her to him firmly as he licked and sucked until she was squirming in his lap, her little mewls getting louder and more demanding.

His kitten needed more.

With his hands still on her back, he lifted her off his lap and laid her on the bed. "Ready to take these off?" He tugged on her leggings.

"Yes." No hesitation.

He hooked his thumbs in the elastic band and pulled down. Pulling off her panties and leggings slowly, one inch at a time, Jackson gave her every opportunity to stop him the moment she felt uncomfortable.

As Tessa lifted her butt off the bed, making it easier for him to continue, Jackson pulled a little faster, hungry for his first glimpse of her fully naked.

His breath caught.

She was completely bare.

Tessa hadn't been the last time he'd touched her under her panties.

"Do you like it?" she asked.

"I fucking love it. When did you do it?"

"Today. I wanted to look pretty for you."

He caressed her moist bare folds with the tip of his finger. "So smooth. Did you wax?" The thought made him cringe. She shook her head. "It was on the spur of a moment, so it's only a close shave. Next time I'll wax."

"Don't. I heard it hurts like hell." Just thinking about someone pulling on her soft and delicate tissues made him wince.

"But you like it, don't you?"

"I do, but not if it causes you pain." He smoothed the tips of two fingers down her center. "If you allow me, I'll gladly shave you here anytime you want." As far as he knew, immortal females had no body hair. But he didn't know if a grown Dormant lost it after her transition. He wasn't going to ask Syssi or Nathalie such an intimate question. As former humans, they might still hold onto human sensibilities. Besides, their mates would not be happy about him sticking his nose where it didn't belong. But he could ask Bridget.

Tessa moaned, her eyelids fluttering shut as an outpour of moisture coated his exploring fingertips. The idea excited her.

"I'd like that," she husked.

CHAPTER 17: TESSA

*T*essa would've never expected Jackson's offer to give her such a delicious thrill. As someone with major intimacy issues, the idea of being exposed and vulnerable to him while he glided a razor blade over the most sensitive place on her body should have terrified her, but it didn't.

It was the sexiest thing ever.

She would be embarrassed, no doubt about it. Nevertheless, when it was time for the next shave, she would let Jackson do it. The ultimate gesture of trust would be the perfect gift for his patience and selflessness.

Hopefully, she wouldn't freak out. In her mind and in her heart she was more than ready, but her subconscious, which still bore the scars of her past, might interfere.

The bed dipped as Jackson climbed on and stretched on his side next to her.

For a moment, his eyes roamed her body, the hunger in them making her feel beautiful, desired. Under his gaze, Tessa didn't feel too small, or too skinny. She didn't feel like a scared little girl. Jackson's burning desire brought out the woman in her.

The one she was born to be—confident and strong.

"I'll never get my fill of looking at you," he said, his fingertips tracing the line from her shoulder down to her arm.

As he reached the inside of her elbow, the sensation part ticklish, part arousing, she shivered in anticipation. Tessa wished for his knuckles to brush against the side of her breast, and then for his warm palms to cover her wet, hard nipples. But he'd done none of that, leaving her aching with need.

Was it deliberate?

A way to ramp up her desire by depriving her of touch?

She arched her back a little, hoping he'd get the message.

Jackson chuckled. "Not very patient, are you?" He dipped his head and took the nipple closest to him between his lips, his fingers closing around the other.

Fire shot from the twin points of pleasure straight to the juncture of her thighs, her butt lifting involuntarily off the bed.

His breathing got heavier, and after a moment his hand abandoned her breast to scorch an excruciatingly slow path down her belly, skimming her hip and sliding around to her inner thigh.

God, would he touch her there already?

As his hand moved up in what seemed like increments of a fraction of an inch, her breathing got more and more ragged.

Jackson hadn't been kidding about going slow, or how good it would feel.

A most exquisite torture.

Tessa felt needy and achy, but there was something to be said for savoring every little touch, every sensation, for being acutely aware of the coil inside her tightening with growing want. The buildup of anticipation.

Instinctively, she knew that the slower he made the climb up to the steep edge of the cliff, the higher and longer she would soar when she leaped off.

When his fingertips finally reached her wet folds, Tessa's

hips jerked up and her eyes popped open, straight into the twin pools of light Jackson's emitted.

"So beautiful." She cupped his cheek.

Drawing lazy circles around and around, he steered clear of her most needy place. "Would you allow me to kiss you there?" he asked.

Kiss her there?

It was something she'd only heard about. Did men actually do it for women? It wasn't another urban legend?

Tessa wondered if Jackson was the one in a million who was willing to pleasure a woman orally, or was it as common as women pleasuring men that way.

In the world of Internet pornography and open talk about sex, she was the anomaly. Ignorant though not innocent. Outside the safe bubble Jackson provided, anything sexual repulsed her.

Tessa didn't read about it and she didn't talk about it.

The downside was that she knew next to nothing about the different ways a woman could be pleasured. She was an expert on the reverse. Tessa knew all about the many ways men derived pleasure from using women with no regard for their pleasure or pain.

Not all men, she reminded herself. Not her Jackson.

"Am I going to like it?"

"I'll make sure you do."

"Then yes," she whispered.

Jackson kneeled on the bed at her feet and put a hand on either knee, applying light pressure to push them apart. "Don't be afraid. You're going to love it." He kissed each knee.

Quivering, her excitement tinged with a little apprehension, Tessa allowed her legs to part.

With a gentle push, Jackson spread them further and lowered his face, kissing the inside of one thigh, then the other.

As he kissed and nipped, working his way down, the

tension inside Tessa coiled tighter and tighter, until she was sure she'd explode the moment he arrived at his final destination.

She was ready to scream when his mouth hovered ever so close over her quivering folds, pushing up to meet it, but he clamped his hands on her thighs and held her in place.

"Patience, kitten." He blew air on her overheated flesh, cooling it down a little before flicking the tip of his tongue to tease her folds, setting them on fire again.

The repeated cooling and heating was the most exquisite torture imaginable. Tessa was torn between begging Jackson to stop and begging him to continue.

It was hard to think when every nerve ending in her body tingled with sensation.

"Please," she begged for something, anything.

The next lick was followed by another and then another, delving between her folds and teasing them gently until suddenly his tongue drove inside her, catching her by surprise.

Tessa's hands fisted the bed sheet. "Oh, God, Jackson... yes..."

She was close. One flick of his tongue over the right spot and she would go off like a rocket.

As his tongue thrust in and out of her sheath, Tessa bucked and writhed as much as his gentle hold on her thighs allowed. The small part of her brain that still functioned realized that he was guiding her rather than restraining her movements and that she should follow his guidance because he knew what he was doing.

She whimpered as he withdrew his tongue, but then as he pressed the flat of it over that most sensitive bundle of nerves, her lower body surged up and she had to bite down on her lip to stifle the scream that built up in her throat.

Not moving his tongue, Jackson let her ride out the initial jolt of finally being touched there, waiting for the tremors to subside before replacing his tongue with his lips and delivering the gentlest of kisses.

So sweet, so loving, and so not what she wanted at that moment.

Or did she?

As she was discovering, Jackson was more attuned to her needs than she was.

The loving touch had brought the intensity level a notch down but provided priceless reassurance and a powerful sense of being cared for.

She probably needed this as much as climaxing, if not more.

His hands on her inner thighs moved to caress the muscles she hadn't known were tensed, and she relaxed even further, letting her buttocks unclench and rest fully on the bed.

The reprieve didn't last long, though. Apparently, Jackson's intention was to move her away from the brink so that he could bring her there again.

Closing his lips around her clit, he sucked gently and pushed a finger inside her. Her opening, which the swollen inner walls had made impossibly tight, stretched, and then he added another one.

Jackson's fingers working in tandem with his gentle sucking, he brought her back to the precipice and held her hovering above it for long moments.

Panting, head thrashing, sweat dripping between her breasts, Tessa was mindless with pleasure and the need to catapult over that edge. Once she did, she was going to shatter into a million pieces.

"Jackson…" she pleaded.

"I've got you, kitten."

He sucked harder and curled his fingers inside her, touching a sensitive spot she didn't know existed, bringing the pleasure to the point of no return.

Tessa erupted with a brilliant explosion of light behind her closed eyelids. It shimmered for a moment then flicked out of existence, and all she saw was darkness.

Later, when she came to, Jackson's lips were trailing a path from the hollow of her throat up to her mouth.

His kiss was gentle, appreciative. "Thank you," he whispered.

She cupped his cheek. "Why are you thanking me? I should be the one thanking you. It was indescribable. I didn't even feel your bite."

He touched her inner thigh. "I bit you there."

"But I climaxed like an exploding volcano before that. You're amazing."

Jackson couldn't have looked prouder if she had handed him a Nobel Prize. "Thank you for the gift of your pleasure. For me, there is nothing more precious. Except for your love, that is."

"Oh, Jackson," she whispered, tears stinging the back of her eyes. "I love you. More than anything."

CHAPTER 18: CALLIE

*Y*esterday, as she'd planned today's escape while keeping her mask firmly in place, must have been one of the toughest days in Callie's life, topped only by the day she'd lost her baby.

Keeping calm and pretending that nothing was going on had been so difficult. She'd pulled out the best acting of her life, but Shawn had been suspicious nonetheless.

The thing was, he was always suspicious, and with how nervous she'd been, Callie couldn't ascertain if he was acting more suspicious than usual or just the same.

She'd been relieved beyond measure when he'd left for work and had told her he would be late because they had a sales meeting after closing. Not trusting him, she'd called the dealership and talked to Shawn's manager. She'd asked him how long he thought the meeting would last because she was planning a surprise for her husband and needed to know when he'd be back.

That way she'd verified that there actually was a meeting, and made sure the manager wouldn't tell Shawn she'd called.

Even if he did, it would be no big deal. Her excuse was good enough to fool Shawn too.

Callie chuckled.

He was in for a surprise all right. Just not a pleasant one.

As she packed her suitcase, it was quite shocking to see how little really mattered to her. She still remembered the care with which she'd chosen the perfect place setting and best bedding she could afford. None of that meant anything to her. In fact, other than the photo albums containing her childhood memories, she could've walked out in the clothes on her back and not missed a thing.

Callie hadn't taken much, packing only the newest and most useful articles of clothing, all of her photo albums, the books she'd purchased for her classes that had cost a bundle, her laptop, the little jewelry she owned, and miscellaneous toiletries.

She regretted not thinking ahead and scanning all those old photographs and storing them on a flash drive. Her suitcase would've been so much lighter.

Now all that remained was to call her dad and Dawn.

The question was which phone to use. It might have been paranoia, but she feared using the house phone or her cell. If Shawn was using her phone to track her location, it was possible that he was somehow tracking her calls as well.

A better idea was to wait and call from the restaurant's landline.

Taking one last glance at the home she'd shared with Shawn for close to two years, she felt nothing but relief as she stepped out the front door and locked it.

At the bank, she took out the seven thousand one hundred and thirty-two dollars that represented half of their savings. Stuffing the cash inside an old makeup bag she'd brought with her just for that purpose, she put it all the way at the bottom of her oversized satchel, then covered it with whatever else was there. Not much of a protection, but it was the best she could do.

Once Brundar picked her up, it would no longer be a concern. Her personal bodyguard was formidable enough to protect her and her money.

Arriving at the restaurant earlier than planned, Callie stashed the satchel inside her locker in the employee lounge.

"Hey, Callie. You're early." Suzan plunked her butt in one of the chairs.

"So are you."

Callie had arranged with Kati to take over her shift, but had asked her not to tell anyone. As far as everybody at the restaurant was concerned, Callie was working her shift as usual.

Paranoid or not, she refused to let seemingly unimportant details give her away.

Suzan stretched her arms. "Yeah. My mom got there early to babysit my kids, and I grabbed the opportunity to have a few quiet moments for myself, put my feet up, and read a raunchy romance." She pulled out her reader and propped it against the napkin dispenser on the table.

"Sounds like a plan. Enjoy."

Crap. Callie was hoping to have the lounge to herself when she called her father and Dawn with the news. Then an idea struck her.

"Suzan, can I borrow your cellphone? Mine is low on power."

"Sure thing. Just don't call China. My plan doesn't cover whatever is beyond the Great Wall." She winked as she pulled her new Nebula phone out of her purse and handed it to Callie. "Be careful with my baby."

"I will."

Now, where to call from?

The bathrooms were too public, and there were always a few tables occupied out on the patio, especially on a hot day like this one. She could either find a shaded spot out in the parking lot, or hide in the storage room.

Given the hundred-degree heatwave, the storage room seemed like a better choice.

Ducking inside, she went all the way to the back and sat on the floor in the little corner niche between the two tall shelving units housing the restaurant's miscellaneous cleaning and paper supplies.

She called her father first.

Huffing like she'd run the marathon, Iris answered. "Callie, how are you? Is everything all right? We haven't heard from you in way too long."

That was Iris's usual line of questioning. It had nothing to do with a sixth sense or anything resembling one.

"I'm fine. What about you? Did you run to the phone?" She didn't want to tell Iris her story and send a nine-months-pregnant woman into hysterics. Her father could relay the news later.

Iris snorted. "Me? Running? I get winded from climbing the stairs. And I'm talking about the five steps leading up to the front door, not the ones going up to the second floor. I regret buying a two-story house."

"Cheer up. Only a little bit longer, and then you're going to be a mommy."

"I know. You should see my ankles, though."

"What about them?"

"It looks like I don't have any. Anyway, I'm sure you didn't call to hear me kvetch. I'll put Donald on the line."

"Thank you."

"Hi, cupcake. How is the world treating my girl? Did you hear back from UCLA?"

Damn, it was going to be hard.

"I got in."

"She got in, Iris!" Donald called out.

"Yay!!" She heard Iris clap her hands. Her father's young wife wasn't best friend material, but she was a good person.

"When do you start?"

"I don't. Not yet, anyway."

"Why? Is it a money problem?"

"That's what student loans are for, dad. It's a Shawn problem."

Her father had never been thrilled about her marrying Shawn, but he hadn't been too distraught over it either. Donald had no idea how bad it had become for her. Not his fault, though. She didn't share her mistakes and failures with others.

Not even her father.

"What's going on, Callie?"

"I left him."

There was a moment of silence. "How did he take it?" By her father's tone, the news didn't come as a big surprise. He sounded worried. Which meant that he wasn't as clueless as she'd thought he was.

"He doesn't know yet. That's why I'm calling. I don't want you to freak out when he calls looking for me."

"Where are you going?"

"A friend is helping me out. I need to go underground, so to speak, until my divorce is finalized. I'm afraid of what Shawn might do to me when he finds out I left him."

"Tell me the truth, Callie, did he raise his hand to you?" Her father's voice quivered with anger.

"No. But he raged a lot and destroyed things. I felt it was only a matter of time before he turned that anger on me. I didn't want to wait around for it to happen. The last straw was when he refused to pay a dime for my studies, as if I wasn't working and had no say in it. He also refused to hear about taking out a student loan. I don't qualify for a scholarship, not with our combined earnings. But as a single woman, I might. And if not, I'll take out a loan."

"Do you need help? Iris and I can chip in for the tuition, and you can come stay with us until the storm passes."

His offer brought tears to her eyes. Just knowing that help was there if she needed it meant so much to her. "I'm good. I took out half of our savings and it should tide me over. But you and Iris need to be careful. I'm afraid that Shawn might go after you guys and after Dawn. He'll try to intimidate you into telling him where I am. Or worse, threaten to harm you if I don't come back to him."

"Don't you worry about us, Callie. I'll buy myself a shotgun and put a hole in that asshole if he comes anywhere near us. You can come here and I'll make sure you're safe."

Callie barely stifled a snort. Her father was incapable of harming a mouse, let alone a human being, and he'd never held a weapon in his life. Still, it felt good to hear him getting so protective.

"Thanks, Daddy. I really appreciate the offer, but it's better this way. As a precaution, I'm not going to call anytime soon, but I don't want you to worry about me. It's better that you don't know where I am. I'll send postcards. You get anything with a picture of a sunset, you'll know it's from me and that I'm fine."

Her father chuckled. "You are really going deep into cloak and dagger territory, aren't you?"

"Better safe than sorry, right?"

"Always."

CHAPTER 19: BRUNDAR

When Brundar arrived at the restaurant, Calypso was already waiting for him on the patio, a cocktail clasped in her hands. He glanced at his watch even though he knew he wasn't late. In fact, he was early.

"Have you been waiting long?" he asked.

"I was impatient."

"Understandable. Are you ready to go or do you want to finish your drink."

"No, I want to get going. The sooner it is done the better."

"Agreed." He offered her a hand up.

She took it, swaying a little on her feet.

Steadying her, he lifted a brow. "Drink or nerves?"

"A little bit of both."

"Are you okay to drive?"

"I'm good."

"Perhaps you should get some coffee to go."

"I have water in the car."

He nodded. "Follow me to the parking lot of the Galleria."

"Okay." Calypso seemed a little dazed.

Had she remembered the fine details of the plan? There

weren't many, but in the state she was in she could've forgotten something important.

"Did you leave your phone behind?"

"Yes. It's in my locker."

"Good." He took her elbow. "Which car is yours?" He knew, but there was no reason to alert her to the fact that he'd been stalking her for months.

She pointed. "The Honda."

He helped her in. "Do you have everything you need?"

She patted the large satchel she'd deposited on the passenger seat. "All my money is in here."

Any thug could snatch it from there while she was stopped at an intersection, taking all her worldly possessions.

"Put your bag on the floor and push it under the seat."

"Yes, sir." She followed his instructions.

Her slurred speech worried him.

"Touch your finger to your nose."

She did just fine. But he was still worried.

"On second thought, I'll follow you. Do you know the way?"

"Sure. Everyone knows where the Galleria is." She rolled her eyes at him as if he'd asked her the dumbest question.

"Drive carefully."

"Yes, sir." She saluted.

As he drove behind her, Brundar was relieved to see Calypso driving steadily and obeying all traffic laws despite her mild inebriation. Still, he was uncommonly agitated until they arrived at their destination and he eased his car next to hers in the sprawling underground parking structure of the mall.

When Calypso popped the trunk, he glanced at her single suitcase. "Is that all?" he asked as she got out and joined him.

"Yeah. I travel light. Most of the stuff in my house isn't worth much. When I start earning money again, I'm going to get rid of the clothes I took and buy everything new. I want to erase that period of time from my life. No reminders."

"A clean slate."

"You got it."

He lifted the suitcase and carried it over to his Escalade. When he opened the passenger door for her, she got in without a second glance at her car and put her large satchel on her lap.

Evidently, his Calypso wasn't a material girl.

Where in damnation did that come from? Brundar shook his head. She wasn't his. Not now, not ever.

She was a human, and even if she weren't, the only thing he could offer her was keeping her safe for a short period of time. No woman wanted an emotionally handicapped male at her side.

Undeniably, he felt something for her, and it was more than he'd ever felt for anyone else, different from the familial bonds he had with Anandur and their mother. But even though it was a lot for him, it was not enough to satisfy a woman's need for love.

The best explanation for what was happening to him was that his protective instincts were kicking in full force. The strong physical attraction might have something to do with it as well.

But the thing was, he liked her as a person, which was significant since Brundar couldn't stand most people.

"Do you have any special abilities?" he blurted out.

Amanda had recently added affinity as a possible Dormant indicator.

Was that what he was feeling for Calypso?

She cast him a perplexed glance. "Like what?"

"Can you tell if someone's lying? Or sense someone else's emotions?"

She shrugged. "Not unless they are very obvious about it. Why?"

"Just curious. I read an article about extrasensory perception. It said that some people have it but are not aware of it. I know a guy who can always tell the truth from a lie."

Calypso chuckled. "I wish I had that ability. If I had, maybe I wouldn't have married Shawn."

Brundar intended to ask her about it, and she'd just provided him with the perfect opening. "Why did you?"

Looking down at the satchel in her lap she shrugged again. "The oldest reason in the world. He'd knocked me up."

That didn't add up. She didn't have a child. Maybe he was misinterpreting the phrase? It happened to him sometimes. "I'm not sure I understand."

Calypso sighed. "I was young and stupid and trusted him to take care of us both. We had never done it without protection, but a condom must've been defective and tore." The bitterness of her tone made it clear she didn't believe it had been an accident.

"Did he do it to entrap you?"

"I have no proof, but I suspect that he did. He was so enamored with the idea of being my first, and he wanted to be my last."

Brundar didn't want to drag up old hurts, but he needed to know. "What happened with the baby?"

"I miscarried six weeks into the pregnancy. It was terrible. I cried my eyes out for months. But I guess it was not meant to be. I never conceived again, though not for lack of trying on Shawn's part. He was obsessed with getting me pregnant. I, on the other hand, thanked God every time my period came on time."

"Did you use contraceptives?"

Calypso shook her head. "When I realized that there was no hope for us, I wanted to but didn't dare. If Shawn found out, I was sure he would lose it and do something horrible to me. So all I did was pray to God not to let it happen. My prayers must've been heard."

It was a surprising revelation. Brundar was under the impression that Calypso's dissatisfaction with her marriage was a recent development. When he'd kicked her and her husband out of the club, she'd seemed embarrassed by Shawn's behavior but hadn't harbored animosity toward him. Brundar would've sensed it if she had.

As far as he knew, the situation had started its downward spiral only a few months back. That's when Shawn began to show more and more of his true colors, and Callie started looking out the window with a sad expression on her face.

"When I first saw you at the club, you didn't look like you wanted to be free of your husband."

She sighed. "I was still hoping to salvage our marriage. Things were good between us for a little while, but then slowly deteriorated over time. At some point I realized that I didn't want to bring a child into the world before I knew for sure that it would be born into a healthy, loving family."

"When did you give up on that dream?"

"It didn't happen overnight. I'm stubborn, and admitting failure is not easy for me. It happened gradually over time. I think the last straw was when he tried to stop me from attending UCLA. I wasn't willing to give up on my dream of becoming a teacher."

Before he knew what he was doing, Brundar reached for her hand and clasped it. "You did the right thing. He is danger-ous. Eventually, he would've harmed you." Or worse. But Brundar couldn't tell Calypso how he knew her husband was unstable and capable of murder.

She would've said he was overreacting.

Her lips twisted in a sad smile. "Do you have special abilities yourself, Brundar? Can you see the future?"

"No, I can't. But I'm a good judge of human nature, espe-cially the rotten side of it. And Shawn is rotten," he bit out.

Calypso tilted her head and gazed at him appraisingly. "Part of the job, I assume? As a bodyguard you probably encounter a lot of bad people."

"I do."

Unfortunately, not only on the job. He'd been exposed to evil way before he'd become the warrior he was now. In fact, that experience had shaped him into who he was today. On that day, he'd vowed never to be a helpless victim again.

Brundar had spent his life honing his skills and ensuring he could cut down anyone who threatened him or his.

"I forgot to ask, where are you taking me?"

Brundar stifled a wince. He didn't like lying to her. Hell, he didn't like lying period. But it was necessary. "My friend is teaching a semester abroad. I told him that you are a trust-worthy house sitter."

The furnished one-bedroom apartment he'd rented for her was a great find. It wasn't fancy, but it was walking distance from the club, and the building had a good security system in place. The front door was always locked, and visitors had to call and show their faces to the camera to be let in, reducing the chances of undesirables making it inside the building without invitation.

"Did your friend leave a car behind by any chance?"

"No. But his place is ten minutes walking distance from the club, and there is a grocery shop nearby that makes deliveries. You don't need a car. I would advise against visiting friends until your divorce is final."

Calypso grimaced. "Other than Dawn, I have no close friends. Shawn made sure none wanted to keep in touch."

His anger rising, Brundar's hands tightened on the steering wheel. It was a classic bully strategy. By isolating her, Shawn ensured she had no one to turn to.

"Brundar?"

He cast her a sidelong glance.

"Promise me you're not going to arrange an accident for Shawn."

He chuckled, because it was exactly what had crossed his mind. "Are you sure you have no paranormal talents?"

"I'm sure. But I'm starting to read the tiny nuances in your expressions. You looked like you had murder on your mind."

"It would solve all of your problems."

She shivered. "I don't hate him so much that I would like to see him dead. I just want to be free. He never actually harmed me, not physically. Suspecting that he was about to doesn't justify harming him."

Brundar couldn't argue with that statement.

His own code of honor demanded the same.

CHAPTER 20: CALLIE

*H*efting her suitcase in one hand like it weighed no more than a grocery bag, Brundar pulled out a key from his pocket and opened the glass door to the building's lobby. It looked old and a bit rundown, but it was clean.

"You see the camera up there?" He pointed before entering.

She lifted her head. "Yes."

"The feed from it goes to each apartment. You can see on the screen who is buzzing you from downstairs." He held the door open for her. "It's an old building. Only one elevator."

"What does your friend teach?" she asked as they entered the lift.

"I don't know." Brundar pressed the button for the third floor.

Callie frowned. How come he didn't know something so basic about a friend who was close enough to entrust him with finding a sitter for his apartment?

Her suspicions only intensified when they entered the apartment. The furniture wasn't new, but then most hotel rooms' furniture wasn't either. And like in a hotel, there were no personal touches to indicate someone lived there, other than a few books that looked brand new, several DVDs and one potted plant. No throw blanket on the couch, and no framed family photos on the mantel. A quick look at the kitchen cabinets confirmed it. A matching service for six, all pieces included and none chipped, was neatly organized on the shelves.

Then again, Brundar's friend might have been a neat freak. Or had OCD about matching place settings. No chipped or mismatched mugs like in her own kitchen.

Not mine anymore.

"Come see the bedroom." Brundar opened one of the three doors clustered in the barely there hallway.

Callie opened the one across from the bedroom. It was a coat closet. The other one led to a bathroom. She peeked inside, then walked in and crossed to the door on the opposite side that opened into the bedroom.

As Brundar pulled the closet doors open and put her suitcase inside, Callie dropped her satchel on the queen-sized bed that took up most of the space. A six-drawer dresser with a flat screen on top leaned against the opposite wall. The remote was on the nightstand.

Just like in a hotel.

Three decorative pillows against the slatted iron headboard and a folded blanket on a chair seemed like a feeble attempt at making this room look more lived in.

The best part, however, were the sliding glass doors that opened to a nice-sized balcony, which the bedroom shared with the living room. It was furnished with a lounge chair and a side table.

"It's a very nice apartment. Thank you."

"It's safe."

It didn't escape her notice that he didn't answer with a 'you're welcome,' or that she should thank his friend and not him.

Pushing her hands into her pockets, she glanced at her rescuer. "What now?"

"Grocery shopping. Then the club."

"When do I start working?"

"Tonight."

That was a pleasant surprise. "Really? So soon?"

He misinterpreted her question. "Tomorrow then."

"No. Today is fine. I don't want to sit around this empty apartment all by myself. I'd rather be working."

Brundar acknowledged her with a nod and headed for the front door.

The grocery store was packed with customers, most everyone casting curious glances at Brundar and basically ignoring her. Callie wasn't a great beauty, but she was used to at least a few appreciative look-overs from guys. This felt like hanging with a supermodel. A male supermodel.

Brundar seemed oblivious to the attention he was garnering, his stoic expression unchanging even when the cashier blushed all shades of pink while ringing up their stuff.

Not theirs, hers, Callie corrected herself.

"Please, let me pay for my own groceries."

Brundar shook his head. "Next time. This one is on me."

Not wanting to make a scene, Callie decided to repay him by cooking him dinner.

But wait, what if he had someone waiting for him at home?

A guy as handsome as him probably had a girlfriend. Or even a wife. Which would explain why he wasn't interested in her. That little speech about being attracted to her had probably meant nothing.

Empty words to make her feel good.

Except, it wasn't Brundar's way. He wasn't polite. He didn't say things just to put someone else at ease. He didn't say much at all.

Callie spent the short drive back to her new apartment

planning dinner. When they got there, Brundar insisted on carrying all the bags up to her apartment, not letting her pick up even one.

"You're a chauvinist," she accused.

He lifted a brow, waiting for her to open the door, then carried the bags to the kitchen and deposited them on the counter.

"Can I invite you to dinner? Or do you need to be at the club?" *Or home with your significant other?*

Brundar looked surprised, but in a good way. "Will it take long?"

Good. He wasn't going home to anyone. "Not at all. I'm a devil in the kitchen."

She expected some witty comeback, but there was none. Instead, he pulled out a stool and sat down on the other side of the kitchen counter.

"I guess that means you accept."

He nodded.

"Do you like Mexican?"

He shrugged.

"I guess it's a yes." Callie wondered if that's how all their conversations were going to be—with her talking and him either nodding or shrugging or grunting in response.

After rinsing the vegetables, she pulled out a cutting board and started chopping onions and bell peppers. "So what exactly am I going to do at the club?"

"Serve drinks."

"Yeah, you said that before. But I couldn't help wondering which portion of the club I will be serving the drinks in. The upstairs or the downstairs?"

"Upstairs. I'm not letting you inside the kink club."

Callie paused mid chopping. "Why?"

"You're too young."

She put a hand on her hip. "I'm twenty-one."

"You need to be twenty-eight."

"Since when? My friend Dawn is only a year older, and she was allowed in."

"It was a recent change."

"Why?"

"To prevent kids with fake identification from getting in. It's harder to fake being twenty-eight than twenty-one."

"But I'm not going in as a participant. As an employee I'll need to provide my social security number, and you can easily verify my age."

Brundar cast her a hard look. "You're not working down there. End of story."

He was such a freaking chauvinist.

Swallowing the arguments that were on the tip of her tongue, she pulled out a skillet and put it on the stove. The man was helping her out of the goodness of his heart. Arguing the terms of that help would be the epitome of ungratefulness.

"What made you come to the club in the first place?" he asked.

Callie felt the blush creep up her cheeks. "I was curious."

Brundar arched a brow. "I remember you telling me that it was your idea, not your husband's."

She turned around, adding oil to the skillet. "He didn't want to go. I convinced him to."

"That's unusual for first timers."

Callie dropped a package of beef strips into the skillet, the sizzling meat filling the small kitchen with an appetizing smell as she stirred them around with a wooden spoon.

"Let me ask you something." She turned to Brundar. "How can I tell the difference between a bully and a dominant?"

His stoic expression revealed nothing. "Respect and consent."

He was driving her crazy with those one- or two-word answers. "Can you please elaborate? Give examples?"

Brundar rubbed a hand over his clean-shaven jaw. "A bully demands your obedience and submission. He thinks of it as his right and doesn't care what you want."

That was a little better, but it still left a lot of questions unanswered. Brundar was like a web browser. She had to ask precise questions to get relevant answers from him. He didn't extrapolate what else he could tell her, or answer questions she didn't know to ask.

"Okay, so if I understand it correctly, a dominant asks for my permission and cares for what I want. Isn't that what any normal guy should do?"

"Yes."

Ugh. He was so frustrating.

"That doesn't tell me anything."

If she had a sliver of hope that Brundar might be interested in her, his cold and detached tone made it clear he wasn't.

"Your meat is burning."

"What?"

He pointed at the stovetop behind her.

She'd forgotten all about the skillet. Snatching it off the burner, Callie tossed the smoking strips around. "I hope you don't mind well-done bordering on charred." She speared a piece on a fork and tasted it. "Still good."

"Smells fine."

Was he being nice? Not likely. Brundar probably found the smell appetizing. Otherwise he wouldn't have said anything.

Callie added the chopped vegetables to the skillet. "I guess I'll have to come to the club and observe how it works. You're not telling me much."

"You can read about it."

"Yeah, I did. But the problem with that is that I don't know how much of it is true."

Brundar pinned her with a hard stare. "Tell me what prompted you to come to the club."

Gah. She'd never talked about it with anyone but Dawn, and even then it was half-jokingly.

"I'm not into pain." She wanted to make that clear. "I'm not a masochist. But dominance excites me. Always has. Ever since I started having naughty thoughts." She turned around and got busy with the wooden spoon, stirring fajita sauce into the meat and vegetable mixture.

"A lot of females are excited by it. It's not unusual."

"I guess."

Maybe not. But she was willing to bet that most of those women enjoyed purely vanilla sex as well.

She didn't.

Unless she added a fantasy of dominance to the act, she didn't get aroused, let alone reach a climax. It didn't have to be anything extreme. Imagining her arms held over her head, or a little erotic spanking would do the trick.

The images her brain conjured up had the expected effect, especially since her fantasy dominant was replaced by the very real Brundar who was sitting no more than four feet away from her.

Her curiosity be damned, this conversation had to end, or she would be forced to excuse herself and make a dash for the bathroom. Callie turned her back to Brundar and got busy with the skillet.

CHAPTER 21: BRUNDAR

She was killing him.

Whatever Calypso was imagining, it was exciting her—the scent of her arousal was overpowering that of the cooking meat.

Was she thinking of him?

Gazing at her shapely ass encased in those tight-fitting jeans, Brundar's own imagination went to work. He would walk up to her and clasp her wrists so she couldn't touch him. With her arms twisted behind her back, her ample breasts would get pushed forward, and he would cup one, then the other, tweaking her nipples through her bra as he kissed her neck. She would melt into him and beg him to take her to bed…

To master her…

Brundar closed his eyes. Not going to happen. He was already too emotionally entangled to risk the intimacy of a scene. The only way to stay detached was to engage with partners who weren't seeking an exclusive playmate.

That wasn't Calypso. He didn't know her well, but a girl

who'd married the first guy she'd had sex with wasn't the type to do casual.

She needed guidance, though. Without it she could fall prey to another jerk like her soon to be ex-husband. The club was a safe place for her to dip her toes. The problem was that he couldn't stomach letting anyone else show her the ropes, literally speaking, and he couldn't do it himself.

"It's ready," she announced with fake cheer as she placed a plate of sizzling fajitas in front of him. "Would you like a beer?"

He shook his head. "Water will do." To an immortal, the Hawaiian beer she'd bought would taste like piss water.

She poured him a cup. "Ice?"

"No."

Calypso put a much smaller portion on her own plate and sat next to him. "Dig in." She grabbed one of the warmed tortillas and heaped some of the mixture onto it, then added a tablespoon of ready-made salsa.

Brundar followed her lead. A home cooked meal was a novelty for him. He and Anandur ate out except for the rare occasions they mooched off Okidu's cooking.

Taking a bite, he wasn't expecting it to taste as good as it did.

"How is it?" Calypso asked.

"Good."

She chuckled. "You sound surprised."

Brundar wiped his mouth with a napkin. "I'm not used to home cooking. I didn't know what to expect."

"Do you live alone?"

"No."

"Oh." She sounded disappointed.

"I live with my brother."

"Oh." The 'oh' sounded peppier. Had she been asking to find out if he had a girlfriend?

Finishing one tortilla, he reached for another. Calypso smiled. So he ate a third and a fourth.

"You were hungry." She collected his plate and took it to the sink.

"I wasn't. But it was really good."

His words brought a bright smile to her beautiful face. A stuffed to bursting stomach was worth the sacrifice.

Calypso finished washing the dishes and wiped her hands with a paper towel. "Ready to go?"

"Yes." *No.* He wanted to stay and have her all to himself, even if it was only to talk or watch a movie on the television. It didn't really matter what.

But that was another lie. What he wanted was to take her to the bedroom, tie her to the bedposts, and show her pleasure like she hadn't known before.

"By the way. What do you suggest I do with the cash? I don't want to carry it with me, but I'm afraid of leaving it here."

"You can use the safe in the club."

She looked unsure.

"Or I can help you find a good hiding spot right here."

She fiddled with the dishrag. "It's not that I don't trust you. I do. But I want access to it whenever I need it."

"Understood. Give me the money."

She went into the bedroom and returned with her satchel. Taking out the bundles of hundreds, she put them one by one on the counter.

Brundar opened the Ziploc box they'd bought and pulled out several bags. Wrapping each bundle in paper towels, he stuffed it inside a Ziploc, closed it, and stuffed it inside another one. When all were done, he opened the freezer and put everything on the bottom of the ice cube compartment, then piled the ice on top of the bags.

"It will do for now. I'll get you a safe tomorrow and install it for you."

She eyed the freezer. "That's clever. No one would think to look under the ice cubes."

He wasn't so sure of that. But he trusted the building's security system to prevent anyone from getting in and looking. "It's a temporary solution. Let's go."

She followed him out and locked the door behind them.

"Are we taking your car or walking?"

"We're walking. I want to show you how close it is."

The walk would do them both good, cooling some of the heat that had been generated in Calypso's kitchen. What he hadn't counted on, however, was how awkward the short walk to the club would be.

As they strode in silence, Brundar had the strange impulse to wrap his arm around her shoulders, but then she would wrap hers around his middle like he'd seen other couples do, and he wouldn't like it.

Except, what if he did?

Better not to test it. He'd lived with his limitations for hundreds of years and managed just fine. There was no need to change a thing.

As it was, the girl had done enough damage already.

A master fighter like him needed to exist in the zone, which was impossible when feelings were battering against the walls he'd built around his psyche. Calypso was dangerous to him.

His Achilles heel.

CHAPTER 22: KIAN

*R*obert's heavy footsteps announced his arrival long before the guy knocked on the glass doors of Kian's office.

"Come in, Robert."

He walked in with a newspaper tucked under his arm.

Apparently, Robert still preferred the old fashioned way of reading the news, as did Kian. But he had a feeling Robert preferred it for other reasons—like using it as a shield when relaxing in the downstairs coffee shop. Reading news on a smartphone wasn't as effective in that capacity.

"I thought you'd find this interesting." Robert put the newspaper in front of him. A story about a new string of murders was circled with a red sharpie.

Frowning, Kian speed read the article.

Over the past week, five women had been found dead. They'd bled to death from twin arterial puncture wounds to the neck. There were no signs of struggle, and autopsies revealed no drugs or high levels of alcohol in four out of the five. The similarities had the authorities suspecting that the murders were the work of a serial killer.

Kian dropped the paper on his desk. "Doomers?"

Robert shook his head. "Doomers don't go around killing women. They are considered too valuable to waste. This is the work of a crazy person. Probably an immortal male, but not necessarily a Doomer. He could be one of us."

It didn't escape Kian's notice that Robert had referred to the clan as us. Should he be glad that the guy was counting himself as one of them?

Kian wasn't sure how he felt about it.

"Thank you for bringing it to my attention. I'll start an investigation."

Robert rose to his feet. "I guess you'll be keeping the paper?" He looked at the thing longingly.

"I don't need the whole thing. Just leave the article about the murders. Unless there is something else you think I should read?"

"Are you interested in sports?"

"Not really."

"Stocks?"

"Shai keeps me updated."

"Then I can think of nothing else." With careful precision, Robert tore out the relevant section, folded it neatly, and handed it to Kian.

"Thank you."

As soon as Robert left his office, Kian called Onegus.

The chief Guardian arrived a few minutes later.

"Doomers." He shook his head as he read the article.

"Not necessarily. Robert argued that even Doomers don't kill women indiscriminately. He thinks it's an immortal male gone insane. Which means the murderer could be anyone. Even one of ours."

Onegus scratched his tight blond curls. "It happened before."

"Vlad."

126

"Yeah. What a clusterfuck that was."

In those days, there had been no newspapers to deliver news almost instantly. News had traveled slowly. By the time they'd become aware of what their deranged relative had been doing, the body count had been staggering.

"I'm putting you in charge of the investigation. If you need help, we can contact Turner and have him send out one of his contractors to snoop around."

"We could use Eva's help."

Kian pointed a finger at the Guardian. "Don't even breathe a word of it in front of her. Bhathian would lose his ever-loving shit if we involved his pregnant mate in an immortal-gone-rogue manhunt."

"I have no intentions of getting her physically on the case. Just as an advisor."

"And you think she'd be satisfied with that? I've dealt with her. Other than my mother and Amanda, she is the most strong-headed female I've ever dealt with."

Onegus chuckled. "I can sweet-talk her like I do every other woman."

"No, you can't. Just drop it. We don't need her help with this. Am I clear?"

"Yes, sir." Onegus saluted with a grimace.

Fuck. The Guardians needed a reminder that he was their leader and his orders were not suggestions or friendly requests.

Kian expected them to be obeyed.

"*L*et's go out." Kian pulled Syssi into his arms. "You need a change of atmosphere."

As always, the feel of his strong, warm body provided a sense of well-being. But even that wasn't enough to improve her mood. Which was probably why Kian was suggesting an outing.

"Where to?"

"How about your favorite, that cheese place?"

"I thought you didn't like how crowded it was."

"I don't. But you like it, and that's good enough for me."

It was sweet of him, but she didn't want him cringing under the hungry gazes of covetous humans. She wasn't happy about those either.

They shouldn't have bothered her. Kian had eyes only for her and patently ignored all others, but when it happened more than once or twice it became annoying.

No wonder movie stars stayed away from public places.

"We can go to By Invitation Only."

His bright smile confirmed his preference. "You sure? I don't mind the cheese place."

"I'm sure. I like the idea of dressing fancy for a change."

The gleam in his eye meant he had something naughty on his mind. "Wear your diamond choker for me."

She smirked. "I thought I was supposed to wear it only in the bedroom with nothing else on."

"After dinner, it will be exactly what you'll be wearing. Or rather not wearing." He cupped her rear and gave it a squeeze. "I've been remiss lately." He slapped her butt playfully.

It was true. With how down she'd been, it was no wonder Kian had been in no mood to play. It started with the vision and had gotten worse after Eva's announcement. The twinkle of hope that the little boy in her dream had brought had been snuffed out, and the disappointment was devastating.

"What else should I wear? Besides the choker?"

Kian shrugged. "Something that's easy to take off."

"You're so romantic…" she mocked.

"Never claimed to be." He kissed her lightly. "Go get dressed." He turned her around and slapped her butt again.

God, she missed it—that delicious tingle and tightening. Tonight they were going to play, and she was going to forget all about the disturbing vision and her silly yearning for a baby.

What had gotten into her anyway?

She and Kian had time in abundance to become parents, and in the meantime she was getting her baby fix babysitting Phoenix. Soon there would be another little one to babysit. Eva and Bhathian would be living next door in the new compound, or village as everyone had started referring to it, and she could enjoy their baby boy whenever she pleased.

As to the visions, she was done with that. No more courting those. She could do nothing about them when they came out of the blue, but there was no reason to actively seek them.

No more visits to the famous medium either.

When Nathalie was ready, she could go see Madam Salinka and learn how to deal with her ghosts. As of late, Mark was her only visitor. Nathalie was perfectly fine with him popping in and out of her head, but his comments about keeping the bad spirits at bay had scared the crap out of her. Not that Syssi blamed her. Mark could cross over at any moment and leave Nathalie exposed. The sooner she learned how to block those nasty ghosts the better.

It didn't take Syssi long to get ready, and an hour later they were sitting in their favorite private enclave and going over the revamped menu.

Syssi shook her head. "Gerard must've gone through another of his culinary crises. I don't recognize any of these items."

Kian seemed unfazed. "He can't afford to become boring or predictable. His finicky clientele would abandon him."

"After the membership fee they paid? I don't think so. It was a brilliant move. Guaranteed repeat business."

A chuckle bubbled up from Kian's chest. "For most of the people here, the cost is insignificant."

She crossed her arms under her chest. "If they are so rich, they should donate that money to charity."

"The world doesn't work that way. Most of them donate plenty. That's what all those charity balls are for. What's the fun of donating extravagant amounts if they can't show off to their rich friends?"

Syssi uncrossed her arms. "I don't mind that. Whatever they get out of it is fine. Fame, admiration, I don't begrudge them these thrills. What's important is that the people who need the help get it."

Kian reached across the table and took her hand. "My sweet Syssi. I love how practical and level-headed you are."

She smiled at her husband and squeezed his hand back.

He would disagree, but Kian was so sweet. He never failed to compliment her on every little thing. So yeah, he was often late to dinner, and sometimes he worked in his home office long after she'd fallen asleep, but his love for her was ever present and unwavering. For a guy that didn't smile much and had a quick temper, the joy he expressed at just being with her was all the more precious.

"Thank you for taking me out. I needed that."

"I should have done so sooner. But you know me, I want to make you happy, but sometimes I just don't know how. Clueless as usual."

"Oh, Kian." She reached for his other hand. "You make me happy just by loving me. You don't need to do anything special. Some things are just beyond your control." She smirked. "I know how hard it is for you to accept that you're not omnipotent and all knowing."

His eyes peeled wide as he pretended shock. "I'm not? I think I'm plenty potent." He waggled his brows.

"You are plenty potent, just not omnipotent."

"I wish I was." His expression got serious. "I wish I could protect you from your visions. And more than anything I wish I could give you the baby you want."

It dawned on her then that she hadn't been the only one suffering. Her misery had been affecting Kian as well.

Time to toughen up, girl.

It was one thing to wallow in self-pity all by her lonesome, but dragging Kian down was another. It was her duty as the clan leader's mate to provide him support, not weaken him.

They were a team.

"We will have our baby. Eva pointed out that she was forty-five when she got pregnant for the first time, and she hadn't been using any contraceptives because she'd thought she was barren. I'm still young, even in human terms. I shouldn't be obsessing about babies yet."

Kian looked as if a weight had been lifted off his shoulders, and he winked. "I don't mind keeping trying."

"Me neither."

"Good. Let's go home and practice."

She laughed. "We didn't eat yet."

"Right. After we eat. You'll need your energy."

When their dinner arrived, Kian wolfed down everything on his plate in record time. The new menu items they'd ordered were unsurprisingly excellent, but Syssi had a feeling his haste had more to do with wanting to get her home than with hunger.

"Gerard is a true culinary genius," she said, wiping her mouth with a napkin.

Kian nodded. "An unparalleled talent with an attitude to match." He leaned closer. "To call him a prima donna is a polite understatement."

True. The guy was a pompous ass. The way he'd treated Carol when she asked for an apprenticeship had been despicable. If Gerard had been more accommodating and less insulting, Carol might have not chosen a new career path as a spy.

It was so scary to think of the pixie blond in the midst of the hornets' nest that was the Doomers' base, alone, with no support and no one to rescue her if needed.

"I worry about Carol. If there is one reason I would consider courting visions again, it would be to try and foresee her future."

"Carol is not going anywhere yet. First, she's not ready. Second, until we figure out how to communicate with her and find a means to extract her if necessary, I'm not green-lighting the mission."

"Good. Please keep me in the loop. I'll sleep better knowing what's going on with her."

"I will."

An uneasy expression flitted across Kian's handsome features, and Syssi wondered what he was trying to shield her from.

"What is it? What are you hiding from me?"

"I don't want to upset you."

She rolled her eyes. "Come on, out with it."

"Robert came to see me today and showed me a news article about a series of murders. Someone is biting women and leaving them to bleed to death."

That was horrible. "Doomers?"

"That was my first thought too, but Robert pointed out that killing females is not their way. He said that it could be any immortal male gone crazy, and I had to agree since it's not the first time something like that has happened."

"Are you talking about Dracula?"

"It was a dark time in our history."

Syssi frowned. "Where were the bodies found?"

"The article didn't say. The police are not releasing much information yet. Why?"

"Maybe the deaths in my vision were of these women? The first victims I saw were all female. After that the vision got blurry, and I couldn't tell anymore. I was so sure the vision was about us, but maybe it was about what's going on now."

"It could be. I put Onegus in charge of the investigation, and Andrew is looking into it as well, trying to dig out whatever information the authorities are hiding. We will know more tomorrow."

As a shiver ran through her, Syssi rubbed at her exposed arms. "Poor women. I hope he is not one of ours."

CHAPTER 24: BRUNDAR

"*W*hat's up with you, bro?" Anandur opened the bathroom door and leaned on the jamb.

His brother had no respect for personal boundaries.

"Get out." Brundar snapped a towel off the hanger and wrapped it around his hips.

"If I do, you'll just slink out like a shadow, and I'll miss the opportunity to bond with my little brother."

"What do you want, Anandur?"

"You're acting strange lately. Let me rephrase. You're acting stranger than usual."

"I don't know what you're talking about." Denial was the best defense. Telling Anandur anything was like announcing it to the entire clan.

To be fair, the guy knew how to keep a secret when it was important, but anything involving Brundar and a woman was too juicy a bit of gossip for Anandur to keep to himself.

"I'm smelling a woman."

Without thinking, Brundar sniffed at his body, searching for Calypso's scent. It dawned on him then how ridiculously he was acting. He'd just stepped out of the shower. Besides, like any other immortal male, he often returned home smelling of a woman. Nothing unusual about that. But the only one who came to his mind was Calypso, even though they never touched more than hands.

He frowned at his brother. "What if I am?"

Anandur chuckled. "I meant figuratively. Wrap a towel over that hair of yours. You're dripping all over the floor."

He was. Catching the long strands, Brundar leaned over the sink and wrung his hair out.

"Want me to blow dry it for you?" Anandur teased.

Brundar ignored the obnoxious oaf and stepped into his closet to get dressed.

Looking at his sparse selection, he wondered what should he wear for his appointment with the judge.

Should he put on dress slacks?

Edna always managed to unnerve him and disturb his equilibrium. Though not as much as Calypso, and for different reasons. Brundar did his best to stay as far away as possible from the Alien Probe.

His secrets were no one's business, and Edna didn't always ask before probing people's emotions and intentions. It was different from thralling, and in her defense, she only did it for the right reasons, but it was disconcerting nonetheless.

When it came to the clan's safety, Edna had no qualms about probing. She'd done it to Syssi without the girl's permission. Worse, she hadn't even asked Kian's. Apparently, even their almighty regent was afraid of reprimanding the judge, because, as far as Brundar knew, Kian hadn't done anything about it. Not publicly. Maybe he'd had words with Edna privately.

Anandur followed Brundar into the closet, eyeing the gray dress slacks he was pulling on. "Where are you going?"

"None of your business." Brundar grabbed a white button-down off the hanger and shrugged it over his shoulders.

Anandur crossed his arms over his chest. "You're neglecting Carol's training."

Brundar stopped with his fingers poised over a button. It was true. Over the past week, he'd canceled three training sessions in a row. Then again, Carol wasn't taking the training as seriously as she should.

Until she was willing to kill, he wasn't going to invest more time in her training and definitely not going to authorize her for any missions. "She needs to make up her mind whether she is in all the way or not."

Anandur frowned. "I thought she was."

"She did too. Until I told her she would need to kill an animal and take its heart out."

Anandur cringed. "Ouch. No wonder she is having second thoughts. Carol is a lover, not a fighter."

"She needs to be both to have a chance in hell to get out alive from where she is going." His dress socks in hand, Brundar glanced at his brother. "No objections?"

"No. You're right. Target practice and real life are two different things. She needs to toughen up."

Brundar pulled a pair of black loafers off the shelf and blew on them to remove the dust. He hadn't worn those since the last wedding he'd attended.

Should he wear a jacket? The only place he could hide knives under his dressy outfit was strapping them to his calves. If he put a jacket on, he could strap some to his back and front as well.

"Feeling naked without your toys?" Anandur knew him well.

Brundar tapped the numbers on the combination lock securing his metal weapons closet and took out only two small blades. Edna would appreciate him showing up practically unarmed.

"Not now, I don't." Brundar adjusted his pants over the hidden weapons.

"Do you want me to help with Carol?"

"Doing what?"

"I can get her to kill something."

Maybe. But Brundar didn't trust the big softie. Anandur would do the killing and give Carol credit.

"No. Kian entrusted her training to me." Using his fingers, Brundar combed his long hair away from his face and secured the long ponytail with a stretchy piece of leather string.

"I promise I won't cheat. It's going to be her kill."

Brundar eyed his brother suspiciously. "What makes you think you'll succeed in convincing her to do it while I couldn't?"

"A little humor and supportive attitude will help ease her into it. The first time is the toughest. The next one is not going to be as difficult. It takes time to turn someone into a cold-hearted killer. Especially a female."

Brundar arched a brow. He'd been turned into one overnight. Except it had been in his nature, and only needed the right catalyst. Carol, on the other hand, had suffered much worse than he had but was still averse to killing. She wasn't born with the right instincts.

It was an interesting thought. "Maybe she doesn't have it in her? If we push her too hard, she'll break. Carol needs to decide for herself."

Anandur scratched his bushy beard. "As unbelievable as I find you having such insight, I have to agree. I'll talk to Vanessa, and ask her if I should bring Carol for an evaluation. We need a professional's opinion."

"Thank you." Brundar passed his brother on his way out.

"You're welcome. You know I always have your back."

Brundar stopped with his hand on the door handle and turned around. "I know."

CHAPTER 25: BRUNDAR

"Come in," Edna called out when Brundar knocked on her office door.

He pushed it open and strode in. "Thank you for agreeing to see me on such short notice." Brundar's tongue twisted in his mouth as he forced himself to address the judge politely. Not only because he needed to ask a favor, but because she'd chewed him out for his laconic speech patterns before. As an attorney, Edna appreciated clarity and exact usage of language.

He'd do all the tongue twisting necessary, including reciting poetry if it helped him avoid the trap of her hypnotic eyes. Even without actively probing, the woman saw too much.

"That's what I'm here for. What can I help you with, Brundar?"

"A friend of mine needs to file for a divorce, and she's short on cash."

Edna's brows lifted in sync with the corners of her lips. "You've got a friend?"

Brundar shifted in the uncomfortable chair. Everyone knew he didn't have any.

Was Calypso a friend?

Probably the closest he'd got to anyone since he was a kid, but that didn't make her a friend. "An acquaintance."

"You need to tell me more, Brundar."

He'd been expecting that. "She is married to an abusive jerk and fears for her life. I helped her make a clean exit, and I'm helping her hide from him. She wants a quick divorce. There are no children involved. She took half of their cash savings and wants nothing more from him. The house they bought together can stay his, and she is not asking for support."

As Edna regarded him with her old, pale blue eyes, Brundar focused his gaze on the top of her forehead.

"What is your involvement with her? Did you influence her in any way to leave her husband?"

He'd been expecting that line of questioning as well. Hopefully, Edna would believe him and not try to push her ghostly tentacles into his head to check his veracity.

"I didn't thrall her. I only told her what she already knew. Her husband is manipulative, controlling, dangerous, and unstable. Up until now he has only taken out his anger on inanimate objects, but that's about to change. I allowed myself a quick peek into his mind. He'd rather kill her than let her go."

Edna nodded. "With no kids and no property to divide it's going to be a simple procedure. I can file the paperwork for her."

"Thank you."

"Naturally, I need her to come see me."

"I can bring her to your outside office." The one she kept for her dealings with humans.

The judge brought up her schedule on the screen. "Can she come at two o'clock?"

"Yes."

"Good." Edna smiled. "I'm glad you finally found someone."

"It's not like that. I'm just helping her out. She is human."

"No special talents?"

He shook his head. "None. She is an ordinary, young human female." Calypso was anything but ordinary to him, but Edna didn't need to know that.

"I'll see you both tomorrow." She rose to her feet, her baggy slacks too long, their bottoms pooling over her sensible Oxfords. "I'm curious to see the girl that managed to penetrate the shields of our most formidable warrior."

Brundar couldn't help the wince that twisted his lips. His strategy hadn't worked, and Edna had read him as if he was an open book.

Unnerving woman.

"As I said, she is only an acquaintance. Someone who needs my help."

Edna patted his arm, her sad eyes getting sadder as he flinched away from her touch. "Sometimes all that's needed is a small initial spark. You deserve to have someone care for you. Other than your brother, that is."

"Goodbye, Edna. And thank you again."

Out in the corridor, Brundar exhaled the breath he'd been holding, his shoulders sagging in relief. The worst part was over. Tomorrow, when he brought Calypso with him, Edna was going to focus on the girl and leave him alone.

The next step was to ask Onegus for a half day off. Filling in the paperwork would probably take up the entire afternoon.

When he entered the chief Guardian's office, Onegus looked him over. "Going to a funeral?"

"I need half a day off tomorrow. I can be here until one o'clock, but someone needs to take over my evening classes, or I can cancel them."

Onegus knew better than to ask what Brundar needed the time off for, but his eyes were full of curiosity. "I don't have anyone to fill in for you. You'll have to cancel."

Brundar nodded. "I'll take care of it." He walked out of

Onegus's office and pulled out his phone to send a message to his trainees.

On second thought, though, there was someone who could teach a couple of self-defense classes for him.

She answered on the third ring.

"Carol."

"Yes, my absentee sensei."

"How do you feel about taking over my classes this evening?" His talk with Edna had left a residual polite tone.

"Brundar? Is that you?"

"If you feel you're not up to it, I'll cancel them."

"It's not that. I can pretend to be you and whip those trainees into shape. But I'm shocked that you asked me how I felt. What happened to you? I'm thinking an alien invasion of the body snatchers."

Brundar rolled his eyes. "Thank you. I'll text you the times and room numbers."

"You're thanking me! I'm about to faint!"

Brundar clicked the call off.

Silly girl.

Carol and Anandur would get along great. The question was whether they would get anything done, or spend all their time horsing around.

CHAPTER 26: CALLIE

*A*s they left Edna's office, Callie felt ten pounds lighter. Heck, it was more like twenty. Brundar's cousin, the woman he'd failed to mention he was related to, seemed super capable. With those smart eyes of hers and her gentle tone, she'd projected calm and confidence that Callie had desperately needed.

"I can't believe the divorce can be finalized in a month." That was what Edna had said, but Callie doubted it would go so smoothly. Shawn would not let her go so easily, not even for her share of their house. Edna had suggested offering Callie's half in the equity in exchange for agreeing to the expedited process.

"If Edna says it will be done in a month, it will be probably done even sooner." Brundar opened the passenger door for her and waited until she buckled up to close it.

He looked so different today in his fancy appointment-with-the-lawyer clothes, like some model from a menswear magazine.

Callie slumped in the passenger chair. It was such a shame

he was uninterested in her. Maybe if she had more experience, she could've done more to seduce him.

Except, he might have responded negatively to her taking the initiative. Dominant men liked to be the hunters, not the hunted.

But didn't all men enjoy feeling wanted?

Was she supposed to play coy and give out hints like a damsel from a different era?

Callie wished she knew the rules of the game, but Brundar refused to tell her even the bare minimum.

Last night, she'd tried snooping around the club to find someone who was willing to talk to her, preferably a woman, but it seemed as if the two portions of Franco's sprawling domain were completely separated.

"Edna liked you," Brundar said.

"She did? How do you know?"

The woman had been accommodating in a professional manner, but she didn't smile enough for Callie to feel comfortable around her. Compared to Brundar, though, Edna was like a fluffy blanket of warmth.

He'd treated his cousin with such cold detachment.

Callie was grateful that he acted a shade warmer with her. She couldn't have dealt with him if he treated her the same way.

"She didn't interrogate you." Brundar turned into the onramp, easing into the freeway's slow traffic.

"Funny you would say that, because I felt like she did. She asked me a lot of questions."

"None of them intrusive. Trust me, Edna could make anyone squirm."

Callie lifted a brow. "Even you?"

He nodded. "Those eyes of hers. They see too much."

Wow, Brundar not only admitted to having a weakness but had expressed a genuine feeling.

He wasn't a lost cause.

She wondered what was he hiding from his cousin's knowing eyes. "Edna can look to her heart's content. I have nothing to hide." It was true. There were no dark secrets lurking in Callie's head and no skeletons hanging in her proverbial closet.

"Must be nice." Brundar stopped in front of her apartment building and killed the engine.

Was he coming upstairs?

God, she hoped he did. Not that there was any chance of him touching her, and it would be pure torture to think about it and imagine it while he was there, indifferent, or at least pretending to be. But she wanted to spend some time with him, have him near.

Was it because she had no one else?

Because she was lonely?

Her yearning for Brundar's company didn't make sense. He barely talked and almost never smiled. He reminded her of an old science fiction story she'd once read. It was about a humanoid robot that was made to look like a very handsome man. The thing was, the robot in the story knew how to mimic human emotions. If the story were about Brundar, the robot would've been a defective one.

Broken.

Was that what was wrong with him?

Was he broken?

Or was he perfect the way he was?

Callie shook her head. She was confusing herself.

"Are you coming?"

She lifted her eyes to see him standing on the sidewalk with her door open, waiting for her to come out. "I'm sorry. I zoned out again."

A big box under one arm, he offered her his other hand.

"What's that?" Callie pointed at the box as she took his offered hand.

"A safe."

"Thank you. I forgot all about that."

"The meeting with Edna must've been stressful for you."

Callie smiled tightly. "Yeah. It was. A life-altering event." A second one. The first one was Brundar walking into Aussie and making her an offer she couldn't resist.

Or perhaps it had happened even before that.

In the club.

Life was funny that way. Something seemingly trivial could lead to unexpected consequences. Alter the course of one's life.

"Your keys." Brundar held his palm out.

Feeling around her purse, she found the jingling pair. One to the building's front door and another to her apartment.

Only two keys, and neither belonging to her.

But those keys were what separated her from the truly homeless. Tears pooled at the corner of her eyes as she pulled them out and handed them to Brundar. Standing a step behind him as he opened the door, she wiped them discreetly on the sleeve of her shirt.

He cast her a curious glance as he held the door open for her. "What's wrong, Calypso?"

She shrugged, her lungs constricting as she watched him press the button for the elevator. Spending even a few short moments with him in such a confined space would be too much.

"Do you mind taking the stairs? I hate that clunky old thing." She wasn't lying. Besides being claustrophobically small, the noises it made were frightening. Going up and down the three flights of stairs was nothing.

"No."

It was good that he headed for the door to the staircase,

otherwise she wouldn't have known if he'd said *no* to the stairs or *no* to not minding them.

Frustrating man.

She followed him up the stairs, getting an eyeful of his fabulous ass muscles moving under the thin fabric of his dress slacks. His movements were so graceful, so fluid. Compared to him she felt clumsy. Callie was glad to be in a good enough shape to not get winded by the climb. It would've been so embarrassing.

Spending long hours on her feet had been good for more than getting paid.

Her keys still in his hand, Brundar opened the door to her apartment. "Go sit on the couch and put your feet up. I'll install the safe in your closet and bring you a glass of wine to relax with."

"Thank you. You're an angel." In more ways than one.

She hadn't been pampered like that in... well, never. Callie had always been the one telling others to relax while she brought them things. Her father, when he would return tired from work, or when he would get sad. And then Shawn, who'd expected her to wait on him hand and foot.

Closing her eyes, Callie heard banging noises coming from her bedroom. A few minutes later Brundar came back with an open wine bottle and two wine glasses.

The man sure worked fast.

"The safe is secured to the floor, and I left the instructions on top." Brundar lifted the bottle with a grimace and poured the red wine into the glasses. "I should get you better stuff than this."

"Thank you." She took the glass he handed her. "What's wrong with that? It's not a cheap wine. I think it was like almost twenty bucks." At home, she used to drink the ones from the Trader's market that went for less than four bucks and were very good for the price.

"Let me spoil you. I think I would like it." He frowned as if he wasn't sure.

She took a sip and looked at him from under her eyelashes. "You sound like you've never spoiled a girl before."

"I haven't."

"Oh." She'd forgotten.

Dominants probably didn't pamper their girlfriends. She should strike that stupid sexual fantasy of hers for just that reason alone. When Callie started dating again, she wanted to be treated like a princess. Not the maid.

Even at the cost of sexual satisfaction.

She could always resort to her fantasies to carry her over. Having a nice guy who treated her well was more important than how she got her orgasms.

Love as thy wilt. She remembered the book that had changed her outlook on sexuality, liberating her from feeling ashamed because her fantasies didn't conform to the norm.

"Next time I'm here, in addition to the wine I'll bring some Chivas for me and cocktail fixings for you. I know you like the sweet stuff."

The wine was starting to work, relaxing more than her muscles. "You're so sweet for noticing."

Brundar winced as if she'd offended him.

Callie laughed. "You're funny."

Now he really looked perplexed.

CHAPTER 27: BRUNDAR

*N*o one had called Brundar sweet or funny other than his mother, and that was a very long time ago. He used to love making Helena laugh. As a little boy, he'd thought his mother's laughter was the most beautiful sound in the world.

Anandur had gotten her sense of humor, her propensity for mischief, and her love of gossip. The red hair and his size must've come from his sire. Brundar had inherited their mother's looks. Her pale blond hair, her slim build, her perfectly symmetrical features. She was a stunningly beautiful woman.

On a male, though, that beauty was a curse.

He should call her.

But what would he say?

Sorry for not calling?

Nah. Anandur was doing the honors for both of them. His brother updated their mother on the latest keep gossip, and she returned the favor by supplying the same about the Scottish arm of the clan.

Every Sunday, on their once a week call, Brundar would hear them talking and laughing.

Yeah, it was better if he didn't call. Ever since he'd been irrevocably changed, talking to Helena only dampened her spirits. She could do without his calls.

According to his brother, Brundar was a dry stick who had no sense of humor.

"How am I funny?" he asked.

Calypso waved a hand. "You got that confused look on your face when I called you sweet. That's funny. You're funny."

She was slurring her words after three-quarters of one glass of crappy wine. The woman was not a lightweight; she was a featherweight.

"Are you okay?" He frowned. "I think you're drunk."

She nodded with a smile. "I am, a little, and it feels wonderful. Don't be mad." She pouted.

The woman was so sexy when she loosened up. Leaning against the sofa's back pillows, Calypso let her head drop back, which had the effect of elongating her creamy neck and pushing her breasts out.

Like a ripe peach, sweet and succulent, she looked ready for the taking.

"Why would I be mad?" His own words came out somewhat slurred, though in his case it wasn't due to inebriation.

She shrugged. "I don't know. You're weird. Difficult to figure out. I don't know what makes you happy, what makes you sad, what gets you aroused… and your eyes glow." She pointed with a finger.

He bet they did. Every part of his immortal male anatomy was responding to Calypso's unintentional come-hither body language.

She giggled. "Did little Red ask the big bad wolf about his glowing eyes? Or was it their size?" She glanced down at his very obvious bulge and giggled again, covering her mouth with her hand. "Do you think it was a metaphor for something else?"

"So now I'm the big bad wolf?"

She shook her head. "You're way too pretty." She appraised him with mischief in her eyes. "You are Prince Charming." The mischief extended to her lips, lifting the corners in a sexy smirk. "But unlike in the fairy tale. I didn't get a kiss, yet." She waggled her brows.

He narrowed his eyes at her. Was she really that drunk from one miserly glass of cheap wine? Or was she angling for a kiss?

Tempting, so very tempting.

But if he kissed her, he would be crossing the point of no return.

After kissing her, he would lift her into his arms, carry her to the bedroom, tie her spread-eagled to the bedposts, and pleasure her until she forgot her own name.

A stupendously bad idea.

"Don't do this, Calypso. You don't know what you're courting."

Swishing around what little remained of the wine in her glass, she took a moment to lift her head and look into his eyes. "I love it when you call me Calypso. I used to hate that name, but not anymore. On your lips it sounds like sex."

Fates, he was losing the battle to this little girl. The mighty warrior was helpless against the charms of a woman barely out of childhood.

She was setting his blood on fire and scrambling his brain.

He watched with morbid fascination as she reached her finger and touched his lower lip, the scent of her arousal drowning out the last vestiges of reason and restraint.

The predator in him surged to the surface, demanding he take over and teach her everything there was about yielding, starting with that impudent finger. Catching it between his blunt front teeth, he bit down gently, then licked the little hurt away.

Calypso didn't cower and pull back as he'd expected her to.

Instead, her eyes hooded with desire, and her lips parted on a moan.

He shook his head, dispelling the momentary loss of control. This wasn't right. She was drunk, and he hadn't explained anything, hadn't laid out the rules. That was not how it worked in his world.

But he couldn't reject her either. It would crush her spirits. The wine had given her the courage to voice her wants, and if refused she might never have the guts to be so forward again.

It would be unforgivable.

He should kiss her, even if it could go no further than that. Just one kiss with no strings attached. Give the girl a taste of how it could be. Give her the courage to seek her pleasure and not shy away from it.

Cupping the back of her neck, he leaned closer, his mouth inches away from her lips. "Sweetling, there is so much I need to tell you, but it will have to wait until you sober up. Remember what I told you about respect and consent? Those are not present when your brain is even marginally incapacitated."

She blushed but didn't shy away from his gaze. "I might not have the courage then. I know what I want, what I need." Her temporary bravado spent, she lowered her eyes. "Sometimes, though, I wonder if it's worth the risk or the consequences. It would be so much easier to leave it as a fantasy. It took me forever to admit my cravings. I don't know why I have them. I wish I didn't. It's hard on my self-respect. I'm not weak, and I'm not a pushover, but that's the first thing that comes to mind."

He shook his head. "This is a misconception. There is a stigma attached to the women and men who enjoy submitting sexually, but those who pity or look down on them should be envious instead. Vanilla, even at its best, can't compare. The heights of pleasure a submissive can climb are unparalleled."

She chuckled and gulped the last of her wine. "So what are you saying? That I'm lucky to be like that?"

"That's exactly what I'm saying. This is a gift, not a curse. Don't deny yourself because of what others think. You shouldn't deprive yourself of the experience. But make sure you do it with a deserving partner. Safety is paramount. Don't bestow this gift on just anyone. The right man should understand that your pleasure and your needs dictate the scene. Not his."

"I don't get it. You make it sound as if it's all about me. What do you get out of it?"

By replacing the hypothetical placeholder partner with him, she was turning it personal and making it extremely difficult for Brundar to leash his raging need.

They weren't talking about him.

This was about her.

He continued as if he wasn't part of the equation. Because he couldn't be. "What people fail to understand is that the dominant partner should serve the needs of the submissive and not the other way around. The pleasure the dominant derives is in direct proportion to the pleasure he or she delivers. I'm not saying that it's like that for everyone, not even the majority of them. But the good ones know that it's their responsibility, and that it should never be taken lightly."

Franco had taught him that. It was that philosophy that had made the place a second home for him as well as for the other members.

For Brundar, there was no greater satisfaction than bringing his partners to the peak of ecstasy, and not by pumping them full of his venom. That came after—an unexpected bonus he ensured they had no recollection of.

By this point in the explanation, most novices' emotions would be all over the place, hovering between lust and embarrassment, even fearfulness. Not Calypso, though. She was still gazing at him with desire in her eyes, and if he was reading her right, determination.

Damn. The lady knew what she wanted, and whom she wanted it with.

"Can I at least get a kiss? I'm sure you don't need a signed contract for that." She didn't even try to hide the sarcasm in her tone.

Was she making fun of him?

Did she think he was making too big of a deal of something that wasn't?

Brundar was tempted to show her the error of her ways. One light punishment would drive the point home. Leaning closer, he whispered in her ear, "I should spank you for not taking this seriously. And for that disrespectful tone."

Instead of jerking away, Calypso closed her eyes and let her head fall back into his loose grip. "Oh, God. Yes. Please."

He nuzzled her neck. "Not shy, are you, lass? Is that the wine talking?"

"It's not the wine. I'm tired of waiting around for what I want."

Brundar had to admire her honesty. "Good for you."

Encouraged by his praise, she lifted her hands to his chest. He could tolerate a female's hands on him; it was only another male's touch that repulsed him, but that didn't mean he was comfortable with it. Gripping her wrists in one hand, he held her hands down on her lap.

She whimpered, her arousal rising.

Damnation. Not taking it further than a kiss was going to strain his formidable self-control to its utmost limits.

Could he survive just kissing her for the next hour until she sobered up?

Or should he give her the one kiss she'd asked for and leave?

That would be the smartest course of action. The problem

was, for a change, Brundar wasn't thinking with his head. His gut and his lust were screaming so loudly for him to take her that he could barely pay attention to what his brain was trying to tell him.

CHAPTER 28: CALLIE

*C*allie should've been shaking like a leaf. How the hell had she summoned the courage to proposition Brundar, the most dangerous man she'd ever met, and goad him into taking the first step?

Was it liquid courage?

Or was she certifiable?

Looking for the baddest of the bad boys?

First Shawn, and now this deadly angel of a man who made Shawn look like nothing more than a sandbox bully.

Where Shawn was quick to anger, making as much noise as possible and breaking things while at it, Brundar's silent control gave the impression of real and mortal danger. The analogy that came to her mind was a bulldog versus a tiger. One raged and barked loudly, the other delivered justice stealthily, swiftly, and emotionlessly.

One was a potential criminal, the other a lawful executioner.

The paradox was that Brundar's leashed power didn't scare her. Not much anyway. She had a strong feeling that if he only let her in, it would be like taking shelter in the eye of the storm. The world could rage around her, but she would be safe.

Naturally, there was a price to pay for that security.

She was more than willing to pay. Ceding control to the only man who could ever live up to her fantasies was no hardship at all.

His thumb stroked the back of her neck where his large hand held her in a loose grip.

"You're a beautiful woman, Calypso," he said as he closed the distance between their lips and kissed her.

As lights exploded behind her closed lids, sizzling energy flooded her body, frying her synapses and making her limbs feel limp.

She'd been waiting for this for so long.

How many times had she fantasized about being held immobile and taken by a man she trusted implicitly?

But the reality of Brundar being that man was so much better than the fantasy. For the next few minutes her choices were no longer hers, but only because she agreed to the transfer of power and was a hundred percent sure she could get it back anytime she wanted to. A contradiction, a paradox, but somehow it all made sense to her.

His lips were firm, but gentle, and as his tongue licked at the seam of her mouth, the fingers holding her nape tightened. On a gasp, her lips parted, granting him entry. Keeping her immobile with a firm yet careful grip on her neck, his other hand holding down both of her wrists, he plundered her mouth expertly, thoroughly.

She was being taken and loving everything about it.

As Brundar possessed her mouth, the fire burning inside her got so hot she felt like she was melting. For a few precious moments, Callie experienced something so new, so different, that it was outside her sphere of reference. Nothing compared to this.

When his mouth abandoned hers, she was ready to cry from disappointment, but then Brundar lifted her into his lap and closed his arms around her, cocooning her in his warmth.

The iceman wasn't cold at all.

But why had he stopped?

The hard length prodding her backside proved that he'd been just as affected.

Callie's experience with guys wasn't extensive, limited to Shawn and what she heard or read about, but it was enough to know that stopping in the middle of something so hot was not what the vast majority of men would do.

To have a willing woman they were obviously attracted to and refuse her?

"Is it because I'm not on the pill?" she blurted. It was something Callie intended on taking care of as soon as she could.

Brundar rested his chin on the top of her head. "No, sweetling. It's because of what I told you before. Alcohol impairs judgment."

"I'm not drunk. I can prove it to you. I can touch my nose with my finger." She tried to release one of her hands, which he had trapped between their bodies.

His arms tightened around her. "Don't."

The edge of command in his tone sent a wave of heat rushing through her.

"Okay," she reluctantly acquiesced.

Were they done?

Would he ever allow her to touch him? Just a casual touch when they were not in what he called a scene?

A chilling thought occurred to her. What if he never did anything with a woman outside of those parameters?

Was he one of those who demanded obedience at all times?

Talk about a splash of ice-cold water.

The disappointment was so deep that it almost felt like grief. Already, she was mourning the loss of him.

Callie could never tolerate a relationship like that. No matter how amazingly sexy the guy was, or how much he'd done for her, her freedom was not something she was willing to barter for a few moments of passion. This was not how she wanted to live her life.

Brundar's hold on her loosened. "What's going through your head, Calypso?" He sounded worried.

She shook her head. For someone who appeared so stoic, he was way too perceptive. He felt her emotions changing even without observing her expressions.

She couldn't tell him, though. It wasn't fair to him. This was all on her.

She'd been the one to initiate, to push him into something he didn't want or would only participate in under strict conditions.

No wonder going over the rules was so important to him.

"I'm sorry. I shouldn't have pushed."

He chuckled. "If I didn't want to kiss you, it wouldn't have mattered how much you pushed."

The compulsion to ask was too strong for her to ignore, even if the answer she was expecting would hurt like hell. "Why can't I touch you? I understand when it's part of a scene. But we are done, aren't we?"

"Yes, we are."

When he didn't continue, she thought he wasn't going to answer her, but then he sighed and put his chin on top of her head again. "I don't like being touched. I don't even shake hands."

Was he talking about his sexual partners or in general? "With no one?"

"No one."

Okay, so it wasn't about sex with him. Some kind of a phobia?

"But you're touching me. You offered me your hand several times."

He chuckled. "I have no problem with touching you. I love having my hands on you."

She could live with that. Maybe not forever, but in the meantime, until she helped him work out whatever issues he had with being touched.

Listen to yourself. After one kiss you're already planning on fixing the guy? What if he doesn't want to be fixed?

Relaxing in Brundar's arms, she rested her cheek on his hard chest muscles, listening to the steady beat of his heart. He was so strong. Yes, he'd just revealed vulnerability, but that required strength as well. It was hard to imagine a powerful man like him having trouble with such a simple thing as a handshake.

"You're a bodyguard. What happens in a fight? Like in hand-to-hand combat?"

"I'm very good with knives, swords, and guns. You name it; I mastered the use of it. No one ever gets close enough to touch me."

Callie shivered. She could totally imagine Brundar with a sword like some medieval knight.

Curiosity demanded that she ask why, but compassion overpowered that need. He didn't know her well enough to share such a personal thing with her. That being said, she could at least sate her curiosity regarding his relationship preferences.

"Forgive me for asking," she started and felt him tense. "What kind of a relationship are you into?"

"What do you mean?"

"I read about the lifestyle and I know some dominants like to be in charge at all times. Are you one of those?" She held her breath as she waited for his response.

And waited.

The guy took his sweet time.

"I don't think so, no."

He'd sounded unsure, which was weird. He either was or wasn't. Brundar seemed to be in his late twenties or early thirties. A guy as handsome as he probably had a lineup of ex-girlfriends. He should have some idea of what he liked in a relationship.

"Think back. What did you like or not like about your relationships with women?"

"I never had any."

That couldn't be true. He must've misunderstood her meaning.

"Your other girlfriends. Did you want to dominate them twenty-four-seven?"

He sighed, sounding exasperated. "I've never had a girlfriend. I only do hookups."

She looked at him. "Do you mean to tell me that all you had your entire life were fuck-buddies?"

"That would be correct."

"So…" she started.

"That's enough, Calypso. Don't try to fit me into a box, and forget all you've read about on the Internet. It doesn't apply to me."

"But you told me to read—" His disapproving expression shut her up.

It was true he'd told her that, but what she could learn from reading about others would tell her nothing about Brundar. Every person was different. The only way she would find out what made him tick, what he liked or disliked, was by getting to know him.

The question was whether he'd ever let her get close enough.

CHAPTER 29: RONI

*T*wo weeks and nothing.

Roni knocked on the glass, letting Barty know he was ready to go.

Maybe Andrew's venom was too weak?

The last time they'd met at the dojo, Andrew had said something about bringing another immortal male. Hopefully it wasn't that scary Brundar guy.

Was he even bigger than Anandur?

Were all immortal males big?

Sylvia was of average height, and none of her girlfriends were huge, so it made sense that the men were of average height too. Maybe Anandur was the anomaly.

He could hope.

Crap. He wasn't looking for a repeat round of getting thrown to the mat and bitten. Then again, now that he knew what was coming it wasn't as scary. The bite had stung like a son-of-a-bitch, and being overpowered so easily by Andrew had been humiliating, but the after effects hadn't been so bad.

Hell, if he cared to be honest it had been fucking awesome.

A psychedelic trip.

Roni wondered if it was what smoking pot felt like.

From movies and books it seemed that his entire generation was doing it and he was the only one not partaking in the fun because he was a prisoner. A pampered and respected one, with a nice crib and all, but not free to do what other guys his age took for granted.

He was beyond lucky that Andrew had agreed to help him get laid, otherwise he would have still been a virgin. And he was luckier still that Sylvia liked him enough to stick around.

"Ready for some ass whooping, boy genius?" Barty asked as he opened the door for him.

"Fuck you, Barty. Put your fat ass on the mat and let's see how well you do."

Barty shook his head. "Touchy, touchy." He slapped Roni's back. "There is nothing wrong about getting your ass handed to you by someone better trained. That's how you learn."

Yeah, if he was training to become a fighter that would've been true, but Roni was fighting a war with a different set of tools. His were much more valuable than the muscles needed for simple hand-to-hand combat.

One day, in the not too distant future, he would be able to topple regimes without firing a single shot. Working for the government, with the best hardware in the world at his disposal, Roni's skill had grown exponentially over the years.

Anandur, Andrew, and their like had nothing on him.

This was the new reality. The world belonged to geeks and nerds, not the strong of arm. The days of might making right were over.

On the drive to the dojo, Roni distracted himself by reading a book. The old fashioned paper kind because his supervisors refused to let him use a smartphone or a tablet outside his secure glass enclosure.

God, he couldn't wait to be free.

"Who's the new guy?" Barty asked when Roni opened the door to the dojo.

"I don't know."

The new immortal they'd brought in looked less intimidating than Anandur, but not by much.

Anandur beckoned him over. "Roni, my man, come meet Onegus. Your new sparring partner."

The guy cracked a smile and winked as he offered his hand. "Don't worry, kid. I'll go easy on you."

"Don't," Barty called from the peanut gallery.

"Asshole." Roni turned around and flipped him the bird.

"Don't mind him." Onegus wrapped his arm around Roni's shoulders and leaned closer. "Let's give him a good show," he whispered.

Roni groaned. It might be a show for Onegus, but it sure as hell wasn't going to be for him. "Yeah. Let's."

Onegus assumed the stance and Roni mirrored it.

"Barty, you're not listening," Sylvia complained.

"I want to watch the new guy." The handler waved for her to move.

That was a problem.

"Pay attention to Sylvia," the one called Rachel said, compelling both Barty and Roni to look at Sylvia.

Onegus snapped his fingers. "Eyes on me, kid."

Roni shook his head and turned to face his sparring partner. There had been something weird in both Onegus and Rachel's voices, a sort of vibration that had an almost hypnotic quality. Was that thralling?

"Last warning, Roni. Pay attention." Anandur said. "Let's start with a warmup, going through the katas you've learned."

"Okay."

"Onegus, you're on the offense."

The guy moved in slow motion, broadcasting his move so

Roni could prepare the appropriate block. They went through several sequences until Anandur clapped his hands.

"Okay, boys. Warm up is done."

Roni glanced in Barty's direction. The handler had forgotten all about him and was giving his undivided attention to Sylvia, who was telling him about her imaginary brother who wanted to become an agent.

The girls must've been thralling Barty all along for the guy not to realize that it was strange they never joined the guys for practice, or that Sylvia was spending most of her time entertaining him with stories instead of training.

"Don't worry about him," Onegus said. "A bomb could detonate next to him and he wouldn't notice."

Roni nodded.

Onegus smiled again, this time flashing a pair of elongated fangs. Interesting. The warm up had been enough to spur aggression in the immortal. There was so much Roni still had to learn about these people. Just as humans, each one was an individual—different and unique. Onegus was nothing like Anandur, and Andrew was nothing like either one of them.

Getting in position, he waited for Onegus to make the first move, but the guy motioned for Roni to start.

Roni attacked, and Onegus blocked but didn't attack back. For a few minutes, he let Roni practice his moves and then started a slow attack. Roni managed to block a few, but the guy was so strong that blocking him nearly shattered Roni's bones. When this match was over, he would be bruised black and blue.

"Finish it," Roni said quietly.

Onegus shook his head. "You have to work for it, buddy."

Crap. The immortal was toying with him.

"Showing off to impress the ladies?" He taunted the guy, hoping to make him angry.

"Always." Onegus smiled again. The guy used that smile of his like a weapon. "But these ladies are my cousins. So no, I'm not showing off to impress them. Come on, boy. Show me what you got. You can do better than that."

Frustrated, Roni forgot all about the damn katas and just charged forward, yelling as he barreled into Onegus.

He barely managed to move the guy an inch, let alone topple him. Roni's miserly one hundred and thirty pounds were to the immortal what a fly was to a wolf.

With a sigh, Onegus grabbed Roni as if he was going to give him a hug, picked him up and slammed him down to the mat, turning him around midair.

The air rushed out of his lungs and his ribs hurt, but Roni didn't stay down. Rolling sideways, he kept Onegus off him for another split second.

The immortal didn't pounce on him. He grabbed him like a rag doll, turned him around and slammed him back face down. A powerful hand closed over the back of his neck. "Stop squirming and make like a possum," Onegus hissed, his hot breath bathing Roni's neck.

Easier said than done.

Roni's brain was telling him to submit and have this over with, but his instincts screamed for him to get away and avoid the mouth with those sharp fangs poised for attack, hovering an inch away from his neck.

"Stay!" Onegus's hand squeezed tight, cutting off Roni's air supply.

Roni bucked harder.

"Oh, for fuck's sake." Onegus loosened his fingers, moving his palm to the back of Roni's head.

A moment later Roni felt the guy's tongue on his neck.

What the hell? He hadn't signed on for any tongue action.

But when the sharp points of Onegus's fangs penetrated his skin, the burn wasn't as bad as when Andrew had done it. Or maybe it was just less of a shock.

"Hey? What the hell are you doing to him?" Roni heard

Barty yell, the cloud of euphoria spreading throughout his body, making his limbs feel as soft as clouds.

"He is fine. Give him a moment," Anandur said.

The venom's effect was milder this time. Roni was aware of what was going on around him but too loopy to respond. It took him a few minutes to regain control of his arms and push himself up to a sitting position.

"Are you okay, boy?" Barty tried to push Anandur aside.

Yeah, good luck with that, buddy. Moving a semitrailer was easier.

"I'm good, Barty. Just got the air knocked out of me for a moment." Roni took several deep breaths, then pushed up to his feet.

He walked over to Barty, his wobbly legs making him sway from side to side as if he was drunk. "I'm touched, old man. You care." He pulled Barty into his arms in a weak embrace. "I love you, man."

Awkwardly, Barty patted his back. "You must've banged your head damn hard, boy." The handler turned an angry glare at Onegus. "Are you out of your fucking mind? Do you know what his brain is worth?"

Barty pushed Roni off him but wrapped his arm around his waist to help him stand straight. "That's it. This class is officially over. These people are morons."

"No, Barty. I'm fine. Really. Ask me something hard."

"How much is sixty-four times seventy-three?"

Roni rolled his eyes. "That's what you call hard? I can do this with half of my brain missing."

"Just answer the question, smart ass."

"Four thousand, six hundred and seventy-two."

Barty pulled out his phone. "Hey, Siri, what's sixty-four times seventy-three?"

Naturally, Siri confirmed Roni's answer.

"Okay, so you can still do head math. But I still think something is wrong with you. You're way too relaxed and mushy. My Roni is a prickly pear."

"Oh, you called me your Roni." Roni leaned his head on Barty's shoulder.

"Well, kid, if getting beat up gets you in such a good mood, I'm willing to slap you around anytime."

"Stand in line," Andrew muttered.

Roni flipped them both off. "I feel the love, assholes."

"And… he's back." Barty clapped him on the shoulder.

CHAPTER 30: KIAN

From his seat at the head of the conference table, Kian glanced at William and Andrew who had joined the weekly Guardians meeting. Their respective expertise was needed.

"What's the status with the cars, William?" he asked.

The poor guy looked like he had lost a lot of weight, but it had done nothing to improve his looks. On the contrary. The dark circles under his eyes had gotten worse, and he looked even paler than usual. Kian was of a mind to send the guy to Bridget for a checkup. Or even better, to Vanessa.

William seemed depressed. Ever since his girlfriend had left, he hadn't been his cheerful old self and had been spending his days and nights in his lab, working. By the looks of him, the guy hadn't slept for days.

"I'm told that the model works fine. The design firm shipped it to us for a test drive, and once we approve it, they'll send a rep to incorporate the technology into our manufacturing process. After that, it's a matter of how fast we can build them."

"Tell them to send the rep right away. I want them to

modify the production line even before the test model gets here. If they say it works fine, then it probably does. If I'm not happy with something, they should be able to make adjustments on the fly."

"I'll let them know." William started typing on his tablet.

"What about the hacker?" Kian asked Andrew.

"Onegus treated Roni to another bite yesterday. I haven't heard anything from the kid yet."

Kian tapped his pen on his notepad. "A young guy like him should've transitioned after the first bite. I think we need to accept that he is not a Dormant."

Andrew shook his head. "Not possible. He has more indicators than all of us newly initiated immortals put together."

"That's true. But it could be a coincidence."

Andrew lifted a brow. "Including the grandmother?"

"Who knows. Maybe there is another explanation for that. In any case, if he doesn't transition in a couple of days, we venom him one last time. If that doesn't work either, it's memory clean time."

Andrew grimaced. "Can we keep him even if he doesn't turn immortal? The kid is a fucking genius. He is going to be a huge asset to us. Besides, taking chances with that brain of his…" He shook his head. "It would be like exposing a masterpiece to smoke. If we damage his brain even a smidgen, it would be unforgivable."

Bracing his elbows on the table, Kian raked his fingers through his hair. "If we do that, we will have to keep him locked up for the rest of his life. That's not a good deal."

"He would be exchanging one prison for another, with the added benefit of being with Sylvia whenever he wants. I think it's a better deal than the one he has now."

"True. But his current imprisonment is temporary. How long does he have left?"

"Don't be naive, Kian. They will not let Roni go unless they find someone better to replace him. They will dig out more charges or make some up as an excuse to keep him locked up. He is too valuable on the inside and too dangerous on the outside."

"Guys," Kri interjected. "This whole discussion is premature. Wait until we know for sure that he is not turning."

"Right." Kian waved a hand. "We'll discuss Roni again at our next meeting." He turned to Onegus. "Any news on the police investigation?"

"There was another murder at the beginning of the week."

"Fuck," Bhathian grumbled.

"The police are trying to keep it under wraps to prevent panic, but they are suspecting a satanic cult or something similar. They're thinking along the lines of ritual sacrifices."

Kian nodded. "What about your investigation?"

"Still working on it. I'm checking every male's alibi for the time frame of the last one's murder."

"Any suspects?" Kian asked.

Onegus smirked. "The only one who sneaks around like he has something to hide is our friend Brundar."

Kri snorted, and all eyes turned to the Guardian.

Brundar crossed his arms over his chest and lifted a brow. "Should I get legal representation?"

Fates, the guy really didn't have a sense of humor. "No, Brundar. Just tell us where you were."

"No."

"Leave him alone." Anandur put a hand on his brother's shoulder, which earned him a deep scowl and a growl. He took it off. "Brundar is seeing some mystery woman. That's all."

Several pairs of incredulous eyes landed on the stoic warrior.

"Is that true?" Onegus asked.

"None of your fucking business."

I'll be damned. Kian stifled a smile.

CHAPTER 31: BRUNDAR

*F*ucking Anandur and his big mouth.

Brundar shook his head as he walked out. It served him right for trying to crack a joke. He sucked at it. Legal representation. It wasn't even funny.

What had possessed Anandur to come to his rescue when none had been needed?

He'd known Onegus hadn't been serious.

His brother was supposed to be the trickster, the funny one; he should've recognized a joke for what it was. But no, he had to do the brotherly thing.

Brundar got in his car and slammed the door shut.

For a few moments, he sat motionless, trying to calm down. Ever since Calypso had reentered his life, not that she'd ever really left, his quiet Zen-like attitude had evaporated. He was restless, agitated, and itching for a fight.

If only he could find someone to offer him a challenge.

It probably had something to do with his self-imposed abstinence. He wasn't like William who could do without. Brundar was only four generations removed from the source, which made him one horny bastard who needed a steady supply of sex.

Normally, it wasn't a problem; he had plenty of willing takers in the club and elsewhere. But he wanted none of them. There was only one woman he wanted, and he couldn't have her.

What a clusterfuck.

Brundar turned on the ignition and backed out of his parking spot. There was a small matter that he needed to take care of, and it couldn't wait.

Tomorrow, Shawn was getting served with the divorce papers. Brundar intended to make sure the guy signed on the dotted line.

He was about to break clan law, and he didn't give a damn. He was allowed one fucking transgression after all his years of service.

No, he wasn't. All the excuses in the world would not make it right.

Brundar sighed. As a Guardian, he had an obligation to adhere to the letter of the law, and until now he had. Thralling was not allowed for personal benefit.

Out of necessity and in the spirit of keeping immortals' existence secret, it was allowed after a venom bite and any other incident which could lead to their discovery. Naturally, everyone cheated a little, and as long as it was harmless no one made a big fuss about it. But as a Guardian Brundar held himself to higher standards. He'd already bent the law when he'd thralled Shawn a year ago. Except, at that time there had been no personal benefit to Brundar. He'd done it to protect Calypso.

Not even Edna, the strictest judge the clan ever had, would fault him for doing so. Or maybe she would. Edna believed that the laws the clan had put in place over its many years of existence were crucial to its continuing survival and the welfare of its members.

It was fine with him if she took that stance. As far as Brundar was concerned she could judge him for that infraction and impose whatever penalty she believed he deserved. But the one he was about to commit was not an infraction, it was a straight out violation. So yeah, in a way he was protecting Calypso again, but Brundar couldn't pretend he had no personal stake in it.

He would do the crime and serve the time, or have it taken out of his hide as the case was. After the deed was done, he would march himself to Edna's office, confess, and get the whipping she would no doubt sentence him to.

Not a big deal. Pain didn't scare him. On the contrary, he would welcome it. The punishment would help clear the guilt.

Nothing was going to deter him from the course of action he'd decided on.

Hopefully, the asshole was home. If not, Brundar was going to wait as long as it took until he got there.

Last night, Brundar had listened to the recordings of Shawn's phone calls over the past week. He owed William a favor for that.

The guy had fumed and raged when Calypso's father had informed him she'd left, and that he had no idea where she was. Shawn had made some threats, but fortunately for him, he hadn't followed through on them.

Calypso's friend had been next. When she'd told him the same thing, Shawn had changed tactics. He'd asked Dawn to deliver a message: to tell Calypso that she was going to crawl back to him and beg him to take her back because she was a worthless piece of whoring shit and no one else would ever want her.

The jerk deserved a slow and excruciating death just for that. But that was Brundar's opinion, not the law's. Not the clan's and not the humans'. Hateful words were allowed by law, and punishing someone for uttering them wasn't.

Brundar only wondered how many victims' lives could have been spared if the law saw things differently.

Shawn wasn't home when Brundar got there, but he didn't have to wait long until the guy arrived and his expensive car pulled into the garage.

A minute later Brundar knocked on the door.

Shawn threw it open, his eyes narrowing. "What do you want?" Obviously, he'd been waiting for someone else. "I don't want to buy anything." He tried to slam the door shut in Brundar's face.

Brundar blocked the door from closing with his booted foot, then gave it a push, sending Shawn staggering back.

"What the fuck?"

"I only need a minute of your time." Brundar walked in and shut the door behind him.

They were more or less the same height, and getting Shawn's beady eyes to focus on his was easier than Brundar had expected.

Weak mind. He was reminded of his first impression of the guy.

"Listen and remember." He took hold of Shawn's suit jacket, which the guy hadn't had time to take off yet. "Tomorrow, you'll be served with divorce papers. You are going to accept all the terms and sign them immediately. You're getting one hell of a deal. Callie is leaving you the house and asks for nothing. You are very happy about that. She is gone, and you get to keep the house. You don't care where she goes or what she does. You don't want to even think about her. After you sign the papers, you will barely remember ever being married to her. Do you understand?"

Eyes glazed over, Shawn nodded.

"Repeat what I said."

"I'm very happy about the deal I'm getting. I get to keep the house, and I don't care what Callie does or where she goes."

"Very good. Now go sit on the couch and repeat that twenty times."

Shawn shuffled to the couch and plopped down. "I'm very happy—"

Brundar let himself out.

That had been one hell of an invasive thrall. Some brain damage was inevitable, but Brundar couldn't care less. With Shawn's twisted mind, anything would be an improvement. The important thing was that it should hold for at least a couple of months. By then Shawn would forget why his wife leaving him had upset him.

The thing was, Brundar still felt uneasy. Killing Shawn would've eliminated the threat not only to Calypso, but to any other woman the guy might get involved with in the future. But the law tied Brundar's hands.

As he drove back to the keep, Brundar debated the wisdom of the laws he followed. Today he'd done the right thing, and yet he was going to get punished for it.

Was it right? Or was it wrong?

Was the law flawed?

Or was his reasoning erroneous?

There were no right answers, and greater minds than his had struggled with these issues. Right and wrong were not black and white, they were many shades of gray.

"*M*iri, I'm taking my break now," Callie told the barmaid.

"No problem, take your time. It's a slow night."

"Thanks."

It was her second week working at the club. Even though she was an experienced waitress, it had taken some adjusting to. The level of noise was deafening. She'd tried wearing earplugs to reduce the damage to her hearing, but it was counterproductive to taking drink orders, and she'd taken them out.

Other than that Franco and his crew were good people who treated her as part of the family from day one, which was very much appreciated given how lonely and isolated she was.

Customers were the same everywhere; some were nice, some were jerks and some tried to flirt with her. But she'd encountered none who had been overly rude or handsy. The tips, as she'd discovered, were much better than at Aussie.

As always, she took her break outside to give her ears a reprieve from the noise.

"Hey, Callie girl, how ya doin'?" Donnie the bouncer closed his massive hand on her shoulder and gently tugged her to stand next to him. Wandering away from the club without an escort was not happening. Neither Donnie nor Salvatore would let her out of their sights.

"Fine." She cast him a glance. "Tell me something, Donnie. Did Brad tell all of you to keep an eye on me or is it standard procedure?"

Donnie added his second hand to her other shoulder and started kneading her sore muscles. "It's the middle of the night, girl, and this is no Beverly Hills. Not that I would've let you walk alone in the dark even if it was."

"Oh, Donnie, this feels great. But you didn't answer my question."

He exhaled an exasperated breath. "I did. Even if Brad didn't ask, I would be keeping you right here by my side."

So he did ask. Figures.

Every night after her shift ended, Brundar walked her home, and if he wasn't available, Franco or one of the bouncers did.

The problem was that it always ended at her door. He never came in.

Brundar had given her a taste with that one kiss and that was it. At the club, he treated her the same as any other employee, and the only one who talked on their short walk to her apartment was her. He was very careful not to give her the slightest opening, keeping her at arm's length.

Donnie let go of her shoulders and pulled out a cigarette. "You want one?" he asked as he always did even though she'd told him she didn't smoke.

As frustrated as she was, maybe the coffin nail would do her some good. She was so sick of being a good girl. Perhaps that was why Brundar was staying away from her. She was too naive, too green, etc., etc.

"Yeah, I'll take one. But you need to tell me what to do. I never smoked before."

He handed her the cigarette and pulled another one for himself. "Easy, it's just like smoking a joint."

"I never smoked pot either."

Donnie chuckled. "Where did you grow up? An Amish farm, or a convent?"

"Stop it." She slapped his arm. "Not everyone does it. I chose not to."

Lighting his cigarette, Donnie shook his head. "I knew there was something strange about you. You're a time traveler from the fifties."

Callie laughed and slapped his arm again. "Doofus. You keep it up, and I'll tell everyone that the big scary Donnie is a sci-fi and comic books nerd."

"See if I care." He flipped the lighter again and held it up for her. "Put just the tip to the flame and inhale. Don't take it in too deep. You'll choke." He winked.

"Pervert."

She followed his instructions and immediately started coughing. "This is horrible."

"I told you not to inhale too deeply. You didn't listen. Try it again and hold the smoke in your mouth. Don't inhale at all."

After two more drags, she dropped the cigarette and stamped it out. "Blah. It left a bad taste in my mouth."

Donnie's massive shoulders heaved with laughter.

"It's not funny." What a one-track mind. Were all guys like that?

She narrowed her eyes at him, her anger giving her courage. "Do you ever work or play downstairs?"

He shook his head. "Not in the way you think. Sometimes I help carry chairs and other furniture down there, but they have their own bouncers, or monitors as they call them." He smirked. "Why? Are you curious?"

"Yes. But Brad won't let me even take a peek. What do they do there that's so bad?"

Donnie waggled his brows. "Maybe he doesn't want you to see because what they do there is so good, eh?" He gently elbowed her side.

"If it is, why aren't you there?"

"It's not my thing. I'm as vanilla as they get, baby. Your boyfriend, however, has quite the reputation."

"He is not my boyfriend."

Donnie lifted a brow.

"He is a friend who happens to be a boy. Not the same. And what do you mean by reputation?"

Donnie shrugged. "He is very popular with the ladies. That's all I know."

Right. Donnie was a terrible liar.

"I know you know more. Spill."

"And get in trouble with Brad? I like my face the way it is, and I like my job."

Okay. She could understand that. Brundar was intimidating as hell. Though for a mountain of muscle like Donnie to fear him, he must've done more than glare.

"Is he violent? Did he ever get into a fight in the club?"

Donnie shook his head. "Not that I know of. He doesn't need to get physical. He just needs to show up. You know what we call him behind his back?"

"What?"

"The Grim Reaper."

She snorted. "He is too beautiful to be evil."

Donnie crossed his arms over his chest. "The Grim Reaper is not evil. He just does his job. And he is God's emissary, which means that he is an angel. And angels are supposed to be pretty."

"When you put it like that... I guess. He might be a little intimidating, but he is a good man. He is helping me, a lot, and expects nothing in return."

Donnie's brow lifted. "You sure about that?"

"Well, yeah. You said it yourself." She grimaced. "He is very popular with the ladies. He doesn't need to go out of his way to get, you know… laid."

Donnie remained silent for a few seconds, which wasn't like him. The big guy was a chatter bug. Taking one drag after the other from his cigarette, he blew smoke out into the cold night air.

"He doesn't look at anyone the way he looks at you."

"What do you mean?" Callie didn't notice Brundar looking at her at all. He'd been avoiding her as much as he could. He didn't look at her even on their walks home.

"He sneaks peeks at you like some teenager with a crush. And when he sees guys ogling you, he treats them to his deadly stare. I haven't seen him do that before. Until you came along, I thought he was made of granite. Like a statue or like that Edward guy from the vampire movie. Super pale face and all." Donnie bent from his considerable height and whispered in her ear. "Maybe he is a vampire. Did you notice his canines? They are fucking huge."

They were a little longer than usual, but a far cry from qualifying as fangs.

Callie patted Donnie's arm. "You have one hell of an imagination."

He shrugged. "Can you blame me? Most of the time I'm so bored standing here that I count the bricks on the building across the street. I have lots of free time to think."

"Why don't you get another job, then?"

"Who says I don't have one," he said in a tone that implied it was something interesting.

"What is it?"

"I draw comics." Donnie squared his big shoulders.

"Really? Which one?" No wonder he'd been telling her so much about them. He probably worked on one.

"Mine is not published yet. But it's going to be. Guess who's my superhero?"

"How would I know?"

"Your boyfriend. Bud, the slayer of rogue vampires."

Callie put her hand over her mouth to stifle a laugh. "He's going to kill you if he ever finds out." She didn't know Brundar well, but he seemed a very private person. Not the type who would appreciate starring in a comic.

Donnie put a finger to his lips. "If you don't tell him, he never will."

CHAPTER 33: BRUNDAR

*E*dna sighed, her shoulders slumping. "I understand why you did it, Brundar. But the law is the law. However, given the mitigating circumstances, I can reduce the severity of your penance. One week of incarceration."

Brundar shook his head. "I appreciate your leniency, but I can't do jail time. We are short on Guardians as it is, and putting me away will put an extra strain on the others. Besides, I need to keep an eye on Calypso. I'll take the whipping."

Edna regarded him with her soul-probing eyes. "Can I ask you a question?"

He nodded.

"Are you a masochist?"

Interesting. It seemed the Alien Probe couldn't read him as well as he thought she could. Good to know.

"No, I'm not."

Her lips lifted in a smile. "Good. I wouldn't want your punishment to be a reward."

Damn rumors. "I know what they whisper behind my back and I don't give a f… fig. I'm not looking forward to it, but I don't tremble in my pants either."

Her smile got wider. "I can't see you trembling in your pants for any reason. You have the strongest hold on your emotions of anyone I know. And it's more than skin deep."

Brundar stifled a smirk. Edna wasn't the all-powerful empath and soul searcher everyone thought she was because for the past two weeks his emotions had been all over the place. It was a daily struggle to drag himself back into the zone.

"Thank you."

"You're welcome, though I'm not sure it's a compliment."

"For me it is."

She nodded. "I bet. Back to the issue of your penance. Because you are a Guardian, only another Guardian can deliver it. But given the mitigating circumstances, I leave it up to you to choose which one. Also, I'll keep it a private affair with only Kian and the Guardians present. The last thing we need is for a rumor to spread of a Guardian breaking the law."

"Right. I appreciate it." He would've hated a public whipping. On the other hand, it could've been beneficial to show that Guardians were not above the law and got punished for breaking it the same as any other clan member.

"Normally, I prefer to execute the sentence immediately, but I'm willing to accommodate you. When would you prefer it done?"

"Tomorrow night if it's okay with you. I want to deliver the papers to Calypso's husband personally and make sure he signs them."

Edna tilted her head. "You know you're compounding your punishment. That's another violation to tag on."

He shrugged. "I want to see this brought to a conclusion as soon as possible, and I'm willing to suffer the consequences. Well worth it for me."

"You need his signature notarized. Are you going to drag a notary with you?"

He hadn't thought of that. "If I must, I will."

"You can use my secretary. She is human, but she knows not to ask questions."

"Good. And thank you."

Edna opened a drawer and handed him a brown envelope. "Everything he needs to sign is in here." She lifted her desk phone and pressed the intercom button. "Lora, could you please come in here? I have a short errand for you."

"Of course."

A moment later a rotund older woman entered Edna's office.

"Lora, this is my cousin Brundar. He is a friend of the lady who I took on as the pro bono divorce case. I need you to go with him to the husband's home and notarize his signature."

Lora shifted from foot to foot. "Hmm, you said he is the violent type. Wouldn't it be better to send a guy?"

Brundar rose to his feet. "That's why I'm delivering the documents. You have nothing to worry about with me around."

Lora looked him over. Once, then again. "You look like someone who can handle himself in a fistfight. But what if the guy has a weapon? A knife or a gun?"

"I'm trained to deal with situations like that. You're perfectly safe."

"Special Forces?"

"Yes. You'll wait in my car until I'm sure he is going to behave. You'll come in only when I call for you."

Lora exhaled the breath she'd been holding. "Okay. That I can do."

He waited for her to get her briefcase, then escorted her out of Edna's office and down to the parking garage of the high-rise.

"Thank you," she smiled as he opened the passenger door for her, then huffed as she climbed up into the seat.

"That's a big car you got," she said as he got in. "Do you have a large family?"

"Huge." He knew she was referring to a wife and kids and not to his extended family. But telling her that would have started another cascade of questions. Like how come he wasn't married and what was he waiting for?

"I have five grown kids and eleven grandchildren." She pulled out her phone and started showing him pictures.

Brundar pretended to glance at what she was showing him, nodding from time to time so as not to appear rude.

"My husband, may his soul rest in peace, he was the silent type too."

Sure he was. With her talking nonstop, the guy hadn't had a chance to stick a word in between.

"I didn't mind." She chuckled. "I talk a lot, as you surely noticed. So it was nice to have someone who was happy to just listen. I miss him dearly." She wiped at her eyes.

Poor woman, she must've lost her husband recently. He should say something. "I'm sorry for your loss."

Lora waved a chubby hand. "Oh, my Larry, God bless his soul, has been gone for more than a decade now. He was a good husband and a good father. The kids and I miss him so."

Surprisingly, Lora's love for her dead husband tugged at Brundar's heart. He'd witnessed his share of misery and loss, but he always managed to remain detached.

So why the hell had this story saddened him?

It wasn't a bad story. Lora and her Larry had had a good life together, which was more than most people got.

Was it because Lora was sitting right next to him?

Was it because she was a nice woman who wore her emotions on her sleeve?

Or was it envy for her deceased husband?

She'd compared Brundar to her Larry, and it made him think. The guy had been dead for over a decade but was still loved by his wife and children. It was something Brundar couldn't even imagine. He never thought of himself as worthy of love.

No, that wasn't true.

As a boy he'd been loved and cherished by his mother, probably still was in some small way. But he'd lost the ability to feel that love.

He didn't deserve it.

He'd been a foolish boy who should have listened to his elders instead of trusting the wrong people. He'd been so fucking naive.

Because of him, his family had suffered.

CHAPTER 34: RONI

tanding by the window, Roni looked out on the night cityscape visible from his building. Not much of a view. A row of office buildings, four to five stories high, one bench across the street with a poster of a smiling real estate agent glued to its back, two lampposts. He'd been staring at the same thing for way too long. And it seemed like he'd be staring at it for a whole while longer.

Fourth day since the bite and nothing. Roni sighed.

It had been a pleasant dream. Freedom, Sylvia, immortality. Maybe even good money so he could buy a car, a convertible, and go traveling.

With Sylvia, of course.

He'd leave the top down. Her hair blowing in the wind, she would be smiling the whole way. Maybe even singing.

Could she sing?

He didn't know.

They would stop for the night at roadside motels and make love for hours, then in the morning get in the car and keep going.

A fantasy.

Turning away from the window, Roni walked over to the couch, grabbed a comic book off the coffee table and lay down. Barty had brought him a stack of them. The agent claimed that he'd found them while cleaning up the attic. Tucked away in a box that had been gathering dust and spider webs, they were beautifully preserved because Barty's nephew had put each one in a plastic sleeve to protect them.

There must've been over a hundred of them, and Roni intended to read until his eyes got tired and he fell asleep. He needed to take his mind off what was not happening to him.

His eyes started drooping sooner than he'd expected. By the second comic his vision blurred and he had to close them. Maybe he needed reading glasses?

It was cold, and Roni covered himself with the throw blanket Barty's wife had crocheted for him. She'd never met him, and yet she'd gifted him with something that must've taken her days or even weeks to make.

The handler and his wife acted more like parents to Roni than his real ones.

What if he was adopted?

Maybe that was why his parents didn't care about him?

That would explain why he wasn't transitioning even though his grandmother almost certainly was an immortal. Other than that the only indicator that he was a Dormant was the fact that Sylvia liked him. True, the odds that a hot girl like her would fall for a scrawny guy like him were slim, but women were strange that way. Maybe she was attracted to his brain.

Could happen. Like Stephen Hawking's second wife. It wasn't as if she'd left her husband and married the dude in the wheelchair, the one her poor shmuck of a husband had designed for Hawking, because the scientist was such a hunk or a charmer. The only thing the guy had going for him was his brain.

Damn, it was getting cold in his apartment.

Too lazy to go get another blanket, or drag his ass to bed, Roni tucked the throw tighter around him and pushed himself deeper into the couch, pressing his back against the cushions.

He was still cold.

Why was his apartment freezing? It was the middle of summer for fuck's sake, and this was Los Angeles. Not a city known for its cool weather. Fucking climate change. It was supposed to be global warming, not cooling.

When the shivers started, Roni realized it wasn't cold in his apartment, but that he must be sick and running a fever.

Wait a minute, Andrew had warned him that the first symptoms of transition were flu like.

Fucking hell. If he was transitioning, it meant that he wasn't adopted, just not lovable enough for his parents to give a damn. True, his legal defense had ruined them financially, but weren't parents supposed to love their kids no matter what?

He hadn't killed anyone for God's sake. And until his eighteenth birthday, his pay checks went straight to his parents' account. That should've compensated nicely for their losses.

They had been relieved when he moved out, taking his handler with him and giving them their lives back. In the beginning, they'd still called once or twice a week, visiting once or twice a month, but soon the phone calls and visits had dwindled down to once every few months.

Fuckers.

Not a nice thing to say about one's parents, but they deserved it for abandoning him like that.

Whatever, he was getting a new family now.

Yeah. Like they were doing it out of love for him. The only reason the immortals were interested in him was his talent.

Did Sylvia really have feelings for him? Or was she bait to lure him in?

Paranoid much?

It was too late to start second guessing things now. He should call the front desk and tell them he wasn't feeling well. For his extraction to work, he had to get transferred to a hospital.

With a shaking hand, Roni picked up the cordless and dialed zero for the internal switchboard.

"What's up, Roni? Want us to order you pizza?"

He groaned. "Not this time. I'm sick. I need you guys to call a doctor or take me to the hospital."

"What's wrong with you?"

"I have a fever, and I shake all over. Please, hurry." He made himself sound more pitiful than he really felt.

"I'm on it. Hold it together, kid. We will take care of you."

"Thanks, man."

Disconnecting the call, Roni slumped into the couch cushions. Hopefully, they would call Barty to come sit with him. Roni doubted they would allow him to use the hospital's phone, while Barty wouldn't mind calling Sylvia for him, which would start the ball rolling.

Images of Sylvia swirling in his feverish head, Roni dozed off, only to wake up when someone pounded on his door.

"Roni, are you alive in there? We are coming in."

About fucking time.

He didn't answer, not because he didn't want to, but because his mouth was too dried out to talk.

The next moment, Jerome walked in. It was good that Roni's door had a keypad and not a regular lock. There was no need to break it down. Jerome could've done it, the guy must've weighed over three hundred pounds. Most of it was muscle, but a good layer of fat provided padding on top.

"I'm taking you to the hospital. Boss's orders." The guy scooped Roni into his arms as if he weighed nothing.

"Kevin, bring the kid a glass of water," Jerome told his buddy.

A couple of moments later the other security guard held a plastic cup to Roni's lips. "Try to drink some, kid."

The water felt heavenly and he emptied the entire cup. "Thanks. Can you get me another?"

"Sure thing, kiddo." Kevin walked over to the kitchen to refill the cup.

"Put me down, Jerome, I'm fine."

Jerome shook his head. "I put you down, you crumple like a rag doll."

Kevin held the cup to Roni's lips. He emptied it as well.

"Okay, princess. Let's get you to the hospital," Jerome said.

"Screw you."

"See?" Jerome turned to Kevin. "I told you he is not as sick as he looks. Roni is still the jerk we all know and love." He hoisted Roni higher. "You always act like such a prima donna, at least now you have a good excuse."

"Just don't mistake me for a football, and toss me to Kevin." Jerome used to play football in college.

"I just might. Doesn't his big head look like a football?" Jerome asked Kevin as he carried Roni out.

"It does. But how do we separate it from that scrawny string attached to it? What is it? Is it a neck?"

They might have had more fun at his expense, but Roni decided that it was okay to check out for at least a few minutes. Everything was working according to plan, and he was on his way to the hospital. His head resting on Jerome's padded chest, he closed his eyes and let sleep claim him.

CHAPTER 35: BRUNDAR

"*A*re you okay here on your own?" Brundar asked Lora, peering at her through the open passenger-side window.

"Perfectly. Better here than there." She pointed at Calypso's house.

"Expect my call in a few minutes."

"Yes, boss." She lifted her phone, showing him she was ready.

"Good."

Once again he was striding up to that house, readying for a confrontation with Calypso's soon to be ex-husband. Hopefully, for the last time and not because he killed the bastard.

Since Brundar had set the divorce papers as the trigger, the thrall he'd implanted in the guy's head was not in effect yet. Once Shawn was served, he would be compelled to agree to all the terms and sign, but until that moment a lot could happen.

Itching for the guy to give him a good reason to beat the hell out of him, Brundar knocked on the door. He couldn't kill the asshole, but beating him within an inch of his life would do.

No answer.

He pressed the bell button.

A moment later the door flew open. "What do you want? I'm not buying anything."

The small additional thrall to forget Brundar seemed to have worked exceptionally well. There wasn't even a shard of recognition in Shawn's booze-shot eyes. By the smell of alcohol wafting off of him, the guy had been drinking for a while.

Brundar rolled his eyes as Shawn tried to slam the door in his face again.

So predictable.

His hand bracing against the door, Brundar was ready this time. "Get inside." He shoved it open.

Shawn swayed on his feet, his balance further impaired by his inebriation. "What the hell? I'm calling the cops," he slurred.

"No, you're not. Sit down." Brundar pointed at the couch. "And turn off the dumb box." He imbued his tone with influence, compelling Shawn to obey.

"What do you want, man? I have no money or jewelry because my fucking whore of a wife left me and took everything with her." The guy's face twisted into an ugly grimace.

Brundar didn't need to delve deep to get hit with the jerk's ugly thoughts. He was practically projecting them like a damn telepath.

I'm going to find her, and when I do, I'm going to beat the shit out of the fucking, cheating bitch until her pretty face is pretty no more. And after I kill the fucker she's fucking, I'm going to rearrange her face, so no one will ever want her. She'll come crawling back to me. I'll take the whore back, but I'll make her pay for the rest of her fucking life.

In two long strides, Brundar closed the distance between himself and the piece of shit, hauled him up by his ratty T-shirt, closed his hands around the guy's thick neck, and squeezed.

Shawn tried to pry Brundar's fingers off, but even though he was strong for a human, he stood no chance against a pissed immortal.

When the guy's face started turning purple, Brundar forced himself to let go, dropping the scum on the couch.

If he killed every psychotic piece of shit for what they were thinking, there would be a trail of dead bodies in his wake. Ugly thoughts and nefarious intentions were not considered criminal until perpetrated.

As the guy wheezed and sputtered, Brundar picked up the yellow envelope from where he'd dropped it on the floor, and pulled the divorce papers out.

"Read, motherfucker." He shoved them at Shawn's trembling hands, then stood over the guy until he'd read every last paragraph.

"I don't have a pen," the jerk wheezed, tears running down his purple cheeks as he frantically looked around for one.

Brundar pulled out his phone and dialed Lora's number. Hopefully, the woman wasn't squeamish and wouldn't faint when she saw the black fingermarks on Shawn's neck and the purple hue of his face.

"You can come in now."

A few moments later, Lora knocked on the door. Brundar opened the way. "I had to use a little persuasion. I hope you're not the fainting type."

"Don't worry about me. Whatever you show me, I've seen worse. I volunteer at a battered women's shelter."

Brundar dipped his head in respect. "Then you'll appreciate my work here. I promise you that he earned it."

She regarded him with a serious expression in her eyes. "I believe you. Lead the way."

Five minutes later they walked out with the signed papers, everything properly notarized.

"Is he going to report you to the police?" Lora asked as he opened the passenger door for her.

"No."

"You sure?"

"I'm sure."

"Do I want to know why you're so sure?"

"No."

"Okay."

Brundar walked around and got behind the steering wheel.

Lora buckled herself in and smiled at him. "You didn't work him up as bad as I thought you would."

He lifted a brow. "What were you expecting?"

"By your grim expression, I was expecting at least a broken nose and plenty of blood."

Was it his imagination, or was this soft-looking grandma of eleven bloodthirsty and vengeful?

"Did you want me to?"

She shrugged. "It depends on what he'd done to deserve it."

Brundar didn't answer because he couldn't. How could he explain that Shawn hadn't committed any crimes aside from bullying his wife, and that he'd earned Brundar's wrath by plotting to do her harm?

Instead, he changed the subject. "Is there a personal reason you volunteer at the shelter?"

"Yes, there is. My sister was abused by her husband for years. She was hiding it, coming up with all kind of excuses for her bruises and her broken limbs. I should've guessed what was going on, but it was such a foreign concept to me that the thought never even crossed my mind. I believed her. The last beating before he was finally arrested has left her with permanent brain damage."

"I hope that monster is either dead or behind bars."

Her lips pressed into a tight line, Lora shook her head. "He did some time, but not enough for what he did. No length of time can pay for that. Not even execution."

"An execution would have at least saved his next victim."

Lora nodded. "You'll hear no argument from me. If we lived in different times, my sister's family could've avenged her and rid the world of that monster."

Brundar nodded. He'd lived in those olden times when family avenged family. Was it a better system than what humanity had devised in modern times? Or was it worse?

The monster behind Brundar, the one he used to call a friend, started thrusting in and out of him to the loud cheers of his buddies.

No!!! A roar sounded from not too far away.

A moment later the body above Brundar disappeared, and a sickening breaking noise followed. After that, there were a few more screams, sounds of pursuit, and then nothing.

Throughout it all Brundar lay with his tear-stricken face to the ground, the pain and humiliation he'd been subjected to making him wish for death. There was no coming back from that. It would haunt him for the rest of his life. Mayhap he could end it before his transition. Before he was doomed to carry on endlessly.

Gentle hands pulled his pants up, and strong arms lifted him up, cradling him against a familiar muscular chest.

As Brundar turned his head to look at the carnage, bile rose in his throat and he tilted his head away from his brother's chest to vomit.

Anandur wiped his mouth with his sleeve. "Dinnae look," he said. "It's over."

A drop of water landed on Brundar's cheek, but it wasn't his. He was all out of tears. Lifting his eyes to his brother's face, he saw that the big man was crying.

"I'm so sorry, laddie. I should've come sooner. I didnae know."

"Are they dead?"

Anandur nodded. "To the last one. They will never hurt anyone again."

CHAPTER 36: TESSA

"**C**an you at least give me a hint?" Tessa asked.

Jackson cast her a mysterious smile, then put the blinker on and eased his car into the quiet Venice street. "Nope."

Pouting, Tessa crossed her arms over her chest and tried to guess. Maybe he was taking her to a Sunday brunch?

It was too early for the movies, and it wasn't the beach because he hadn't said anything about a bathing suit or towels.

"I don't like surprises."

"You'll like this one."

Ugh, she was discovering that her sweet, accommodating Jackson had a stubborn streak a mile long.

Over two weeks had passed since he'd kissed her and licked her into her most powerful climax yet, then refused to take the final step and go all the way.

She was more than ready, but he insisted on waiting. Not that she'd been deprived in the meantime. Jackson had been treating her to more of those mind-blowing orgasms nightly.

Tessa had to admit, though, that his caution wasn't baseless. Even though she pleasured him with her hands and her tongue, she still couldn't take him into her mouth. And if she couldn't do that, Jackson wasn't off base assuming that she wasn't ready for intercourse either.

Distracted by her thoughts, she hadn't noticed that they'd exited the freeway at downtown. Was he taking her to the keep? Was someone throwing her a surprise party? But it wasn't her birthday, and no parties started at nine in the morning on a Sunday.

"Are you taking me to the keep?"

"Just a stopover. We need to change cars."

"Why?"

"If I tell you, it will ruin the surprise."

Ugh, she hated not knowing what was coming. Even if it was a good thing.

Jackson parked his car next to a fancy black limousine and got out.

"Hi, Okidu. Thanks for taking us," he greeted the driver, who rushed to open her door for her.

"Madam." He offered his hand.

She recognized him as the same guy who'd served refreshments on her first visit to the keep. Kian's butler. Was he his driver as well?

"Thank you." She let him help her up.

The butler opened the limousine's passenger door, and as she got in, Jackson followed her inside and sat next to her, grinning from ear to ear.

"Why are the windows opaque?" Limousine windows were darkened, so the interior wasn't visible from the outside, but she'd never heard of one with windows that made the exterior invisible from the inside.

He wrapped an arm around her shoulders. "To keep where we're going a surprise."

The partition between them and the driver was raised, and it was opaque too. Given the impressive soundproofing of the cabin and the lack of visuals, the interior felt like a luxurious sealed container. Tessa's stress level began climbing, and all the self-talk trying to convince herself that she was safe with Jackson, and that Kian's driver wasn't aiding in her kidnapping, wasn't helping.

Tessa felt the limousine climbing up the ramp from the underground garage level and then turning into the street. Sensing the movement helped to reduce her anxiety, as did Jackson's warm body pressed against hers.

"I don't like not seeing where I'm going."

He leaned closer and nuzzled her neck. "I can distract you."

As much as she liked him touching her, Tessa was too stressed to enjoy it.

As always, Jackson was attuned to the slightest of her responses. "Or we can watch a movie." He pressed a button, and a screen rose from the panel separating the passengers from the driver. "You can pretend we are in a movie theater."

Tessa let out a breath. "What movies do you have?"

"Anything your heart desires. This thing has all the streaming channels."

"Do they have *Guardians of the Galaxy* number two?"

"Let's see." Jackson got busy on the tablet that apparently served as the remote for the screen. "Found it." He selected the movie. "It's not long enough of a drive to see the whole thing."

"We can watch some on the way to your surprise, whatever it is, and then on the way back. If it's still not over, we can ask Okidu to let us stay in the limo until it ends."

A few minutes into the movie, Tessa got so immersed in it that it felt like no time at all had passed before the limousine stopped and Okidu opened the door for her.

Jackson paused the film and followed her out.

"Where are we?"

They were in a parking garage similar to the keep's, just much larger. The question was where.

Jackson ushered her into the elevator. "Count to twenty, and you'll see."

The doors opened before she reached fifteen, and she stepped out. Outside, beyond the glass sliding doors of the building they were in, she saw lush landscaping and several buildings that looked as if they were in the last stages of construction, with the scaffolding still attached.

Jackson waved a hand toward the glass doors. "Welcome to the village, Tessa."

"I feel so stupid. The car switch and the limousine with its opaque windows should've clued me in." Jackson had promised to arrange a visit to the village weeks ago.

A wide grin on his handsome face, Jackson circled her waist with his arm and led her toward the exit doors. "I'm glad I was able to surprise you."

"Have you been here before?"

He shook his head. "I asked Kian if we could see the place, and he said he'd let me know when he had time to show us around. I kept reminding him, but he was too busy and finally told me we could go by ourselves. He gave me a schematic of the layout so we could find our way around. I could've asked Okidu, but I thought it be would more fun to explore by ourselves."

Pulling out a folded printout from his back pocket, Jackson straightened the page and showed it to her. "The houses that are already taken are marked with a red X, and Kian even wrote next to each one the initials of the couple it's assigned to. All the rest are up for grabs." He smirked. "We can choose the one we want."

For a moment, Tessa was speechless. He wanted them to choose a house? Together? Wasn't it a little premature?

Apparently, Jackson wasn't kidding about the fated mates thing. He truly believed that they were it for each other. Forever.

The thought was wonderful and scary at the same time.

"Didn't you say that young bachelors would be the last ones to pick?"

"Yes. But couples get first dibs."

"We are not married."

"We don't have to be. Amanda and Dalhu aren't married either, and they got to choose a house already."

Tessa rolled her eyes. "You can't compare us to them. First of all, Amanda is Kian's sister and a member of the council, and second of all they have been living together for a while."

His face fell, but then he lifted his head with a mischievous glint in his eyes. "That's true. But to be considered an official couple all we have to do is pledge our love and devotion to each other in front of two witnesses. According to clan law, that's a lawful marriage."

That didn't sound right. Marriage required someone to preside over the ceremony to make it official, legal documents to be filled and signed, a blood test, and maybe more. She never had reason to look into it, and wasn't sure about what exactly was involved in the process, but it was certainly more than pledging love in front of witnesses.

Tessa arched a brow. "Really?"

Jackson dipped his head and kissed the top of her nose. "Really. That was what Bhathian and Eva did."

A stab of hurt pierced her heart. Eva hadn't told her anything. "Are you sure? Eva said they were planning a big wedding."

"They are because they want to celebrate their union, but it's not required."

What was going on?

Was he seriously talking about them getting married? So they could get a house?

No, no, no. First of all, they were way too young to be even talking about marriage, and second of all it was the least romantic proposal she'd heard of.

Tessa stopped and turned to face him. "Is that your round-about way of asking me to marry you?"

Jackson shrugged. "What if it is?"

Tessa lifted her eyes to the sky, praying for patience. "Don't you think this is too early to be talking about it?"

"Why?"

Casting a glance at the Chinese construction workers, who for some reason were eyeing her with open hostility, Tessa lowered her voice. "There are a few things that need to happen first. Like sex and me transitioning before we can seriously talk about getting married. But even if, or rather when both those conditions are met, you're still eighteen, Jackson." She waved her hands in the air. "This is crazy talk. I'm not willing to take such a huge step just because you want dibs on a house."

CHAPTER 37: JACKSON

*J*ackson shook his head and pulled the bristling Tessa into his arms. "Don't get all worked up over nothing. We don't have to even make a pledge to be considered a couple. Everyone knows we are together."

She punched his chest. "So why did you start with that whole thing if you knew it wasn't necessary?"

He kissed the top of her head. "Sheath your little claws, kitten. I'm the one who should be upset. As far as I'm concerned I already pledged myself to you, the only thing missing were witnesses. But your refusal to do the same hurts."

She stopped her struggles and wrapped her arms around his neck, stretching on the tips of her toes to reach him. "I love you. Never doubt it. And I pledge that I always will. But I'm not ready for any official announcements just so we can get priority on a house or any other material benefit. It cheapens what we feel for each other. Don't you agree?"

He didn't. One had nothing to do with the other. The house was a side benefit, and he saw no reason not to take advantage of their status as a couple to secure it for them. "It doesn't matter if I agree or not. The only thing that matters is how you feel about it. We will do whatever you want, Tessa. I'm not pressuring you into anything."

She sighed. "I know. Let's forget about this whole discussion and look at houses just for the fun of it."

"I'm all for it."

As they walked down the winding pathway between the buildings, Jackson couldn't shake the tinge of unease Tessa's rejection had caused. She loved him, he didn't doubt that, but she still wasn't one hundred percent committed the way he was.

Why?

Looking back, he couldn't think of a single thing he'd done wrong. He'd been gentle, patient, supportive, and loving. Everything women supposedly wanted.

Had he gotten it wrong?

Jackson had always made fun of the guys who couldn't figure women out. He'd believed himself an expert, priding himself on knowing exactly what women wanted and needed but were too coy or too confused to ask for.

The problem between most men and women was communication.

Men accepted things at face value, listening half-heartedly beyond the first sentence or two. They ignored subtle clues like the tone of voice and the body language, which betrayed so much more. Women were more attuned to those clues, and they expected their men to be as astute, getting upset when the poor schmucks didn't get it.

Apparently, he wasn't getting it either.

"Is that one taken?" Tessa pointed to a two-story house with a wrap-around porch.

Jackson checked his map. "Yes. That one is Nathalie and Andrew's."

They walked down the lane with Jackson checking each house. "This one is available." He pointed to a one-story ranch style house with a front porch.

"Then let's take a look." Tessa marched toward the door pulling him behind her.

For someone who'd just a few minutes ago bashed him for wanting to secure a good home for them, she was sure eager to explore.

"Nice," he said as they walked inside. He loved the open plan combining the living room, dining room and kitchen into one big space. A perfect layout for hanging out with friends.

"How many bedrooms does it have?" Tessa asked while pulling the pantry door open and peeking inside.

Jackson looked at the printout. "Two bedrooms, two bathrooms and a study that can be converted into a bedroom."

Tessa closed the pantry door. "Perfect." She strode toward the hallway and opened the first door. "It's gorgeous. Come take a look."

He followed her into the master bedroom. Long and narrow, it was big enough for a king-sized bed against its narrow back wall, and a sitting area in front of it, facing a fireplace. But the nicest part was the private patio and the French doors leading to it. Jackson could imagine Tessa and him drinking their morning coffees out there.

"We can hang a television screen above the mantel." Tessa pointed.

She was already taking ownership of the house. Funny girl. Jackson opened the double door to the bathroom and smiled. "A whirlpool tub, a glass enclosed shower for two, two sinks." He opened another door. "And a separate room with a toilet and a bidet. I'm in."

"I love it." Tessa turned in a circle, then opened the next set of double doors. "Look at this closet, Jackson. We can make an office out of it. It's huge."

He walked up to her, wrapped his arms around her front, and pulled her back into him, resting his chin on the top of her head. "We can't. Where are you going to hang all the sexy outfits I'm going to buy for you?"

She turned around in his arms, a happy smile brightening her small face. "I could manage with less than half of the space, but there is no window, so no office."

"Hmm, no window, you say. So if we close those doors we will have total privacy." He didn't shut them, leaving a wide crack to admit some light. Tessa didn't like total darkness.

She narrowed her eyes at him. "What do you have in mind?"

He picked her up, waiting for her to wrap her legs around his waist before carrying her to the nearest wall. "Just a little necking." He kissed her neck.

"Just a little?"

"Hmm, let's see." He pulled her T-shirt up, exposing her bra-covered breasts, and kissed the tops before unhooking it and pushing it up as well.

Perky breasts topped with small puckered nipples made his mouth water. Jackson licked his lips. "Sweet berries." He dipped his head and treated one to several long licks.

On a moan, Tessa let her head drop back, her hands coming up to fist his hair and hold him to her.

"Lift your arms, baby."

When she did, he pulled her shirt and bra off. "That's better." He swiped his tongue around her other nipple.

"Jackson."

It was a throaty whisper that could've meant so many things. After their previous argument, he was no longer sure he could guess what she wanted.

"What, kitten? Tell me what you need."

She cupped his cheeks and brought his mouth to hers, kissing him with passion and abandon that a few weeks ago he would've never believed she could summon.

Her spark hadn't been extinguished; it had remained

hidden somewhere beneath the wreckage, under the scars and the fears. Freed, it was burning bright.

Had it been his gentle coaxing that had nurtured that spark into a healthy flame? Could he at least take partial credit for that miraculous transformation?

Yesterday, he would've claimed it as his doing without batting an eyelid. Yesterday, he would have said that he was born to be the best lover of women a man could be.

Today, he wasn't so sure.

CHAPTER 38: TESSA

"What, kitten? Tell me what you need."

Tessa didn't know.

She wanted so many things.

She wanted to kiss Jackson until he forgot the hurtful words she'd hurled at him because she was afraid to hope too much.

She wanted this house to become their home.

She wanted to raise children with the man she loved even though they were both too young to even think of such things.

She wanted Jackson to lower her to the carpet-covered floor and make love to her and plant a baby inside her right now.

Tessa wanted a lot of things she couldn't have.

Not today and not tomorrow, but maybe someday.

There was one thing she could do today, though. She could give back at least a fraction of what he'd given her.

"I love you, Jackson, and I want to spend the rest of my life with you. I'm sorry if what I said before hurt your feelings. That wasn't my intention."

He sighed and rested his forehead on hers. "You know that I

love you and that I'll wait as long as it takes. I'm an immortal. Time and chronological age have little meaning to me."

She hadn't thought of that.

Of course he would have a different perspective than her.

But even if the thought had crossed her mind, she would've thought that an immortal would feel like a teenager at sixty, not that an eighteen-year-old would feel mature enough to commit to a lifelong relationship.

Maybe it really wasn't about chronological age. Maybe Jackson's soul was old. Some people were like that. Sometimes children possessed wisdom that the adults around them lacked.

Perhaps he was really ready, and she was too close-minded to see that, blindly following society's inflexible rules, when she was the last one who should feel bound by them. Society hadn't been kind to her. The rules governing what was decent and what was not hadn't been applied to her.

She should make her own rules to live by. Simple ones. The first rule she'd follow was to give back as much as she was given. Vengeance for wrongdoing, love for love, and pleasure for pleasure.

"Put me down."

Jackson frowned but did as she asked.

He always did.

Tessa continued her descent until her knees touched the floor, then reached for his belt buckle.

He caught her hands and pulled them away. "What are you doing?"

She smirked. "What does it look like I'm doing?"

"I don't want you to."

"Oh, yeah? You don't like oral sex?"

"Of course I do, but not like this. Not on your knees." He whispered the last words with a pained expression on his face.

She pulled her hands out of his grasp and stroked his thighs. "I know you think this is degrading, but it's not. Not with you, not when you've only ever shown me love and respect. We have no bed to lie on, no couch to snuggle on. And this works. Can you let me do this?"

He nodded, even though given his pinched expression he was still unsure.

Sweet guy. Jackson was the universe's way of righting the wrong, rewarding her after screwing her over so badly.

Leaning against the wall, Jackson let his arms fall at his sides, submitting to her and what she wanted to do to him.

Even before she unbuckled his belt and pulled on the zipper, it was quite obvious that his arousal was gone. Her suspicion was confirmed when she pulled his pants and his boxer shorts down.

He hadn't been kidding when he'd said he didn't want it like this.

Jackson must've been the only healthy male alive who went limp at the prospect of a blow job.

She regretted pressuring him into something he felt uncomfortable about. He'd never done it to her even when he'd thought she'd enjoy it. But it was too late to retreat now. Tessa had a point to prove—more to herself than to Jackson.

First, she kissed the tip to let him know she was doing this out of love. Then she kissed another spot and another until he hardened in her hand. When she treated him to a long lick, starting at the tip and going all the way down to the base, Jackson groaned and got even harder.

She got him.

At first, Tessa just licked and pumped, stopping only to pepper him with small teasing kisses before resuming her ministrations. It wasn't the way she'd been taught to do this, but that was the whole point. Nor was it the first time Tessa had been on her knees in front of a man, but this was the first time she was doing it because she wanted to and not because someone was forcing her.

Tessa intended to make it as different of an experience as possible, wiping the slate clean by doing it her way.

His palms glued to the wall behind him, Jackson held himself still as a statue. The only signs that he was enjoying this were his harsh breaths and the hard length pulsating in her hand.

Lifting her gaze to him, she took the tip into her mouth.

He sucked in a breath, his hooded eyes blazing with an inner light that was enough to illuminate the darkened interior of the closet.

There was no more doubt that Jackson loved what she was doing.

For a few moments, Tessa sucked, licked and pumped, enjoying the taste and the feel of him in her mouth. Sweet and tangy, hard but covered in velvety softness, he was perfect in every way a man could be.

Jackson groaned, his strong thigh muscles straining against his need to thrust.

Should she take him all the way to the back of her throat?

Could she?

Tessa had done this countless times before, but then it had been part of her torture. Could the same act bring about different sensations when done willingly?

Could it actually turn her on?

It was time to find out.

Bracing a hand on Jackson's hip in an instinctual attempt to hold him in place, preventing him from thrusting before she was ready, Tessa closed her eyes and took him a little deeper. Then a little deeper yet.

Jackson's breathing became ragged, but he still didn't move an inch.

Filling her lungs with air, Tessa loosened her throat muscles and took him as far as he would go.

Jackson jerked, trying to pull back, but with his butt against the wall, he had nowhere to go. His next move was the least expected of all. He went flaccid, his erection shrinking inside her mouth.

Why?

Did she accidentally scrape him with her teeth?

Letting go of him in a rush, she expected to see a scratch. But there was nothing. He was as smooth and as perfect as always.

"What happened?" she asked.

Jackson glided down until his butt hit the floor, then reached for her, cradling her in his arms. "A bad thought." He hugged her closer.

What kind of a bad thought could've ruined his mood like that?

Had he remembered a bad experience?

Had some nasty girl bitten him?

Then it dawned on her. It wasn't about something Jackson had experienced himself. It was about what she'd experienced. What she'd done wasn't something a novice could do. It had taken a lot of practice and beatings to conquer her gag reflex. Was he disgusted by her? Had her expertise driven the point home that she wasn't clean?

How could he hold on to her with such ferocity while being disgusted by her?

"Let me go, Jackson," she croaked as tears started running down her cheeks.

His arms around her tightened even more. "I'm not letting you move an inch."

She struggled even though she knew it was futile. "Let me go! I'm disgusting to you!"

"What?" His grip on her loosened just enough so he could look at her face. "What are you talking about? And why the hell are you crying?"

God, what had happened to him? Why did he want to humiliate her further by forcing her to spell it out?

"You went soft on me. I thought I hurt you, scraped you with my teeth or something, but that wasn't the reason. You finally internalized how soiled I am. Didn't you?"

Jackson crushed her to him with a force that had the air in her lungs leave with a whoosh. "Oh, baby, you're so wrong, I could never think that of you. You're my love and my sunshine. You're everything to me."

He sounded so sincere that she had to believe him. "So what happened?"

Jackson sighed. "You're so tiny, Tessa. I've been with girls a foot taller than you who were experienced as hell and still couldn't take me as far as you did. I couldn't help thinking about what you had to go through to be able to do that. I can't think about you suffering and stay aroused. I'm just not wired that way."

"I know."

She put her head on his chest, and as he held her close, the tears kept coming, and there was nothing she could do to stop them.

"I'm sorry," she hiccupped. "I can't stop."

Jackson stroked her hair. "It's okay. Let it all out, kitten, I got you."

CHAPTER 39: BRUNDAR

*H*er hands braced on her hips, her head lowered to avoid Brundar's eyes, Kri shook it from side to side. "Please don't ask me to do that. I've never even held a whip in my hand."

He'd expected her to balk at his request, but she was his only option. Only another Guardian could deliver his penance, and she was the only female Guardian.

Having a male at his back might override his logic circuits and lead to disastrous results. Some reactions were instinctive and too powerful to control.

If he wasn't capable of tolerating even a casual touch from his own brother, there was no chance he could tolerate a male with a whip executing his punishment.

Brundar would never forgive himself if he attacked a fellow Guardian. He wasn't sure anyone could pry him off the guy before he delivered a deadly dose of venom.

"I'll show you how."

She shook her head again. "Why me? Why not Bhathian? He's done it before."

Damnation. Revealing his true reasons was not an option.

No one other than Anandur knew what had happened to him. But he had to tell her something to convince her. Perhaps his reputation would come in handy for once.

"I prefer a woman with a whip."

Kri's face twisted in a grimace. "Ugh, Brundar, that's gross. I'm your cousin. I'm not going to help get your rocks off."

That hadn't come out as intended. "Get your head out of the gutter, Kri. This is not a sex game."

"So what is it? You have to give me a reason to do something I really don't want to do."

Brundar held her gaze. "If a male delivers the punishment, I'm afraid the pain would cloud my reasoning and evoke an instinctive, aggressive response. I don't want to kill one of my friends."

"How do you know you're not going to attack me?"

"The instinct is not going to kick in with a female at my back."

"You sure about that?"

"A hundred percent."

Kri let her head drop down. "Fine. But don't blame me if you end up with a back that looks like ground meat. You really should pick someone experienced."

"I'll take a shredded back over a dead friend any day."

Taking a deep breath, Kri exhaled through her mouth. "Where do you want to train me?"

"Same place you're going to do it an hour from now."

With a groan, Kri nodded.

"Thank you."

"You owe me. And if after this I can't sleep, you owe me more."

"Think of it as an exercise in toughening up."

She waved a hand. "Yeah, yeah."

An hour later, Kri had mastered the basics of wielding a whip, but she was still far from skilled. It didn't matter. Where Brundar prided himself on never breaking the skin, Kri was expected to do just that. She was supposed to deliver a punishment, not satisfy a kink.

She looked like she was going to a funeral. He owed Kri a big favor for this.

"Don't overthink it." He patted her shoulder. "Remember that I asked for it. I could've taken jail time instead and refused because I didn't want to waste time. Besides, I'm going to be as good as new in forty-eight hours or less."

She squared her shoulders. "Don't worry, I'm not going to faint on you."

"I know you won't."

Edna entered the chamber followed by Kian. Trailing behind them were the rest of the Guardians, including his brother who looked even more pissed now than during Brundar's earlier sentencing.

Per Brundar's request, Edna omitted the details of his personal involvement in the matter, only stating that he'd confessed to using an unlawful thrall, and the punishment appropriate for such transgression according to their law.

"No mitigating circumstances?" Anandur had tried to argue in Brundar's defense.

"Declined by the offender." Edna hadn't elaborated, protecting Brundar's privacy.

When Anandur's attempts to drag the details of what he'd done out of him had failed, he'd made it clear in so many words that he was done with Brundar and his shitty attitude.

He'd get over it. Even though Brundar didn't deserve it, his brother always forgave him.

Taking his shirt off, he dropped it on the floor, then disarmed, pulling out every one of the knives he carried on his body and putting them down on the shirt. When he was done, he wrapped them into a tight bundle and handed it to Anandur. "Keep them safe and try not to cut yourself."

Anandur growled. "Now you're making a joke? Screw you."

Brundar turned around and faced Edna. "I'm ready. I chose the Guardian Kri to deliver my penance."

Edna nodded. "Proceed. Ten strokes."

Given his repeat offense, it was a merciful number, and he'd made the mistake of pointing it out to Edna.

Never a good thing to piss off the judge.

With a chilling smile, she'd informed him that she could still slap a week of incarceration on top of the whipping. That had shut him up.

Bracing his hands against the cool stone, Brundar closed his eyes and slipped into the zone. The soft murmurs of the Guardians faded away, and all that was left was quiet. Ready, he dipped his head once, giving Kri the signal they'd agreed on.

CHAPTER 40: CALLIE

*W*orking at Franco's, Callie's schedule consisted of waking up at ten in the morning, two hours of studying, and then lunch. After that, she was free to do as she pleased until her shift started at eight in the evening.

Plenty of time to do nothing.

She'd downloaded a bunch of books on her tablet, spending several blissful afternoons curled up on the couch reading. But the novelty of having so much free time had worn off soon.

Callie was bored and lonely.

No one ever came in.

Brundar, Franco, and the bouncers who sometimes walked her home after her shift never crossed the threshold of her apartment.

When her buzzer went off at four in the afternoon, it was a pleasant surprise.

She padded barefoot to the monitor by the door and pressed the intercom.

"Hi, Brundar." She tried to sound casual even though her heart started thudding in her rib cage the moment she saw who it was.

"Let me in, Calypso."

"Of course."

For a few seconds she couldn't tear her eyes away from Brundar, watching him push the lobby's door open and walk in until he disappeared from the camera's view. Only then did she make a mad dash for her bedroom to brush her hair and put a bra on. There was no time to change out of her pajama pants or look for a better T-shirt.

He'd never just popped in before. But at least he'd given her a few moments' notice by buzzing her intercom. Callie was sure Brundar had another set of keys, but it was decent of him not to use it.

Her stoic, indifferent protector was a man of honor.

She wished he had a little less of all three qualities. Less stoic and more feeling, less indifferent and more interested, less honorable and more forward.

It should've been illegal to be so attractive and so cold at the same time.

He hadn't been cold that one time he kissed her, though.

Callie sighed and rushed back to the living room to open the door.

"Hi," she said as she let him in.

Brundar smiled, actually smiled, showing a little bit of teeth. It was so shocking that she had to ask, "What are you so happy about?"

"I have a present for you." He handed her a large envelope.

"What is it?" She started opening the flap.

"Your freedom."

Her hands trembled as she finished pulling out the stack of papers. "How?"

It had been only two weeks since Shawn had been served. She hadn't known he'd even signed them, interpreting the silence from the attorney to mean nothing was happening yet.

"A little persuasion."

"Did you beat him up to have him sign so fast?" She leveled Brundar with a hard stare. Not that she minded terribly if he had, but she did mind that he hadn't told her about it.

Brundar shrugged. "I didn't have to beat him up to have him sign. As I told you before, I can be very persuasive."

He wasn't lying, but he wasn't telling her the whole truth either. "Is he okay?"

"That depends on what you consider okay."

She rolled her eyes. A question addressed to Brundar needed to be precise. "Is he in the morgue? Or in a hospital with broken bones?"

"No."

Exasperated, she threw her hands in the air. "Please, just tell me what you mean without me having to drag every freaking word out of you."

He seemed taken aback by her outburst, his pale blue eyes widening for a moment. "Shawn's mind is twisted. The world would be a better place without him. But my hands are tied by the law and by your request not to harm him."

Letting out a breath, Callie let her head drop. She felt so bad for snapping at him. It was no way to repay the guy after all he'd done for her. "Thank you. For everything."

He nodded.

"Please, would you like to take a seat?" She pointed at the couch.

Without answering, he walked over and sat down, his back straight as an arrow, his legs crossed at the knee.

"Can I offer you a drink? Coffee?" He'd never made good on his promise to bring her a good wine. After their kiss, Brundar had turned from cold to icy. Not in an angry way, or dismissive, just remote and indifferent. He might as well have painted a sign on his forehead saying, 'I'm not interested.'

"Do you want to have dinner with me?" he asked.

It took a great effort not to let her jaw drop. Brundar was asking her out?

Impossible.

Maybe he wanted her to make him dinner? He liked her cooking. "Would you like me to whip up something quick for us instead?"

His eyes brightened. "Your fajitas were exceptional."

Callie guessed it was a yes. "I don't have the ingredients for fajitas, but I can make something else. If you'd given me advance notice, I would have cooked you a gourmet five-course meal."

"You can do that?"

She chuckled. He was so literal. "I'm a good cook, but calling what I do gourmet is a slight exaggeration." To demonstrate, she put two fingers together with barely any space between them.

Brundar smiled again.

Wow, at this rate she might make him laugh. Wouldn't that be a great achievement? Worthy of a mention in *The Guinness Book of World Records*?

"Let me see what I have to work with." She turned around and headed for the refrigerator.

Brundar followed, taking a seat on the same barstool he'd sat on the other time she'd cooked for him.

Maybe that was the ticket.

Wasn't there a saying that the way to a man's heart was through his stomach?

"I could make lasagna, but it would take too long. Do you like Thai?" Holding the fridge door open she turned her head around, catching him ogling her ass.

If he was embarrassed about getting caught, he didn't show it. Brundar's austere, handsome face was expressionless as ever.

"I will like anything you make."

It was such a nice thing to say, and if it were anyone else she would have interpreted it as flirting. But Brundar meant it literally.

Either way, she knew it was a compliment. That didn't mean, however, that she couldn't tease him about it.

"Did you mean to say that you think I'm a good cook and that you're sure everything I make tastes good, or that you're not particular about what you put in your mouth?" She pulled out a few ingredients from the fridge, then opened the pantry in search of a can of coconut cream.

"You know the answer. I told you I liked your fajitas."

Callie winked. "I'm just teasing you. Trying to loosen you up a bit."

He pinned her with a hard stare she couldn't decipher, sending shivers of desire dancing along her spine. She waited for him to say something, admonish her for suggesting he wasn't loose enough, or for teasing him, but he remained silent.

Oh, well.

Pulling out a cutting board, she started chopping vegetables into large chunks. The way Brundar was following her every move, as if he was her apprentice and was trying to commit every detail to memory, it was a miracle she didn't slice off a finger.

Having his undivided attention was doing strange things to her. She'd never had anyone focus on her like that. Even during the good times with Shawn, when he'd still been charming and attentive, the focus had always been on him, not her.

He'd talked and she listened, he'd told jokes and she'd laughed.

In a way, it had suited her. To be with Shawn hadn't taken much effort on her part. Not in the beginning. But then he'd changed, or maybe she'd just started seeing him more clearly. Being around him had felt like being next to a black hole—he'd sucked the life out of her.

With Brundar it was the opposite. It was all up to her. With laser-like focus, he listened and he watched as she talked, as she made jokes. Being around him was like getting hooked to an electrical outlet, the sizzling current between them filling her with energy, with life.

The powerful vibe he exuded wasn't stifling, it was like pure oxygen to a smoldering fire, igniting a dangerous flame.

CHAPTER 41: BRUNDAR

*H*e shouldn't have stayed.

It was pure torture pretending he didn't know Calypso wanted him, ignoring the scent of her arousal. But she'd looked so relieved, with her beautiful face relaxed and happy for the first time in months, that he wanted to gaze at her for a little longer.

Brundar's idea had been to celebrate Calypso's freedom by taking her out to a nice restaurant, but when she'd suggested cooking for him, he could not bring himself to refuse.

Being alone with her, watching her do this for him, was too precious to squander. For a couple of hours, he could pretend she was his. That he was normal. That he was sharing his life with her.

That he had a mate.

Brundar shook his head. A human couldn't be his mate. And hoping Calypso was a Dormant was like hoping to win the lottery by buying the first ticket.

She had none of the indicators. Not unless cooking could be considered a paranormal talent.

"Do you think I'm safe from Shawn now? Do you think he could still come after me?"

Not in the very near future, but unless Brundar thralled the jerk every couple of weeks, the last thrall he'd put over him would eventually fade. Regrettably, other than Annani none of the clan members had the ability to place a permanent compulsion on a human, and the goddess couldn't be bothered with every abusive asshole. She would end up doing nothing but.

"No."

Calypso arched a brow, indicating his answer wasn't satisfactory. It wasn't. But he was so used to brushing everyone off with his terse answers that he had to relearn how to talk to someone he didn't want to push away. "His mind is not right. I don't know how long he is going to hold a grudge against you, but I don't expect him to forget about it anytime soon."

She nodded, satisfied with the completeness of his answer, but not with the implication. "What am I going to do in the meantime? I want to get my teaching degree, maybe even continue and get a Master's. I can't do it if I can't attend classes."

"You can. With caution."

She lowered the flame under the wok and leaned against the other side of the cooktop. "Meaning?"

Brundar's lips twitched. He was starting to rub off on her. Did she notice that she had just used a one word sentence?

"To start with, you'll need to change your name."

She shook her head. "I was admitted as Calypso Davidson."

"I'm sure the university's administration will have no problem with a new name once you explain the circumstances. I can get you a legit new identification. I know a guy."

"Sure you do. You know a lot of people in the right places."

"It's my job."

"And other than changing my name?"

"A few small changes in appearance. Different hair color and cut, large glasses, different style of clothing."

She pondered his suggestions for a moment, then nodded. "It won't fool Shawn up close, but it might from a distance."

"That's the idea."

Calypso let out a breath and uncrossed her arms. "I can live with that. And with a different name, I can open a new bank account, and Franco can start paying me with checks. I can even get myself a car, a cheap, used one I can buy with cash."

She took out two clean plates from the dishwasher and heaped them with what was in the wok.

"What would you like to drink with that? I only have Diet Coke and orange juice."

"Water is fine."

She put the plates on the counter, took out a can of Coke from the fridge and poured him a glass of water from a pitcher she'd kept there.

"Thank you."

He waited to take the first bite until Calypso sat next to him.

"I hope you don't mind tofu," she said.

"I don't."

Calypso watched him as he forked a cube together with a few pieces of vegetables and stuffed it in his mouth.

"How is it?"

"Very good." It was the truth. He wasn't crazy about tofu, but the dish was so full of flavor it compensated for the tofu's bland taste.

Calypso chuckled. "I would've never pegged you as someone who eats tofu. Not after the steaks you wolfed down at Aussie."

"My cousin is vegan, and his butler cooks vegan dishes for him. Sometimes my brother and I invite ourselves for lunch."

She shook her head. "You have a cousin who has a butler? Who has butlers these days? Is he royalty?"

In a way, Kian was royalty. But it would be difficult to explain without revealing too much. "He is a businessman."

"A very successful one, I assume."

"Yes." Brundar stuffed his mouth with another forkful before Calypso threw more questions at him. In the short time he'd spent with her, he'd talked more than he usually talked in a year. It was tiring. He wasn't used to that.

Thankfully, she dug into her own plate and for a few minutes they ate in blissful quiet.

It didn't last long. Calypso put her fork down and wiped her mouth with a napkin. "I should start looking for an apartment. Your friend will want this one back."

Brundar scrambled for a passable lie. He remembered telling her that his made-up friend was teaching a semester abroad. "He is not coming back anytime soon. They offered him a two-year stint. He is very happy that you're staying here and making sure his place doesn't get vandalized."

She narrowed her eyes at him. "He told you that?"

Brundar nodded. Fates, he hated lying.

"When you speak with him again, please tell him I'm grateful and that I'm more than happy to pay him rent."

If she knew how much the rent was, she would have thought twice before suggesting it. She wasn't making that kind of money at the club.

"He doesn't want a tenant. He wants a house sitter. And besides, you need to save up the money you're making to pay tuition."

She lowered her head. "Right. I forgot about that."

Her embarrassment made him uncomfortable. She'd seemed so upbeat and hopeful about her prospects until he'd mentioned the tuition. Maybe what she was making at Franco's wasn't enough.

"If you need help with that, I can loan you the money. Interest free."

She lifted her eyes to him. "Thank you, but I'll manage. I'm living rent free." She ran a hand through her hair. "God, Brundar, how will I ever repay you for all this?"

Brundar could've said that it was nothing, and heaped on more lies about his nonexistent friend, but he didn't want to. Instead, he changed the subject. "I would advise against visiting your father and your friend. If Shawn is plotting revenge, he will keep tabs on them, waiting for you to show up."

"Yeah. I know. Maybe I can get them to meet me somewhere."

"Wait a few months until you do. Don't call them from here or the club either. I'll get you a burner phone."

"I have one."

Not the kind he was talking about. "I'll get you a safer one. You can trust me to know which one is best."

Her green eyes pinned his with an unreadable expression. "I trust you with my life."

CHAPTER 42: CALLIE

*B*rundar gazed at her as if she'd grown horns. But Callie had meant it.

"Don't look at me as if I'm missing a screw. I still don't know why you're doing all of this for me, but I know that without you none of this would have been possible. You gave me my life back. If not for you, I would've been still trapped with Shawn, and one day he might've snapped and beaten me to death. So yeah, I trust you with my life. Deal with it." She grabbed his plate and hers and carried both to the sink.

She'd never met a more frustrating and confusing man.

He was her angel, but there was palpable darkness in him. It was leashed and contained, but for better or worse it was there. She could deal with it, even embrace it, because without it Brundar would not be who he was—her fierce protector.

That wasn't the problem, though. She needed to understand his motives, she needed him to open up to her, she needed to have him.

It was a need more than a want. On some primitive level, she felt that he belonged to her, and she was more than willing to give herself to him. The attraction didn't make sense. So yeah, he was criminally handsome, and right now he was her only friend, but it was like falling for a robot. A capable, helpful creature like one of the cyborgs she'd read about in her sci-fi romance novels.

"Why are you angry?" He seemed truly perplexed.

She dropped the plate she was rinsing into the soapy water and turned around to glare at him. "You want to know why I am angry?"

It was a rhetorical question, but he answered it anyway. "Yes. I just asked you that."

God, what was wrong with this man?

"I'm frustrated."

"With me?"

"Yes, with you." She walked up to him, invading his personal space. "Are you attracted to me, Brundar?"

He swallowed. "Of course I am. Who wouldn't be?"

"Good." She took a step closer, crowding him. "Then you won't mind this." She cupped his cheeks and kissed him.

He stiffened, not responding to her kiss, keeping his lips tightly pressed and not allowing her tongue inside.

Crap. What the hell had gotten into her? Was she trying to dominate a dominant?

No wonder he didn't want that.

Callie took a step back. "I'm sorry. I shouldn't have." She turned, intending to flee into the bedroom and bury her flaming face in a pillow.

He caught her elbow. "Wait."

Embarrassed, she closed her eyes as he turned her around, refusing to look at him.

"Look at me, Calypso," he commanded.

She shook her head.

His fingers closed on her chin.

"Open your beautiful green eyes and look at me," Brundar repeated softly.

He thought her eyes were beautiful? Gathering her courage, she opened her eyes.

"I want you. But not like that."

"Not like what?"

"I have to be in total control. Do you understand?"

She nodded.

"I can't have you kiss me. I can't even have you touch me."

"I know you don't want to be touched, and I'm sorry I did. Well, I'm not. But you know what I mean. It was an impulse. But are you going to touch me? Because I really need you to. Is that okay for me to say? Or is it not allowed either? You never told me the rules. I don't know what's okay and what's not. It's all so confusing. You're so confusing. I don't know what you want from me—" She was blabbering, but she was so sick of holding it all in.

He put a finger to her lips to shush her. "Yes. I'm going to touch you. But you might not like my rules. And that's okay. The only way this works is if your rules and mine don't conflict."

Callie let out a breath. That made sense, and it made her feel more in control. Somehow she'd managed to push him a tiny step closer. "Tell me."

He sighed. "First rule. No emotional entanglement. Not because you're not great but because I can't. There are things about me I can never tell you that make a relationship impossible."

He might as well have stabbed her heart with a knife. The pain of his rejection was sharp and all consuming. She needed to at least understand why.

"Is it something personal? Something about me? Am I missing something?"

He shook his head and parted his legs, wrapping his arms around her and pulling her closer.

She remembered he didn't want her to touch him, and even

though her hands itched to burrow into his beautiful blond hair, she fisted them by her sides.

"You're perfect. And if I were free to do as I please, I would make you mine and never let you go. But I'm not."

He had told her that he lived with his brother. Had he lied? "Are you married? Do you have someone?"

He chuckled. "I'm married to my job and my duties."

An excuse if she'd ever heard one.

"A lot of people have demanding jobs."

"My job prohibits a relationship with a—" He stopped. "A woman."

She humphed. "Does it allow a relationship with a man?"

He smacked her butt, igniting her arousal. "Don't be a smart ass, Calypso."

She narrowed her eyes at him. "Or what? You'll spank me? I'm shaking in my proverbial boots."

Another smack followed, harder than the first. "At this rate, you won't be able to sit by the time I finish the list of rules."

She shrugged.

Brundar shook his head. "You're enjoying this too much for it to be effective."

He had that right. If she could think of another smart-ass remark, she would make it. "I'm listening."

"Good girl." He patted her behind. "Rule number two. You're not allowed to touch me, which brings me to the last rule. If we get intimate, you'll be tied up and blindfolded. That's the only way I play."

Callie frowned. It required a lot of trust, especially since all they had done until now was kiss. What if she got scared? She'd never been tied up or blindfolded before. Still, his list of rules was surprisingly short.

"That's it? I don't have to call you sir or anything?" She could deal with calling him sir, but she was never going to call him master.

A smile tugged at one corner of his lips. "Only if you feel like it."

"How about treating you with respect and stuff like that?"

"You already do. Most of the time. But that has nothing to do with playtime. I expect respect from everyone I come in contact with, and provided they do, I respond in kind."

Funny he would say that. Apparently, Brundar didn't realize how his curt answers could be perceived as rude. His definition of respectful was very different than hers.

"I like that. Being polite is important to me."

"Good, any other questions? Anything you disagree with?"

"No. I'm game. But what if I get scared? Or overwhelmed? I like you, and I trust you, but we've never done anything aside from kissing. Which by the way, was amazing. But it's difficult for me to leap from that straight to bondage. Do you know what I mean?"

CHAPTER 43: BRUNDAR

*B*rundar knew exactly what she meant. A newbie wasn't ready for bondage. Not with someone she didn't know well and didn't spend a lot of time with.

Telling her that it was the only way he did things would hopefully deter her from her tenacious pursuit of him. Brundar wasn't strong enough to keep pushing her away. It was difficult enough to control his attraction to her, doing it on two fronts was impossible even for a fighter like him.

The only way to stop that thing between them from moving forward was for Calypso to realize that he wasn't what she wanted. The other option was him walking out the door and never coming back.

He'd tried to distance himself from her, but it didn't work. The pull was too strong.

"I know, sweetling. You're not ready for someone like me."

Eyes cast down, Calypso chewed on her lower lip. "I want to try. If I tell you to stop, will you?"

Fates, why the hell was he so relieved that she still wanted him?

He could've said that he wouldn't, scaring her off. Instead, he told her the truth. "Yes. Immediately."

She nodded, then sighed. "I know you don't like to talk a lot, but there is so much I don't know, and so much you can tell me."

Sweet girl. She was so brave.

Calypso deserved so much more than he had to offer. The least he could do was sate her curiosity. For her, he would make an effort and talk. Hell, if it made her happy, he would talk from now until next morning.

The thing was, he wasn't sure he could answer all of her questions.

Brundar didn't dwell on the psychology of the various kinks people engaged in. He couldn't explain them to her even if he tried. He wasn't even sure if his particular kink was the result of what had happened to him as a boy, or if the need for control was just a part of who he was, his genetic makeup.

Pushing to his feet he took her hand, walked her over to the couch, sat down, and pulled her onto his lap.

The world righted itself.

Calypso leaned against him, her body molding into his. Without him having to remind her, she tucked her hands between her thighs.

Good girl.

"I'll do my best to answer your questions. But the truth is that I'm not an expert."

"You're not?"

"I know a hundred ways to tie a woman up, and just as many to bring her pleasure. I'm also an expert with the whip."

Callie shivered, and he tightened his arms around her. "I know how to use it correctly, but it's not something I enjoy doing. I'm not a sadist."

She let out a breath. "Thank God. I can't even imagine the pain. Why would anyone want that?"

He chuckled. "That's one of the questions I'm not qualified to answer. For myself, I know that a punishment like that can be cathartic, but it's not something that excites me sexually."

She frowned. "Have you ever been whipped? Or are you talking hypothetically?"

He shifted, the almost healed scars on his back more itchy than painful. Kri had tried her best, but she had a lot to learn about wielding a whip.

"The first one."

She looked at him with horrified eyes. "Why? Who did it to you?"

Fates, how could he explain this to her in a way she could understand?

"It was ceremonial."

"What do you mean? Like hazing?"

Not exactly, but it would do. "Yeah. Something like that."

She shook her head, her eyes blazing with anger. "God. Men are such morons, always coming up with crazier and crazier ideas to prove worthy of their dicks."

He smacked her flank. "Watch it. That wasn't cordial or respectful in the least."

Calypso wiggled on his lap. "I don't remember spanking on your very short list."

It wasn't, but the scent of her arousal intensified after each smack. Sweet Calypso enjoyed a little playful spanking.

"It's not on mine. But it's on yours."

A deep blush bloomed on her cheeks. "How do you know what's on my list?"

Another thing he couldn't tell her. "An educated guess. You just squirmed on my lap, and it wasn't because you were in pain. I didn't smack you hard enough for it to hurt."

She pouted. "It did."

He might need to add another rule. Honesty was not something he required from his playmates, but he needed it from

236

Calypso. It was hypocritical of him to demand truth from her while he piled lie after lie, but that was different. He lied to protect his people; she lied because she was embarrassed to admit what turned her on.

It wasn't going to work unless she talked to him.

"Don't lie to me. That's another rule."

She wiggled again. "What are you going to do about it?" Her voice got husky.

"I'm going to turn you over my knee and spank your cute little ass until you admit the lie, say you're sorry, and mean it." He teased her, knowing it turned her on.

"What if I like it?"

"I promise you will not."

"You'll punish me? For real?" She looked worried.

"Only if you want me to."

Closing her eyes, she put her head on his chest. "This is all so confusing. Why would I want you to punish me?"

"The why isn't important. Only the what. You make your own rules, and it's okay to change them and make adjustments as you go. You might think you like something and then realize you don't, or the other way around. But you won't know until you try."

"It's all a big game. Isn't it?"

"That's why I call it playing."

"Is everyone in the club like that? Or is it just you?"

He shrugged. "As with every type of game, some take it more seriously than others. Some like to play twenty-four-seven, while others like to play once a month, and everything in between."

She seemed confused. "I don't know what my rules are. And what happens if I refuse one of yours or you refuse one of mine?"

"There are hard rules and soft rules. The rules I laid out for you are my hard rules. If you refuse, we don't play, and the same goes for you."

"Is there a chance your hard rules will one day become soft rules?" she whispered.

Fates, there had been so much hope in that whisper, he knew he was going to disappoint her no matter how hard he tried not to.

It wasn't that he hadn't harbored the same insane hope, a hope that one day he would find his fated mate and would crave her touch as much as she craved his. But Calypso could never be that mate. All she could be was a transitional lover he would have to abandon sooner rather than later.

The only reason he was succumbing to her was that she needed guidance and he hated the idea of her falling into the hands of some pervert who might hurt her. He would teach her the right way to go about it, help her explore her needs and once she was ready he would disappear from her life.

"Not likely. If you can't accept them, we'd better stop right now."

She lifted her eyes to him. "You're not getting rid of me that easily. I'll take whatever you can give me and love every moment of it."

He lifted a brow. "And you know this because?"

"I just do. Call it a woman's intuition."

Right. A woman's intuition. Calypso's was obviously malfunctioning. If it were working right, she would not be sitting in his lap, hoping for a future that couldn't be.

His phone buzzed, and he pulled it out of his pocket.

"It's not a good time, Anandur."

"We need you at County. Roni is transitioning."

Damnation. They needed him for the extraction. Other than Yamanu, his shrouding and thralling abilities were the strongest. "Take Yamanu."

"Are you serious? And miss all the fun?"

Yeah. It was a rare opportunity to practice his skills, but he had more important things to do.

"Yes. Is he okay to go?"

"Of course he is. I just wanted to save this for you."

"Some other time."

"There won't be another time."

"There always is." He clicked the call off.

"What was that about?" Calypso asked.

"My brother wanted me to take part in a prank."

She lifted a brow. "You? Pranking someone? Boy, did he choose the wrong man."

"My thoughts exactly."

CHAPTER 44: BRUNDAR

*T*he phone call had been a most welcome pattern interrupt. Brundar had allowed himself to get carried away.

What the hell was he thinking, sitting with her in his lap as if they were lovers?

She needed information and he was more than willing to provide it, but he shouldn't have done it in such an intimate setting. Calypso's arousal was playing a number on him. He was hard as a rock, and it hadn't gone unnoticed.

Calypso's cheeks were flushed, her eyes glazed in desire. They both needed a splash of cold water to break the spell.

"Come on." He lifted her off his lap and helped her to her feet.

She looked confused for a moment, then glanced at her watch before lifting her gaze to him with a frown wrinkling her forehead. "It's not time for my shift yet."

"I know. You need a tour." He stood up.

Her breath hitched. "You're taking me to the club? I mean to the lower level?"

"Yes."

"I thought not being twenty-eight I wasn't allowed in there."

"Not as a member and not as an employee, but there is nothing prohibiting me from taking you on a tour. There is no one there this time of day during midweek."

She swallowed. "I need to get dressed first."

"Take your time." He sat back and crossed his legs. "I'll wait."

"I won't be long." She hurried off to her bedroom.

As he waited for Calypso to get ready, Brundar wondered what would scare her off. He could show her the various rooms and the equipment they housed. Some of them were set up for those with darker tastes, the instruments of torture sure to terrify her.

Calypso wasn't a masochist, and she seemed fairly empathic. Just imagining what went on in those rooms should cool her off.

By the time the tour was over, sex would be the farthest thing from her mind.

Which was his goal. The scent of her arousal was scrambling his brain. It was impossible to be around her and resist such a powerful and blatant invitation.

"I'm ready." She came back, the strap of her purse slung over her shoulder, wearing the club's informal uniform of black jeans and black T-shirt with Franco's logo embossed in red on the right breast.

Don't look at her breasts!

Brundar stood up and headed for the front door, opening it and waiting for her to step out before closing it. "Lock it."

"Yes, of course." Calypso pulled out her key, her hand a little unsteady as she tried to fit it inside the lock.

"Let me." He took it from her.

She was unsettled. Exactly as he wanted her to be.

They took the stairs, the short burst of activity clearing his mind. He walked over to his car and unlocked it with his fob, then pulled the passenger door open for Calypso.

They passed the short drive in silence, with Calypso sneaking surreptitious glances at him when she thought he wasn't looking.

Poor girl, he was confusing her with the mixed signals he was sending her. Letting his cold mask slip had been an unforgivable mistake. It wasn't her fault he couldn't give her what she needed. Stringing her along had been cruel.

The thing was, Brundar was swimming in unfamiliar waters. Calypso had a way of infiltrating his shields and bringing about sensations that were completely foreign to him.

Most of which had nothing to do with sex.

If it were only sexual attraction he could've dealt with it just fine, satisfying his needs and hers.

But it wasn't.

Calypso felt like home. When he was with her, watching her cook, talking with her, sharing a meal with her, he didn't want to leave.

Ever.

As he pulled his car into the club's parking lot, Brundar took stock of who else was there at that time of day. Franco's red pickup was there, a delivery van that belonged to the laundry service they used, and two other cars he didn't recognize. Hopefully, those didn't belong to members. He didn't want anyone to interrupt the tour he was about to take Calypso on.

He frowned as she opened the passenger door before he had the chance to open it for her. "I was about to do that."

"I can open my own door and get out of a parked car without assistance," she gritted. The lady wasn't happy, and he couldn't blame her. He'd been the worst kind of a tease, getting her all worked up and then dropping her like a sack of potatoes.

"I know you can. That's beside the point. It's okay to let others do nice things for you even if you don't need them to."

"Look who's talking," she murmured under her breath, thinking he couldn't hear her.

She was upset. He would let it pass this time.

Damnation. Once again he was losing his focus. This was about driving Calypso away, not thinking about an impossible future with her.

He strode in the direction of the club's back entrance, leaving her to stomp behind him.

Calypso was getting angrier by the minute. Perfect. The angrier she got, the easier it would be for her to walk away from him.

He didn't waste time looking for Franco before crossing the club's main level to the locked door that led to the basement. A few clicks on the keypad opened the way, and he waited for Calypso to go in before letting it snap closed.

There was no elevator to the lower level, only a narrow staircase. The basement used to be a storage area before Franco converted it into his sprawling playroom.

"It's dark in here," she said, reminding him he'd forgotten to turn the lights on.

He flipped the switch on, and a lineup of shaded sconces bathed the staircase in soft light. "Better?"

"Yes, thank you." Her voice betrayed a slight tremble.

Without thinking, he offered her his hand. "It's not scary. The main room looks like a giant living room, with a bar in the middle and a bunch of soft couches thrown around."

She exhaled the breath she'd been holding, letting him lead her down the stairs.

At the bottom of the staircase, he flicked another switch. "See? Just as I told you, a bar and a lot of couches."

She glanced around nervously. "What happens when there are people here?"

"Same as at any other gathering. Drinks, snacks, chitchat, and gossip."

"You mean to say that no one is, you know, getting busy on those couches?"

He chuckled. "I didn't say that. There is a lot of necking going on. But Franco doesn't allow nudity in here. That's what the private rooms are for. If anyone is into public play, there is a larger private room where they can invite guests."

"Can you show me? I mean a regular room. Not the one for exhibitionists."

Well, one more thing he was certain of. Calypso wasn't into public play. "Sure. I promised you a tour."

Leading her out of the main area into a hallway lined with doors on both sides, Brundar opened the first one using his master code.

She took a look around and exhaled. "This doesn't look so scary. There is only a bed and a couple of nightstands in here. Is that a bathroom?" She pointed at a door."

"Yes. Each room comes with a basic bathroom. Nothing fancy." He opened the door. "A shower, a sink, and a toilet."

"Does it cost to rent a room?"

"There is a cleanup fee."

"I see."

Brundar closed the door, walked over to one of the night-stands, and pulled out the first drawer. "There is a price for each of the toys. For health reasons, if you use them you buy them." He pulled out a wrapped paddle and smacked it against his palm. "Even this."

Calypso jumped. "Oh."

"Would you like to take a peek?"

She hesitated for about two seconds, then came closer and leaned to take a look, her hands clasped behind her back as if she was examining a museum display.

Her eyes widened. "Wow. That's... yeah..." She stepped back. "I think I've seen enough."

Brundar stifled a chuckle. If a paddle, a flogger, and a strap were enough to scare her off, he wouldn't even need to show her the other rooms. His work was done.

"Do you want to go upstairs and have a drink?"

She shook her head. "Not yet. Are all the rooms the same?"

"No. This is the tamest one."

She blushed. "I want to see."

"Are you sure? You just said you'd seen enough."

Calypso waved a dismissive hand. "Of what's in the drawers. I want to see what's in the other rooms."

"Okay." She had only seen the contents of one drawer. The one below her would have made her blush several shades deeper.

The good thing was that he could scent no arousal on her. Brundar wasn't sure he could've been so nonchalant otherwise.

"Let's get a look at another room."

She waved a hand again, pretending bravado she didn't feel. "After you, sir."

CHAPTER 45: CALLIE

*I*t was meant as a tease, a joke, but calling Brundar sir had caused something to shift inside her, washing her in a wave of arousal Callie had managed to hold at bay until now.

The spanking implements inside that drawer had helped. There was nothing sexy about those instruments of pain. The most Callie could conceive of was a light, erotic hand spanking, but not paddles, floggers and the like. Just thinking about it made her shiver and not in a good way.

How could anyone enjoy that?

You're such a hypocrite, she admonished herself. Others would think the same about her deviant desires, tame as they were. It reminded her of a funny definition of a religious fanatic—*anyone more religious than me*.

Change the subject, and that definition would work perfectly for kink as well.

Opening the next door, Brundar cast her a questioning glance. "Ready?"

She nodded and stepped in.

He closed the door behind them.

This room was larger than the previous one. The four-poster bed was taller, and the bedding was a different color, blue as opposed to the white in the other room. The night-stands were also taller to fit the bed, narrower. But the thing that stood out the most was the bench. She'd seen one of those on the Internet—a spanking bench.

As an image of her bent over the contraption with Brundar behind her skittered through her head, Callie felt her core clench. He wouldn't use any of the implements from the other room, just his hand, caressing her heated flesh after every smack...

Next to her, Brundar sucked in a breath. Had the same image flashed through his mind? Or had it been an image of a different woman bent over the thing?

A wave of intense jealousy washed through her, constricting her airways. She fisted her hands, digging her nails into the skin of her palms, hoping the sting would chase away the other hurt.

"What's the matter, Calypso? Is it too much? Do you want to leave?"

What was his game plan? Why did he keep asking her if she wanted to leave? Was he hoping to scare her off? Was it a test to see if she was serious about this?

"You said something about contracts."

"What about them?"

"Shouldn't I sign one? You're showing me all of this, and I didn't even sign a confidentiality agreement. Isn't it against the rules?"

"It is if anyone were here. But it's just the two of us. The confidentiality agreement is to protect the privacy of our members."

She turned to face him. "What if someone walks in while we are still here?"

Brundar frowned, his eyes boring into hers. "Follow me." He turned around and left the room.

"Where to?" She had a hard time keeping up with his long strides.

"You wanted paperwork. I'm just fulfilling your wishes."

Behind his back, Callie rolled her eyes. If he were into wish fulfillment, he would strip her naked, tie her to that four-poster bed, and give her the best sex of her life.

Brundar typed the code into another keypad and opened the door to an office. One desk, two chairs, a filing cabinet. An old style desktop computer that had seen better days sat on top of the neatly organized desk, the keyboard yellowed from years of use. Apparently, Franco was still struggling financially. Or maybe he just didn't care about having the latest technology.

"Does that thing even work?" She pointed at the bulky screen. "It belongs in a museum. Or a junkyard."

Brundar shrugged. "I think Franco keeps it as a desk ornament. It's not really needed here since the contracts are done on paper and kept in the filing cabinet. Franco is old school. Computers can be hacked, and members' privacy could be compromised. Paper is still the safest way to go." He pulled a folder out of one of the drawers and dropped it on the desk. "Have fun."

Callie draped her purse on the back of the chair, sat down and opened the folder. The confidentiality agreement was on top, and she skimmed through it before signing on the bottom and putting it aside. The next several pages explained about consent and limits, and what was permitted in the public areas of the club and what was not.

From the looks of it, Franco's main concern was ensuring members' privacy and safety. Very few things were explicitly disallowed in the private rooms, which left an overwhelming variety of options, some of them quite shocking. Most sexual activities were disallowed in the public area, but there was no restriction on what could be discussed there.

Must be interesting to be a fly on the wall in that room.

The next section contained a long list of activities, three boxes to check off next to each. Okay, soft limit, and hard limit.

She lifted her eyes to look at Brundar who had taken a seat on the other side of the desk, watching her intently.

"Do I need to fill in all of this? There are like five hundred items here."

"Do you want to play, Calypso?" His voice had never sounded so deep.

She swallowed and nodded, the words sticking in her throat. For the first time since she'd met him, Brundar intimidated her. His pale eyes seemed to glow in the poorly illuminated office, and the shadows painted his austere features even harsher.

"Then fill it out." Sensing her trepidation, Brundar softened his tone. "When you are done, we will go over it together. Going through all these items will clarify things for you."

God, she had no idea. When she was done, the hard limit row had most of the check marks, the soft limit a few, and the okay one even less. As far as kink went, she was just a darker shade of vanilla. If this club was as tame as Brundar had said it was, she shuddered to think what went on in others.

This whole idea, which had been fueling her sexual fantasies for years, suddenly seemed extremely foolish.

Turning the folder around for Brundar to read, she leaned back in her chair and crossed her arms over her chest. She wouldn't be surprised if he told her she shouldn't be there. That she didn't belong.

He would be right, of course.

But if not here and not in the vanilla world, where did she fit in?

A sinking feeling in her belly whispered that she didn't fit in anywhere.

It wasn't the end of the world, though. Sex wasn't all that important. In fact, she would be better off forgetting this silly quest and focusing on more important things like getting the education she needed to fulfill her dream, or finding a decent guy to share her life with, complete with the house with a white picket fence and two and a half kids.

The thing was, Brundar was a guy who walked in the shadows. He didn't fit in that sunny picture.

For reasons she couldn't fully understand, Callie felt that she would be better off in his dark and stormy landscape than under the bright sun.

Perhaps her company would make his landscape just a little bit sunnier.

CHAPTER 46: BRUNDAR

*B*rundar wasn't surprised as he looked over Calypso's list. It was exactly what he'd expected. What he hadn't expected, though, was for her to remain seated and gaze at him with hope in her eyes.

While going over the questionnaire, her arousal had slowly dissipated, until the scent was completely gone. He'd been sure she would get up and leave as fast as her legs could carry her.

"Any questions?"

"I'm all out. There is some scary shit in there." She pointed at the papers. "I know it's supposed to cover everything, but I didn't know half of it even existed. Probably more. I feel like such a fool for entertaining the notion that I could belong in here." She waved a hand around.

Her honesty and courage impressed him. It hadn't been easy to admit that she was in over her head. On the other hand, he didn't want her so completely discouraged.

"It's okay, Calypso. I didn't know more than half of it either when I first discovered this world."

With a sigh, she slumped in her chair. "Thank you for telling me that."

Brundar rubbed at his jaw. Calypso deserved better than what he was doing to her.

Hell, whom was he fooling?

If he wanted to be honest with himself, he should admit he was looking for an excuse to backtrack from his previous decision to stay away from this woman who was pushing all of his buttons and tugging at all of his strings. For the first time in his adult life, Brundar felt he was more than a weapon. Not an automaton, but a man who was flesh and blood and, most surprisingly, heart.

He pulled a blank piece of paper from the drawer and handed it to the amazing woman gazing at him with eyes that saw him clearer than he saw himself. "List your rules, Calypso. Now that you have a better understanding, you should know what you want."

She took the blank page, looked at it for a moment, than looked up again. "I can't. It's too embarrassing."

"Do you want me to do it for you? You can cross out anything that I've gotten wrong and add anything that I've missed."

"Yes, please."

Brundar went through the motions of checking her answers again, even though he had them seared into his brain from the quick scan he'd done before.

Calypso was perfect for him, and he was going to let her know that before he touched her in any way.

"You're okay with bondage." He glanced at her and she nodded.

"You're not so sure about a blindfold, but you're willing to try." She nodded again.

"You're okay with a light spanking, but only with a hand." He chuckled as he added, "Paddles, floggers, and straps are all hard limits." She might change her mind about that once she got a taste.

Nodding, Calypso blushed deep crimson, the musk of her arousal perfuming the air.

"You have no problem with obeying orders as long as they don't breach any of your hard limits." Which was almost everything. Calypso didn't belong in the club. Her tastes were too tame even for Franco's soft-core establishment.

She nodded.

"You chose red as your safe word." He looked up and smiled. "Given your short list, I don't think you need one."

She smiled sheepishly. "I know. But it was one of the few questions I could actually answer positively."

Brundar turned the page over to her. "Feel free to make changes, then sign at the bottom."

She looked it over and then scribbled her name. "My list is just as short as yours," she said as she handed him the page.

He took it, adding it to her file. "Which is perfect."

"I agree." Calypso smiled, her facial muscles losing some of their tension.

He rose to his feet and offered her his hand.

She took it, letting him pull her up and bring her flush against his body.

He stroked her hair, then kissed her lightly, not wanting to overwhelm her when she was already overwhelmed.

His courageous girl.

He was done fighting a losing battle. She was his. Not to keep, that was impossible, but at least for a little while. He was too weak to deny himself the rare pleasure of a kindred soul.

"Are you taking me to one of the rooms?" The quiver in her voice betrayed both hope and anxiety.

"Would you prefer I took you home?"

She shook her head. "No. I'm afraid you'll change your mind again."

Poor girl. He'd toyed with her enough. "It's not that I didn't want you. I did, from the very first time I saw you, but you were married."

"Is that why you helped me get free?"

"No, sweetling. I did it for you. Now, same as then, I have nothing to offer you except a few nights of passion. I wish things were different, but that's still true. Are you okay with that?"

"I'll take whatever you can give me. I need you."

Fates, I need you too.

He took her to the one room with a private exit to the outside. Soon, the regulars would start arriving, and she would be embarrassed to be seen walking out of there when they were done.

Hell, whom was he fooling? He didn't want anyone seeing her with him and imagining what they'd done. Calypso and everything about her belonged to him. No one other than him was allowed to have sexual fantasies about her. Not while he was around.

Walking into the room, Calypso took a quick glance around, her eyes lingering on the specially designed contraption in the corner.

"What is that?" She pointed.

He wrapped his arm around her waist, holding her to his side. Not because he was afraid she'd bolt—Calypso had made her decision, and nothing short of an explosion was going to deter her from it—but she was scared and unsure and physical contact would make her feel safer. "I think you can guess."

"Are you going to tie me up to this?"

He scented her anxiety, but it was overwhelmed by the scent of her desire. This was turning her on.

"It's either that or face down on the bed. Your choice. But I think you'll enjoy the bench more."

Resembling a weight-lifting bench, the front part was raised to its maximum height, while the back was lowered. Dangling from the other side of it, the leather straps that were lined with fake fur would secure her comfortably in place, while the extra padding on the almost vertical support would ensure she was comfortable enough for an extended play.

Trying to look at it through her eyes, Brundar didn't think the piece of equipment looked particularly ominous. But assumption was the mother of all fuckups, and it was always better to ask.

He stroked her hair, gentling her. "You're okay with that? Or does it scare you?"

"I think it's fine," she whispered.

CHAPTER 47: CALLIE

*T*hat was not how Callie wanted her first time with Brundar to be.

The first time was supposed to be tender, explorative, which wasn't going to happen while she was tied up and blindfolded with her back turned to him.

She wasn't scared, trusting him to be gentle with her and lead her slowly into this new world of darker pleasures. But she yearned for the intimacy he couldn't give her.

His rules prohibited that.

"Calypso." Brundar pulled her into his hard body, his warmth and his strength easing her turmoil. A finger under her chin, he lifted her head, so she was looking into his smoldering eyes. "Don't think so much, just feel." His large palm stroked small circles on her back as he lowered his head and kissed her.

His gentle hold on her contrasted with the ferocity of his possessive passion as he took her mouth, his lips firm, his tongue stroking and gliding against hers.

Lost to the passion, to the kiss she'd been dreaming about since that first time he'd kissed her and had left her with a taste for more, Callie moaned. Her hands ached to thread through the curtain of his silky hair, but she had to respect his hard limits, the same way she expected him to respect hers.

There was so little she'd agreed to. Would it be enough?

Any moment now, he could demand her to strip for him, and she'd have to do it, with grace, because she'd given him that power. She'd promised to obey as long as he respected her rules.

The thought mortified and excited her at the same time.

Callie wasn't shy, but to strip on command for a man who was going to see her nude for the first time would mean stretching her courage and determination to the max.

Brundar deepened the kiss, a growl rumbling in his muscular chest as his hand, which up to that moment had been so gentle on her back, fisted her hair and pulled her head back, opening her for him.

The dominance of the act more than the slight sting had her nipples pebble and moisture gather in her panties, which hadn't been dry since he'd shown her the room with the spanking bench.

She rubbed her achy peaks against his chest, hoping it wasn't against his rules, and if it was, she didn't care. Worst case scenario it would earn her a spanking, and that wouldn't be bad at all.

But given the tightening of his hold on her and the way he rubbed his erection against her belly, it seemed Brundar was fine with that.

Lost to the sensations bombarding her starved body, Callie felt her legs go soft, and if not for Brundar's firm hold on her, she would've collapsed into him.

With one last swipe of his tongue against her kiss-swollen lips, he made sure she was stable enough to stand on her own before catching the bottom of her T-shirt and pulling it over her head in one swift motion.

"Thank you." She was so grateful he wasn't forcing her to strip.

He chuckled, though she wasn't sure he'd caught her meaning. "You're welcome." He unzipped her jeans and pulled them down. She stepped out of them.

If she weren't so embarrassed, she would've thanked him again for not stripping her in one go, leaving her in her bra and panties.

His palm splayed on the naked expanse of her belly, warm, possessive, reassuring. His other hand stroked her hip, his fingers curling around the curve of her ass.

"You're beautiful, Calypso."

"Thank you," she blurted, feeling foolish for sounding like a broken record. Where was the rich vocabulary she prided herself on? But her mouth was dry, and the words were swirling in her head in an incoherent jumble she couldn't make sense of.

Her breath hitched as the hand on her belly stroked up, reaching the bottom curve of her breast. Panting, she looked up at Brundar, startled at the intensity he regarded her with.

Slowly, he ran a finger at the bottom of her breast, the sensation electrifying but far from what she needed. With a light squeeze, he abandoned her butt cheek, his hand reaching for the back clasp of her bra. He didn't snap it open right away as she'd expected. His fingers caressing the skin around the clasp, he looked into her eyes and waited for her acquiescence.

Callie might have not known much about dominants, but she very much doubted they sought approval before every move. Wasn't he supposed to order her to do things? Take what he wanted as long as it wasn't against her rules?

Not that she was complaining. This was perfect, exactly like it should be between a man and a woman. It just didn't fit the profile she'd imagined.

Except, Brundar wasn't like anyone she'd ever met. He

didn't fit into any neat category. He was different in almost every way.

Snapping the clasp open, he hooked his fingers in the shoulder straps and lowered them down in slow motion, treating her as if she was a spooked little kitten he didn't want to scare off.

Which made her aware that her initial anxiety was gone. With his slow and careful treatment of her, he was easing her into the scene. It was exactly what she needed to loosen up.

Brundar sucked in a breath when he bared her breasts, letting the bra slide down to the floor.

As he stared at her practically nude body, Callie forced herself to stand straight, her hands fisted by her sides to remind herself she wasn't allowed to touch this incredibly handsome man who was looking at her as if she was special, beautiful.

With her shoes gone, she felt tiny next to him even though she wasn't short. Callie couldn't help feeling a little intimidated by Brundar's sheer size. He wasn't bulky or heavily muscled. But his height and the breadth of his shoulders were impressive. That he was powerful, she had no doubt.

If she were allowed to touch him, Callie would've divested him of his shirt and run her hands all over his taut muscles— the six-pack she'd felt when he'd held her close.

"Beautiful," he hissed, lifting his hands to her breasts and stroking his thumbs over both of her nipples, running lazy circles around the pebbled peaks.

Involuntarily, her back arched in a silent invitation for him to take more, to cup her breasts, knead them, lick and suck on the achy twin points of gnawing need.

When his thumbs finally brushed over the tips, the moan she'd been trying to hold in escaped her throat in a rush, and she closed her eyes.

God, it was becoming impossible to keep her hands off of

him. If he didn't tie her up soon, she was in danger of breaking the rules. Maybe he wasn't going to do it after all? He didn't seem to be in any rush.

"I'm proud of you, sweetling," he whispered in her ear, a moment before nuzzling her neck. "Such a good girl for keeping your hands at your sides."

His words of praise elicited another soft moan, and she tilted her head, giving him easier access. "If I promise to keep my hands to myself, can we forgo the bondage?"

"Nice try." He tweaked her nipples hard, the small pain sending a zing of desire straight down between her legs.

"Turn around, Calypso," he commanded.

She obeyed in an instant.

His thumbs hooked inside the elastic of her panties, pulling them down past her hips and letting them drop to the floor.

Her cheeks flared with heat as she imagined him seeing how soaked through they were, grateful for having her back to him.

"Look at you, sweetling, so wet for me."

His finger sliding over her sleek folds from behind, she almost came right there and then, her impending climax halted only by the sharp smack he delivered to her naked ass. "Not yet."

Unbidden, the words she'd never imagined uttering of her own accord in a sexual situation left her mouth. "Yes, sir."

"Good girl." His palm caressed the sting away, making her hungry for more.

"Get on the bench, Calypso." He tapped her butt cheek lightly.

Here it comes. Callie closed her eyes for a split moment, then took in a fortifying breath and stepped closer to the contraption Brundar was about to strap her to.

"Don't be afraid." He kissed her neck as his hand on her shoulder guided her onto the thing.

The pose was awkward to say the least. On the top, the bench reached only up to under her breasts, supporting her torso but leaving them exposed. On the bottom Brundar pulled out two knee supports and guided her to kneel on them, her thighs spread wide lewdly. In seconds, he had her strapped in, fiddling with the buckles to ensure she was secured but comfortably so.

Her thighs were strapped to the supports, her torso to the bench, and her arms to the strap that secured her torso. Her range of motion was limited to less than an inch in each direction.

"Okay?" Brundar's warm hand caressed her back.

Surprisingly, it was. She was comfortable, nothing pinched or pulled, and Brundar's hand on her was reassuring, as was his soft tone.

"Uh-huh."

"Words, sweetling," he leaned over her, pressing his front to her back.

"I'm good."

He dangled a long piece of black silk in front of her eyes. "I'm going to blindfold you now."

She took in a long breath and closed her eyes. "Okay."

CHAPTER 48: BRUNDAR

"*O*kay, sweetling?" Brundar asked after tying the end of the black silk scarf at the back of her head.

"Perfect," Calypso husked.

The entire room was perfumed with her arousal.

Brundar still couldn't get over how trusting she was with him. Did she feel the same deep connection that had battered at his shields, bringing him to his knees?

Was she as helpless against the irresistible pull between them as he was?

Looking at her golden hair spilling in soft waves down her slender back, he felt like an awestruck boy, flummoxed that a beauty like her found him worthy of her trust, her surrender.

She shivered when he lifted the golden strands, shifting them to the side and exposing the long expanse of her back. She was slender, but not thin, small-boned, as his mother would have described her.

Calypso was a tapestry of contradictions. She was soft yet firm, her skin the softest silk spread tight over taut muscles honed by long hours of working on her feet. She was delicate yet strong. She was determined yet flexible, demanding yet yielding.

He loved the many facets of her.

It would take a lifetime to learn all her nuances, discover all her passions, test all her limits—soft and hard. He would have gladly committed himself to the exploration. Unfortunately, Calypso's lifespan was painfully too short for him to unravel all of her secrets.

He'd better remember that before letting the ice shields surrounding his heart melt for her.

Closing his eyes, he made a decision that was going to cause him agony in the short run but save his heart from shattering in the long run. Brundar could not afford a meltdown. He wouldn't survive it, and the clan would not survive without him.

For the foreseeable future, he was indispensable. Until new blood fortified the Guardian ranks, the clan needed him.

He would pleasure Calypso until she forgot her own name, but he would hold back. It wasn't an impossible task. He'd done it before. His overriding need was to bite, and he could do it without taking his pleasure inside her.

Caressing her back, he kissed her neck, nipping the soft spot where it connected to her shoulder, then circling his arms around her to cup her breasts. She moaned and bucked as much as her restraints allowed, while he tweaked and pulled, torturing her hard nipples and ratcheting her desire to a fever pitch.

"Please, Brundar, I can't, please..." She wasn't coherent in her pleas, but then he wasn't expecting her to be. He knew what she wanted, what she needed better than she could articulate in her current state.

He cupped her breasts, his warm palms easing the ache he'd caused, letting her catch her breath.

However, the reprieve he granted her was short. Now that

her front was soothed, he intended to warm her backside—one of the few things she'd listed.

The first smack caught her by surprise.

"Ow, that hurt."

He rubbed the small ache away. "Do you want me to stop?"

She shook her head.

"Words, Calypso." He delivered another smack to her other butt cheek, immediately rubbing the sting away.

"No. More."

He chuckled. "I didn't understand that." He teased. "Is it no more, or give me more?"

"Give me more."

"That was what I thought. But I wasn't sure."

She snickered, which earned her a harder smack.

"Ouch. Was that your hand or did you switch to a paddle?"

The impudent remark earned her a volley of smacks, leaving her heart-shaped behind slightly pinked, and her sex blooming with desire.

His Calypso wasn't much of a submissive, but that was perfectly fine with him. He didn't need her to submit to him, just yield for the duration of their playtime. In fact, her sass was making the game more fun.

He leaned over her, pressing his aching hardness to her warmed behind. "Do you still doubt me, little girl?"

He heard her stifle a chuckle. "No, sir. I wouldn't dare. I'm sure my fanny bears your paddle-like handprints."

"Hmm, let's see." He rubbed one cheek and then the other. "I don't think you've had enough."

Calypso shivered at the loss of his body heat as he pulled back and delivered another volley of light smacks. She was panting now, not because she was in any real pain, but because she was on the verge of climaxing.

"Not yet, sweetling."

"Please, I'm so close."

"I know, just a little bit longer. Can you do that for me?"

She nodded.

"Good girl. Wait for my permission." He kissed her neck, his palm caressing her warmed cheeks.

She stiffened, his command apparently not sitting well with her, nevertheless when his finger brushed over her drenched folds, she groaned but held herself back.

He rewarded her by pushing his finger inside her wet heat, then pulling out and coming back with two, slowly stretching her sheath. She was so tight, it must've been a while for her. He wondered how she'd managed to avoid her asshole husband's advances.

It had been a while for Brundar as well.

Ever since he'd revealed himself to Calypso, he hadn't been with anyone else. His abstinence didn't make sense since he'd had no intentions of having any kind of a relationship with her, but the thought of being with another woman had felt like a betrayal.

Which meant that even though he was still fully dressed, and his painfully stiff cock was still imprisoned inside his jeans, he was just as close to climaxing as she was.

In two quick moves, he freed himself. The fingers of one hand still pumping in and out of Calypso's drenched sheath, he palmed the hard length with the other, stroking it in sync with his thrusting fingers.

Unable to resist, he rubbed the tip in her wetness, coating himself in her fragrant cream before pumping into his fist.

"Brundar…" She whispered his name like a plea.

He wasn't going to last and neither was she. After pining for one another for weeks, they were both too close to the edge to try to prolong this first time.

"I've got you, sweetling," he hissed through protruding fangs and pressed his thumb to the seat of her pleasure.

Her sheath convulsed around his fingers, the loud keening

moan leaving her throat sounding tortured and euphoric at the same time.

Pressing himself to her, his seed shot out, covering her ass and her back in one hot stream after another. He gripped her hair, pulling her head back and elongating her neck before sinking his fangs into it.

She climaxed again, and so did he, bathing her backside in more cum.

As he'd expected, she blacked out, going limp under him, the first venom bite the most potent of all.

Giving himself only a moment to catch his breath, Brundar untied Calypso and carried her to the bed, laying her down on her belly. She was a mess. The sight of her back and her ass and the back of her thighs covered with his seed brought him a sense of odd satisfaction. He hadn't come inside her, but he'd marked her as his nonetheless.

Where had that primitive response come from? It was like nothing he'd experienced before. Nonetheless, he wasn't embarrassed by it. On the contrary, he felt like pounding his chest caveman style and shouting 'mine.'

An odd feeling, but not unpleasant.

Calypso was changing him.

For the better, Brundar decided.

A caveman was a marked improvement over an iceman.

In the bathroom, he wetted several washcloths in warm water, then went back and gently wiped the evidence of his possession off her.

To the naked eye, she might've appeared clean, but his scent was all over her, warning any immortal male to stay away because she belonged to him.

It was a nonsensical sentiment, as no immortal male would care if Brundar claimed a human as his own, but it was significant to him, as was the fact that for the first time ever he'd bitten a woman's neck instead of the inside of her thigh.

"*B*rundar." His name was on Callie's lips the moment she woke up.

No longer tied to the bench, she was lying face down, tucked inside the blankets burrito style. Brundar was next to her on the bed, sitting with his back propped against several pillows, his eyes trained on her with that unwavering focus she was becoming accustomed to.

"Here." He lifted a water bottle off the nightstand, unscrewed the cap, and held it out for her.

Freeing one arm from the tight bundle of blankets he'd wrapped her in, she took the bottle and lifted it to her parched lips. After the first few gulps wet her dry throat, she wiggled out of the burrito style wrapping and sat up, holding a blanket to cover her nakedness while she drank the whole thing up.

"Thank you." She handed him the empty bottle. "Do you happen to have another one?"

"I do."

She drank half of the second bottle before her thirst was finally sated. "Thanks." She handed it back.

"You're welcome." He reached to cup her cheek, then leaned and kissed her lips chastely. "How are you feeling?"

A sheepish smile lifted the corners of her lips. "Like a woman who had the best orgasm of her life." Amazing, considering that he hadn't even been inside her. Which raised the question, why?

Had Brundar remembered what she'd told him about not using birth control with Shawn? Or had it been what she'd told him about getting pregnant because of a defective condom?

Brundar smiled, a real smile and not the slightest lifting of lips that barely passed as one. "I'm glad."

It seemed that pleasuring her into oblivion made the guy not only happy but proud. His male ego had probably inflated to the size of a zeppelin.

"I'm sure you are. I never passed out from one before."

Callie had been so out of it that she hadn't felt him cleaning her up, which he obviously had done because she didn't feel sticky. She hadn't heard him showering either, but it was obvious that he had. Brundar's long hair was swept away from his face and tied at his nape, the wet ends leaving water spots on the pillows behind him. She must've slept for a while.

"How long was I out?"

"About an hour."

"Shit." She lifted her other arm and glanced at her watch. "I'm late." She slid off the bed, dragging the blanket with her.

Brundar caught the end of it, fisting the fabric and twisting it away from her. "You're not late. I told Franco you're off tonight."

Yanking on the blanket, she turned around, the sharp movement making her head spin. "Why? I need the hours, Brundar."

"Because you need to rest more. He'll give you another shift."

"I'm not tired."

He lifted a brow. "Are you steady on your feet, Calypso?"

About to answer in the affirmative, she remembered his new rule about lying. As fun as the erotic spanking he'd given her had been, she didn't want another one right away.

Tomorrow? Heck, yeah.

"No, I'm not. You're right." She wrapped the blanket around her, tucking one corner in. "It's so weird. I'm tired and dizzy as if I ran a marathon when I did basically nothing." She chuckled, lifting her fingers. "I didn't move an inch."

"Come here." He patted the spot next to him.

She did, snuggling up close and almost purring when he wrapped his arm around her and brought her even closer. She needed the intimacy. That's what had been lacking before. As hot as it was, it had been a scene, a sexual experience, a physical coming together of desires, not souls.

Resting her head against his pectoral, Callie sighed. The only thing missing now was her touching him, but she wasn't even going to mention it. He obviously had a problem with that, and she was in no position to ask when it would be okay for her to do so just because they'd had sex.

Sort of.

As far as the simple mechanics, what they had done was heavy necking. Except, they had both orgasmed, which in her opinion counted as sex.

"Scening is intense. That's why you're exhausted."

Hmm, he might be right. "Was it for you? Exhausting, I mean?"

"Less so. It's always more intense for the one on the receiving end."

She lifted her head to look at him. "You mean the submissive?"

He shook his head. "I don't like the term, the same way I hate being called a Dom. People don't fit into neat categories or same size containers, and words have power. Your sexual preferences do not define who you are. You're not submissive,

Calypso. In fact, you're quite bossy. But you enjoy yielding sexually."

Lifting a finger, he rubbed it over her lower lip, awakening her desire. "If I order you to do my laundry, or pick up my stuff from the dry cleaners, it's not going to turn you on, and you're not going to obey. But if I order you to strip, you probably will. Do you get the difference?"

The small touch and the desire she saw in Brundar's eyes were playing a number on her. Her nipples tight beneath the blanket, she wanted him to kiss her, to fondle her. In the sexual haze of arousal, Callie had a feeling she would've agreed to do a lot more than wash his dirty clothes. She wanted to do things for him, to please him.

Was it wrong?

"If you ask nicely, I might do your laundry and pick up your stuff from the dry cleaners. People do nice things for each other when they care." She'd meant to say it teasingly; instead, her words came out sounding throaty and needy.

He tugged at the blanket, and she let it drop, her breasts exposed to his smoldering gaze.

Cupping one, he lazily thumbed the nipple. "And I would do the same for you. If you ask nicely." He bent his head and flicked his tongue over her other nipple.

"Oh, God." Callie moaned. Crossing her legs, she clenched her core in a futile attempt to relieve the ache that had started down there.

But all too soon Brundar sat up, taking his talented tongue and fingers away. "At this rate, we will never get out of here. Get dressed. I'm taking you home."

Bossy man, ordering me around.

Disappointed, Callie felt like reminding him of his little speech from before. It wasn't that she didn't agree they should leave the room. Franco probably needed it for his members, and whoever did the cleaning needed time to replace the bedding and the towels and to wipe all the surfaces clean. But a different phrasing would have made all the difference, turning an order into a request.

Perhaps, though, such subtleties were lost on Brundar. He was a military man, used to issuing and taking commands. For him, it might have been the only way he knew how to communicate.

She knew so little about him, especially about his past. Had he been in the service? And if yes, doing what? A Marine? A navy SEAL? A demanding physical fitness trainer?

Their shared experience didn't give her the right to question his aversion to being touched, but it did allow for at least a few questions as long as they weren't overly intrusive.

Once they got back to her place, she was going to lull him with a good meal and start a carefully worded interrogation.

CHAPTER 50: BRUNDAR

"*C*an you stop by the supermarket?" Calypso asked when Brundar backed out from the club's parking lot.

"Sure." He stifled a smile.

The girl was more resilient than he'd given her credit for. He had underestimated her and her resolve. Apparently, when Calypso set her eyes on a goal, nothing and no one was going to deter her from it. Not even him.

She'd wanted him, and she'd had him.

Case closed.

He'd been mistaken thinking he could scare her off by showing her a few spanking implements or letting her read the long list of kinks Franco allowed in his club. It was by no means exhaustive, but it should've been enough to send a newbie with tastes as mellow as hers running.

Not Calypso.

She'd cornered him into doing exactly what she'd wanted. Obviously, he hadn't been a helpless victim, nothing would have happened if his restraint had held, but he wanted her too much to keep fighting on both fronts.

"I'll be just a moment." Calypso opened the door as soon as he parked next to the small neighborhood supermarket.

"I'll come with you."

"No, it's okay. I know what I need. Give me three minutes."

"If you're not out in five, I'm coming in."

She rolled her eyes and closed the door.

Why did he have the sense she was plotting something? But what the hell could it be that required a trip to the supermarket?

It wasn't as if the place had a lingerie section, and she was planning the next step in her seduction by getting herself something sexy to wear. But even if it weren't the stupidest idea that had ever crossed his mind, and she really was going to buy sexy lingerie, he could have told her that she didn't need anything special to entice him.

Calypso could've been wearing a potato sack, and he would've found her irresistible.

Especially if it was one of those made from a thin plastic mesh…

Her small nipples peeking through the weave…

Fates, he was a goner.

The iceman had melted. The tin man had gotten a heart, or as was the case, a hard-on. Brundar cursed under his breath and adjusted himself in a failed attempt to relieve the pressure. What was the last part? Something about a lion and courage?

As promised, the passenger door opened a few minutes later, and Calypso slid inside holding a brown paper bag.

With his acute sense of smell, Brundar didn't need to ask her what she'd gotten. There were steaks in that bag, rib-eye, his favorite. By the heft of it, though, there was more in the bag, but he couldn't smell anything other than the meat. Maybe she'd bought several pounds of it and was planning a block party to celebrate her victory.

"What's the smirk for?" Calypso asked.

He shook his head. "Nothing I care to share."

With a humph, she crossed her arms over her chest and murmured, "Nothing new there."

Her building was only several hundred yards away from the store, and a few moments later Brundar was sitting at her counter, watching Calypso unpack her groceries.

"I hope you're hungry. I got four steaks. Three of them are for you."

"Feeding me to ensure I have my strength for later?" He lifted a brow.

Calypso stopped and looked up at him, amusement making her green eyes sparkle. "Brundar, did you just make a joke? Are you okay?"

He hadn't. He'd been dead serious, questioning her motives for treating him to another meal in the same day. But if it made her happy, he could play along.

Maybe. He was rusty, but once upon a time he'd had a sense of humor. "It's a legitimate question. I have a feisty, lustful redhead cooking me dinner. Can you blame me for being suspicious?"

A soft scent of guilt wafted from her. Had he been right?

"I'm not a redhead."

An evasive answer if he'd ever heard one. "What do you call the color of your hair? Gold?"

"Light brown with red undertones." She unwrapped the steaks, spreading them over a cutting board.

"That's too complicated for me."

Calypso salted and peppered the meat, then pulled out a head of lettuce and a few tomatoes from the fridge.

"I like cooking for you. You enjoy everything I make, and it's a pleasure to watch you eat. But the truth is that I had an ulterior motive for splurging on steaks."

With a fake frown, Brundar crossed his arms over his chest. "I knew it." If the woman wanted to fortify his energy level so

274

he could pleasure her again, there was nothing wrong with that. But he was glad she felt the need to be honest with him.

"I know so little about you." She dropped the steaks on a large skillet.

"I know that you're of Scottish descent, but I don't know if you were born there or here. I know you have a brother you live with, a cousin who is a superb attorney and another one who is some big shot businessman who has a butler, but nothing about your parents or other family." She rinsed the cutting board, the lettuce and tomatoes, and then started chopping the vegetables for a salad.

"I know that you work as a bodyguard, but I also know that you have a lot of connections in law enforcement and other government agencies, which leads me to believe that you're much more than a simple bodyguard." She flipped the steaks to the other side.

The woman had been listening to every little morsel of information he'd told her. Should he feel flattered?

"I thought if I fed you, you'd be more inclined to talk."

Brundar didn't like where this was going. He would either have to lie or tell her half-truths. He pinned her with a hard stare. "Did it work on Shawn?"

Calypso blushed. "I knew all there was to know about him. I knew his parents. I knew where he went to school. I knew the people he worked with. There was no reason for me to butter him up for information."

Brundar hated that she had anything positive to say about the sick bastard. "What about other things? Did you cook for him so he wouldn't throw tantrums and scare you?" He was hurting her with those questions, and he didn't even know why he was doing it. Was he trying to push her away again?

Calypso wiped her hands with a kitchen towel and then threw it on the counter. "So what if I did? You have a problem with how I survived a marriage that was becoming more and more hellish? Are you going to lecture me about it?" Her voice quivered with unshed tears, tearing him apart.

Brundar pushed the stool back, strode to the other side of the counter, and pulled her into his arms. "I'm sorry. You don't deserve me treating you like that."

Forgetting she wasn't supposed to touch him, Calypso pounded her fist on his chest, not hard, her aim wasn't to hurt, just to make a point. "You're damn right I don't deserve that. Not from Shawn, not from you, and not from anyone else. I don't care if talking about yourself scares the shit out of you. If you can't treat me with respect and kindness, you'd better leave now."

She couldn't have hurt him more if she'd plunged a serrated blade into his black heart.

"You're right. I'd better go." He released her.

The best thing he could do for Calypso was to walk out the door and never come back.

CHAPTER 51: CALLIE

*W*hat?
He thought he was leaving?

The coward.

Callie fisted Brundar's T-shirt and pulled him back. "I can't believe you, Brundar. You're not going anywhere. You're going to apologize and promise to be nice and mean it. Then you're going to eat the dinner I cooked for you, tell me about yourself as much or as little as you want, and then you're going to make love to me. And I mean the real thing. Is that clear? Sir?"

Wow. What had gotten into her?

Callie had never talked like that to anyone. Ever. Not to her father, not to Shawn, not to her friends, and not even to any of the pissy customers who'd been rude to her. She was too polite, too reserved to raise her voice and make demands.

Why the hell had she goaded Brundar?

But the ease with which he was willing to give up on her had made her so angry that her head had started pounding from the stress of it.

The thing was, she wanted this strange, broken man with a passion and an obsessive need that was terrifying in its intensity. There was nothing she wouldn't do to make him hers, but it was going to be on her terms. She would give him her body, her heart, and her soul, but only if he gave the same back.

Deep in her gut she knew they belonged together, and she was going to do everything in her power to make that happen.

In the end, he might still walk away, but not before she'd given it her best. Callie wasn't going to spend the rest of her life wondering what if she'd tried harder. If he walked, it would hurt like hell, but at least she'd know it was not for lack of effort on her part.

Brundar was doing a great impression of a pillar of salt, frozen in place with his eyes peeled wide and mouth gaping. Apparently, no one had ever spoken to him like that before.

Calypso reached behind herself and turned the burner off, then snapped her fingers in front of Brundar's face. "Did I shock you? Do you need smelling salts?"

A moment later his palm landed on her butt with a loud smack. "Watch it, young lady. That wasn't very respectful of you." He wrapped his arms around her and dipped his head to look into her eyes. "I apologize. I promise no more snide remarks or questions. I'm going to eat the dinner you cooked for me, and then I'm going to make love to you until you pass out again. Is that clear? Ma'am?"

The relief his words brought about was so profound that it made her feel lightheaded. She wanted to laugh, or cry, she wasn't sure. Instead, she buried her face in his T-shirt.

"But." Brundar put a finger under her chin and lifted her head, his pale blue eyes boring into hers. "It's gonna be my way —with you tied up and blindfolded. Are you okay with that? Because that's not negotiable."

She nodded enthusiastically. "Yes. Definitely yes."

His lips twitched. "Aren't you going to tack on the 'sir'?"

Callie straightened her back and saluted. "Sir! Yes, sir!"

"Good. Now let's eat. I'm starving." He rubbed at the flat expanse of his stomach.

"How about we take our dinner to the dining table? The steaks deserve a more formal setting than the counter."

"No problem."

Brundar helped set the table, while she arranged the steaks on a platter and tossed the salad with some olive oil and lemon juice.

A bottle of mango-flavored vodka, a container of lemonade, and a bottle of Chivas completed the setup.

"Thank you for the Scotch." Brundar pulled the bottle closer to him. "What are you going to do with the vodka and the juice?"

"Mix them, of course. The recipe says one shot of vodka to two shots of lemonade, but I double on the lemonade. As you've noticed, I'm a very light drinker." She reached for the vodka.

He grabbed the bottle with a speed that seemed almost unnatural. "Let me mix it for you."

"Oh, I forgot the mint. I'll be right back." The drink wasn't the same without that last finishing touch.

When she got back, she dropped the leaves inside the drink he'd mixed for her, and for the next few minutes, they ate in silence.

Watching Brundar eat was fascinating. He was so methodical and precise. Every cut was the same size, and each forkful of salad had the same precise combination of lettuce and tomatoes. She wondered what it said about him. Was he as meticulous in everything? Was the apartment he shared with his brother pristine?

"You never told me your brother's name."

"Anandur."

"Can you tell me a little bit about him?"

Brundar halted with a piece of steak speared on his fork. "Imagine the opposite of me and you get Anandur."

Callie smirked. "You mean ugly, short, and talkative?"

That got a smile out of him. "You got the talkative right. If you want a rumor to spread at maximum velocity, tell it to my brother. He isn't ugly or short. He is bigger than me and covered in way too much crinkly red hair. Beard, mustache, legs, chest, he looks like a Viking."

She would've liked to meet Brundar's brother. Anandur sounded like fun. "Is he in the same business as you? Personal protection?"

Brundar nodded. "We work for our cousin, the big shot businessman with the butler."

That explained how they got to share the guy's vegan meals. If they were his bodyguards, they were spending a lot of time with him.

"Your cousin is smart to employ family. I'm sure you guys are more dedicated to his safety than some random security firm."

Chewing, Brundar nodded again.

"Why does he need bodyguards? Does he conduct business in Third World countries or other dangerous places?"

Brundar hesitated, taking a moment to formulate his answer. "Sometimes. His dealings are confidential. I can't share details."

That was reasonable. "What about your parents?"

"When Anandur and I moved to the States, our mother remained in Scotland."

"What about your father?"

"Fathers. Anandur and I each had a different sire. They died a long time ago."

Sire was a strange way to refer to one's father. It sounded like a sperm donor. Maybe it was a cultural thing, and all Scots referred to their fathers as sires? She wondered if Brundar's mother had been widowed twice.

"How is she doing? Did she get married again?"

Brundar finished chewing. "She was never married. Anandur and I are both bastards."

Callie's hand flew to her chest. "Oh my God, Brundar. What a nasty thing to say. Why would you talk about your brother and yourself like that?"

He shrugged. "It's the truth. Nothing nasty about it."

"You can say that you're a lovechild, or that you were born out of wedlock. You told me yourself that words have power. Why use a derogatory term like that?"

He pinned her with his pale eyes. "When I was growing up, those euphemisms didn't exist. We were simply bastards."

That had to have been another cultural difference. No one called children born to single mothers bastards anymore. She found it hard to believe that things were all that different in Scotland.

"Did you grow up in some small mountain village?"

Brundar dropped his fork, his eyes hardening, and his pale, austere face darkening as if night had descended above his head. "How did you know?"

"Just a guess."

There was a story there, but Callie sensed it was better left alone.

CHAPTER 52: BRUNDAR

*C*alypso was asking too many questions. At first, Brundar tried to humor her, telling her details that revealed no dangerous secrets or even hinted at them, but enough was enough. He wasn't comfortable talking about himself, especially not about his childhood. It was a subject best left buried.

"Why do you keep your hair so long? Not that I don't find it beautiful and sexy, I do, but it's uncommon. You don't strike me as a guy who likes to attract attention to himself." She chuckled. "Though I don't think you could avoid it even if you shaved your head bald. You're strikingly good-looking."

She'd gotten that right. Even without the hair, his good looks had been the bane of his existence, but no more. No one could touch him. No one could get close enough to hurt him. He dared anyone to try.

Brundar put his fork and knife down and wiped his mouth with a napkin. "Thank you for dinner, Calypso. It was very good." He pushed his chair back to lounge more comfortably.

"You're most welcome." She rose to her feet and collected her plate, and then reached for his.

He caught her wrist. "Leave it."

She looked up at him with questioning eyes.

"Put the other one down too."

Without taking her eyes off him, she did as he'd asked. Under his thumb, her pulse sped up. Her breaths became shallow.

Brundar grabbed her other wrist and pulled her onto his lap. Transferring both into one hand, he threaded the fingers of his other one in her hair and kissed her—the taste of the sweet drink she'd had with dinner mingling with her own sweetness.

In moments, the scent of her desire permeated the room.

It didn't take much to arouse Calypso. She was the most responsive female he'd ever been with. Brundar wondered whether it was his effect on her, or had she responded the same way to others.

Her husband had been her first, but that didn't mean she hadn't snogged with others before him.

Had other males touched her intimately before she'd surrendered her virginity to that asshole?

Had she responded to any of them with such lustful abandon?

One thing Brundar knew for certain: No other woman had ever affected him the way Calypso did. He couldn't conceive of her responding to anyone else the way she responded to him.

Jealousy washed over him like hot acid, scalding, scarring, blurring his vision.

As his fangs punched over his lower lip, his venom glands pulsing with venom, he tightened his grip on her hair, pulling her head back to expose her neck. The need to bite her, to possess her, was overwhelming—a primitive urge he fought with every last bit of reason he had left.

Thousands of years of civilization were no match for the powerful animal instinct gripping him. A less disciplined man would have succumbed.

"Close your eyes, Calypso," he hissed.

She tried to turn her head and look at him, but he tightened his grip on her hair until she whimpered. He let go. "Don't argue. Keep them closed." He used his most commanding tone. Her obedience was not negotiable this time. She couldn't see him like that. He'd already thralled her once today; another thrall so soon might cause damage.

"Yes, sir," she breathed without a shred of mocking in her tone.

Letting go of her wrists, one arm around her waist and the other under her thighs, he lifted Calypso as he pushed to his feet and carried her to her bedroom.

"Keep your eyes closed, and don't move," he reminded her as he laid her on top of the comforter, face down.

"Okay," she murmured, sounding a little scared.

He didn't want her afraid of him, but right now it was better that she was. It would keep her from trying to peek at him, which would force him to thrall her again if she did. He treasured her mind even more than he treasured her trust. He could regain the latter, but damage to the former was irreversible.

Rummaging through her drawers, he found a silk scarf in one and an unopened hosiery four-pack in another.

He blindfolded her first, then helped her out of her clothes.

"Back on your stomach, sweetling," he commanded when he'd divested her of the last article of clothing.

Sitting naked on the bed, her sight obscured by the colorful silk tied around her eyes, one leg folded under her delectable ass, Calypso worried her lower lip. "Do I have to?"

Stocking in hand, Brundar paused, letting it dangle from the bedpost he was tying it to.

But before he could make up his mind, she continued. "I can't see you, and you're going to tie me up so I can't touch you either. Can I at least have the intimacy of chest to chest?"

In a last ditch effort to keep up his crumbling shields, Brundar had planned to keep intimacy to a minimum, but he couldn't deny Calypso her request. "You may."

Exhaling a relieved breath, she lay down on her back and stretched her arms over her head.

Spread out before him, trusting him, she was all woman, perfect in every way, and all his. He had to spend a moment just drinking in the sight of her. "You're beautiful, Calypso."

She smiled. "Thank you."

"No, thank you." He wrapped a stocking around one wrist, tying it loosely so she was comfortable, then repeated with the other. Stroking the inside of her arms, he went all the way up to her bound wrists then entwined their fingers. "I left a lot of give in the bindings. If you really want to, you can get free. The ties are meant as a reminder to keep your arms up."

She nodded and let out a breath, the little trepidation that still lingered in her expression vanishing.

Good. Brundar wanted her aroused and hungry for his touch, but not afraid.

He kissed her parted lips, sliding his tongue for a quick taste before getting up to continue his work on the other side. Wrapping his palm around one slender ankle, he pulled it sideways and secured it in place with a stocking, then did the same with the other one.

Spread-eagled, pliable and obedient, Calypso was a wet dream come true. For the next hour or two, this beautiful, strong woman was going to give herself over to him to do with as he pleased, trusting him with her pleasure.

Was there anything sexier than that?

Nothing compared to this.

His prowess as a fighter and a swordsman was legendary, but his prowess as a lover who could bring a woman to the highest possible ecstasy was what Brundar prided himself on most. It didn't matter that none of his clan members would ever know this about him. It was enough that he knew. And now Calypso would know that too.

Like a master musician, he tugged at the strings until he found the right combination of touch and pull to bring the most out of the particular instrument he was playing. Because no woman was the same as another, and each deserved her particular code deciphered.

Just like his swordsmanship, it required singular focus and dedication, prohibiting the intrusion of any rambling thoughts about his disturbing past or his uninspiring future.

Except, Brundar had a feeling that all his prior performances were nothing but practice runs, preparing him for the masterpiece that was Calypso.

CHAPTER 53: CALLIE

*C*allie might have been deprived of sight, but she could sense Brundar watching her. For long moments he just stood at the foot of the bed.

What was he thinking about?

Was he admiring his handiwork?

Was he admiring her?

Callie wasn't shy, but she wasn't an exhibitionist either. She had a healthy body image, knowing she wasn't too thin or overly padded, nor was she flabby or overly muscular, and even though her proportions weren't perfect, they weren't bad either. With the right clothes and the right bra, she could hide the fact that her butt was too scrawny and her hips too boyish in proportion to her bust, or that her breasts were too big for her delicate frame.

Naturally, she couldn't hide those imperfections while in the nude, but it was nothing she felt embarrassed about.

Not with the way Brundar looked at her.

Callie had never felt as beautiful and as feminine as she did under Brundar's gaze. It was so intense that even now, blindfolded, she felt it as if it was a physical caress.

It infused her with power.

"I can't get enough of looking at you," he admitted.

"You can look as much as you want, touch too." She reminded him that she wasn't an exhibition piece but a hot mess of sexual need that couldn't wait to be sated.

Warm and strong, his palm wrapped around her calf, the small touch sending a zing of desire straight to her center.

She was already starved for his touch, even though he'd brought her to the heights of pleasure only a couple of hours ago.

This man was turning her into a nymphomaniac.

"What's that mysterious smile for?" he asked.

"I can't get enough of you either."

He chuckled. "That's good because you're going to get a lot of me, and I'm not sure you can handle it all."

"Try me," she issued a challenge.

He caressed her knee, circling to her inner thigh, his touch feather-light, stopping an inch from her moist folds and moving to her other thigh, feathering his way down.

Calypso shivered, her arms tugging on her bonds.

"You need to learn patience, sweetling. All good things come to those who wait."

Not in her experience. "Do you actually believe that?"

Brundar's hand stilled on her thigh. "No, I don't. Not out there. But in here, you can bet on it." He continued his lazy caress.

Could she?

Brundar had proven to be a man of his word. Except for the wine bottle he'd promised and must have forgotten about, he'd come through for her on every front, not asking for anything in return.

He was her savior, her guardian angel, and she trusted him without reserve—as evidenced by her current state. There was no one else she would've ever let tie her up and blindfold her.

It was a huge step for her. Life had taught Callie not to give her trust lightly, and lowering her shields for Brundar was her biggest leap of faith yet.

And her last.

If Brundar ever betrayed that trust, she would never give it to anyone again. "I bet on you, Brundar. Don't let me down."

He groaned. "I'll make your body sing for me, Calypso. That's a promise, but it's the only one I can make. No entanglement, no strings."

She stifled a smirk. "I expect nothing more."

For now.

CHAPTER 54: BRUNDAR

*T*hat was a lie.

Calypso wanted so much more from him—things he could never give her.

It didn't matter that he'd never promised to stay or be anything other than a guide on her journey of sexual discovery. She wasn't the only one caught in an emotional whirlpool, either. They were both trapped and sinking fast.

When it was done, and he was gone from her life, Calypso would hurt, and so would he. But at least he would know the reason why.

She would be left wondering what she'd done wrong.

The only thing he could do to mitigate her pain was to show her that she was perfect, and teach her to reach for what she deserved.

Later, he would come up with an excuse for why he couldn't stay—fabricate a story that would leave no room for her to doubt herself. Like a deployment to a Third World country on some secret mission he would never come back from.

She'd mourn him for a while, but eventually she'd get over

it and move on with her life, secure in the knowledge that she was desirable and worthy of love.

With that plausible scenario alleviating some of his guilt and his worry, Brundar returned his focus to the naked beauty sprawled before him, her sex slick and glistening with the evidence of her desire.

He'd made her a promise that he would make her body sing for him.

It was time he delivered on that promise.

It had been so long since Brundar had pleasured a woman with her front to him and not her back that he had to stop and think for a moment how to go about it.

Calypso wanted chest to chest contact.

It seemed that he would have to learn some new bedroom skills.

Pulling his shirt over his head, he dropped it on the floor, then climbed on the bed and knelt between her spread legs.

Calypso parted her lips, her heartbeat speeding in anticipation.

He lowered himself gently over her, careful not to crush her under him as he dipped his head and kissed her.

She moaned into his mouth, wrapping her tongue around his as soon as he penetrated her mouth.

His torso still braced on his elbows, he threaded his fingers through her lush hair, cradling her head and lifting it for his kiss.

Arching into him, Calypso groaned in pleasure as soon as their chests touched. The hosiery tying her to the bed limited her range of motion, but the things stretched enough so she could rub her tight nipples against his chest.

The pose must've been extremely uncomfortable to maintain.

"My poor girl, her sweet little nipples so desperate for my attention." The words that had tumbled out of his mouth surprised him. Brundar wasn't much of a talker in general and during sexual play in particular. But he was starting to realize that being with Calypso was changing him in more ways than one.

She wasn't letting him get away with his Spartan speech patterns. She demanded he talk to her, tell her things, and little by little he was getting better at it. It no longer felt like such a tremendous effort to form whole sentences, to express his thoughts and what little feelings he had.

No one had challenged him in so long. Even Anandur had given up on coaxing him out of his shell. But Calypso refused to back down. Refused to accept that it was all he had to give.

She mewled in agreement, rubbing against him one last time before collapsing back down on the bed.

Untangling his fingers from her hair, Brundar moved his hands down to her breasts. For a moment, he just cupped both, enjoying the heft of them filling his hands to overflowing. Her hard nipples poked his palms, reminding him where his girl needed his attention most.

She was sensitive there; he remembered it from their previous interlude that day. Nevertheless, she wasn't averse to a little rough play. A tiny dose of pain was a sure way to ratchet her pleasure.

He started with his thumbs, circling round and round and barely touching the turgid nubs. When his fingers finally closed on them and pinched, Calypso's chest pushed up on a strangled moan.

Sliding down, he licked the small pain away, first one, then the other. When she relaxed, lowering her back, he pinched and tugged again.

"Aw," she complained.

He didn't let go. "Do you want me to stop?"

Biting on her lower lip, her eyelids pressed tight, she shook her head, the scent of her arousal intensifying and proving him right.

When she started thrashing her head from side to side, he knew she'd had enough. Letting go, he plumped her breasts and licked her nipples, alternating between the two until he soothed the pain away.

He had only just begun, and Calypso was already on the cusp of climax.

Trailing small kisses down her belly, he slid further down until his mouth was level with her molten heat.

Fates. How had he thought of denying himself this pleasure?

Spreading her folds with his thumbs, he treated her to a long lick that had her arching off the bed again. She had such a small ass that Brundar could keep her spread with his thumbs, while cupping it with his other fingers and holding her down.

She wiggled in his possessive grip, but it wasn't because she was sore from the light spanking he'd treated her to earlier. There was no trace left of it. Calypso was just loving what he was doing to her.

After a venom bite, even a harsher spanking would've left no residual soreness or marks, which was one of the main reasons he was in such high demand at the club. Those who enjoyed the spicier spectrum of tastes couldn't understand how he did it, only that he was the only one who could.

Brundar had a feeling that his former partners were going to be very disappointed. He was no longer on the market.

For the near future, he belonged to Calypso.

CHAPTER 55: CALLIE

*T*his was the most intimate sexual act imaginable, and Callie was glad Brundar was the first one she was sharing it with.

Shawn had made a half-hearted offer to pleasure her this way, once, but his lack of enthusiasm had made it far from appealing. It wasn't something she'd craved anyway. Too intimate of an act with a man she'd never fully trusted—not even when she'd been still trying to make their marriage work. Subconsciously, or even consciously, Callie had known all along that he wasn't the right man for her.

Only later, she'd also realized he was mentally unstable and dangerous.

And here she was, blissful in her surrender, unafraid even though she had been tied up and blindfolded by a man she knew very little about, who was kissing and licking the most intimate and vulnerable spot on her body.

At first, she'd agreed to the blindfold as a concession to Brundar, but she was discovering that by depriving one of her senses, she was feeling everything more acutely with the others.

Callie could hear Brundar smacking his lips as if he was tasting something delectable, feel the reverence with which he held her open, his thumbs gentle on her folds, his tongue rimming her trembling flesh in slow, careful licks, applying the exact pressure to bring her the most pleasure.

At the same time, his other fingers were digging into her ass muscles, possessive and strong.

The combination pushed all of her buttons—physical and mental.

Or were they one and the same?

A self-feeding loop of sorts?

"Okay, sweetling?"

She loved that he checked with her at every stage even though her body's responses were telling him all he needed to know.

"Amazing. More."

He chuckled, smacking his lips again.

Was he doing it on purpose to let her know he was enjoying eating her up?

Brundar spread her even wider, his thumbs parting her folds and holding her open for his tongue. As he speared it inside her, the need to move and undulate around that penetrating tongue was overwhelming. But the iron grip Brundar had on her buttocks prevented even the smallest of movements. She was helpless and open for his ministrations.

Damn, it was hot.

Giving her bindings a small tug, Callie reassured herself that she truly was at Brundar's mercy.

God, it felt so good to surrender everything and just feel.

In the back of her mind, she was well aware that it was all an illusion. One word from her would stop Brundar immediately. And the binds were loose and stretchy enough for her to pull her hands out without much effort.

She was learning. It was all a game, and perception was everything.

Would it feel different if it wasn't?

What if she really was at this man's mercy with no safe word and ties she couldn't get out of?

Arousing as hell and just as dangerous. The fear would have been too intense to enjoy anything. It was like parasailing for real versus a ride in an amusement park. Same sensations but without taking a risk.

One thick finger replaced Brundar's tongue, filling her in a different way. Then he added another, curving both to massage a particularly tender spot.

The coil inside her getting tighter, Callie moaned, her involuntary undulations thwarted even though Brundar was holding her down with only one hand.

"More," she groaned.

Pressing his mouth over her pulsating clit, he drew it between his lips, detonating an explosion that sucked a scream out of her throat.

Brundar slowed down, planting a gentle kiss on her clit, his fingers moving in and out of her in a slow rhythm, letting her catch her breath.

"You're magnificent when you come."

His words of praise pleased her to no end. So much so that she didn't even come back with the snarky remark that was on the tip of her tongue. He'd given her too much for her to repay him with anything less than profound gratitude.

She was about to say something to that effect, when Brundar resumed his assault, driving away any and all coherent thoughts.

The only movement available to her was thrashing her head from side to side. She tried to form the words to tell him that it was too much, that she was too sensitive and couldn't take any more, but something inside her didn't want him to stop, trusting him to know what she needed. If he thought she could come again then she would.

She wasn't wrong. In moments, she was once again climbing toward another climax.

"Brundar!" Callie keened as another explosion rocked through her.

Her body trembling from the aftershocks, she had a vague impression of his fingers on her ankles. A moment later her wrists were unbound, and he was holding her to him in a fierce embrace.

Warm in his arms, Callie stopped shivering, and her mind's frazzled gears came back online. Brundar was shirtless, but his jeans were still on, and she was no longer bound.

Which meant that as far as he was concerned sex was over.

"What's wrong? Why did you stop?" She hated how needy she sounded.

"I didn't bring a condom."

God, she was so stupid. She should've bought a pack while at the supermarket.

On the one hand, she was touched that he hadn't presumed anything when he'd brought her home. Most guys Brundar's age carried at least one condom in their wallet just in case they got lucky.

"You didn't ask if I have one."

He chuckled. "I know you don't."

She hated for their time to end like that. Being on the receiving end of pleasure was fun, but it didn't sit well with her not to reciprocate.

"Can I return the favor?" She wasn't nearly as good at oral as Brundar, but she would give it her best.

Gentle fingers removed her blindfold, and he leaned to plant a chaste kiss on her lips. "Not tonight. You're exhausted."

It was true. Callie felt as if she'd just finished running a marathon and could sleep for two days straight. Who knew

297

that orgasming several times in the same day would be so tiring?

After all, she hadn't done anything other than cook two quick and easy meals.

"Tomorrow, then?"

"Maybe." Gazing at her as if he wanted to memorize every detail of her face, he leaned and kissed her forehead. "Sleep. I'll see you tomorrow at the club." He slid out of bed.

Callie wanted to reach for his hand and stop him, but then remembered she wasn't allowed.

"Please, can you stay a little bit and hold me?" He didn't seem like the type of guy who cuddled, but she was desperate for the closeness.

He looked conflicted, standing beside her bed and looking at her with hungry eyes.

Of course, he did. He hadn't climaxed. Brundar was considerate, but that didn't mean he had no needs of his own. He probably couldn't wait to get home and jerk off to relieve the pressure.

"I would understand if you couldn't stay." She let her eyes glide over the bulge in his pants. It must be painful.

His jaw muscles hardened and he nodded. "I'll stay."

"Thank you." She burrowed under the blanket and lifted it for him to get in.

Brundar eyed the space she'd made for him as if it was dangerous territory.

"Do you want to stay on top of the blankets?"

He shook his head and got in, pulling her into his arms.

Heaven.

Callie belonged inside those strong arms. Her cheek pressed against his hard chest, she listened to the steady beat of Brundar's heart for as long as she managed to keep herself awake. Every moment was precious, and she refused to squander even one. Eventually though, sleep won.

CHAPTER 56: BRUNDAR

$\mathcal{B}$rundar couldn't refuse Calypso's plea. The temptation to hold her in his arms as she fell asleep had been too strong.

He'd never held a woman in bed, never had anyone fall asleep in his arms. Before today, he'd never felt the need. To want something, he had to be aware of its existence first. Otherwise, how would he know he lacked anything?

Calypso was showing him a lot of things he hadn't known were missing from his life.

Relationships between men and women were not only about sex and procreation. There was more to it than that. There was partnership, companionship, and togetherness.

A simple thing like sharing a meal with Calypso was so much more than just a meal. It wasn't the same as having dinner with his brother, or the other Guardians.

Except, he could have none of those things with Calypso. Not long term.

One day, Amanda might find him a Dormant, and he could try and recreate what he had with Calypso, but Brundar had a feeling he could never feel the same about another female.

Fates knew he tried to keep himself from sinking deeper. But each time he managed to distance himself, Calypso pulled him right back, and he was helpless to deny her anything.

If he'd thought of bringing a damn condom, he would've been inside her a moment after she'd climaxed on his tongue. He carried no diseases, and getting her pregnant was a one in a million chance. But he'd already thralled her once that day, and he couldn't thrall her again to make her think he had protection.

As much as she wanted him, Calypso would've panicked. Especially given what her ex-husband had done to her.

It was better that way.

Brundar would survive a case of blue balls.

The question was what was he going to do tomorrow. Continue from where they'd left off?

Put in motion the story about getting deployed on a mission and cut his ties to her before they were impossible to sever?

Or claim her as his own and keep her locked up in the keep?

No one needed to know. He would ask Ingrid to arrange a new apartment for him, sneak Calypso in, and never invite anyone over.

Would she mind?

Yeah, she would.

Calypso had dreams and aspiration beyond being his pet.

Dear Fates, I could use some divine intervention.

CHAPTER 57: RONI

*L*ifting his eyelids was a struggle, so Roni didn't. It felt as if they were glued shut with sticky slime.

Trying to remember what had happened to him, he couldn't manage to distinguish between what had really happened and the dream he'd woken from. In the dream, he'd been abducted by aliens. One of them had carried him off, and the bastard must've spat on Roni's eyes, gluing them shut. They were playing irritating alien music to get Roni to talk. All that clicking and beeping was giving him a headache.

"I'm not telling you anything, you alien slime," he murmured through cracked lips and dry throat. Part of the torture must've been water deprivation.

"He's delirious again, dear. Should I call the nurse?" It was an unfamiliar kind voice. Grandmotherly.

Was that another torture tactic? An alien disguised as a friendly grandmother who Roni would trust?

"He is getting intravenous. He's fine, Mildred. Stop fretting."

Mildred; the name sounded familiar, as did the gruff voice belonging to the guy she'd called dear.

"How are you doing, kid?" Dear's coffee breath smelled very human. Had Dear and Mildred also been abducted?

"Eyes," Roni croaked. "Sticky."

The coffee breath shifted away. "Mildred, get me a wet washcloth from the bathroom. Cold."

"Of course, dear."

A moment later Roni felt Dear wipe his face, careful around his eyelids.

"Open them now, kid."

At first, everything was blurry, but soon Dear's pudgy face came into focus. "I know you." Roni tried to lift a finger. "Your name is not Dear."

The pudgy face got closer. "It's Barty, you moron. Don't you recognize me?"

There was a shocked intake of breath from behind Barty's bulk.

"Bartholomew Edward Gorkin, don't you talk to the boy like that. He is sick with a high fever. Be kind to him, you hear?"

Barty smirked. "That's my wife, Mildred. Thirty years she is trying to make me into less of an ass. Unsuccessfully, might I add, but she never stops."

"He is a lost cause, Mildred," Roni said.

"I know. But I love him anyway." Mildred brought a cup of ice water to Roni's lips. "The doctor said you can drink a little when you wake up."

Roni lifted his neck and took a few grateful sips, wetting his chin, some of it dripping on his hospital gown. "How long have I been in here?"

"A little over eight hours. The doctor says you have pneumonia."

Crap. As the cobwebs of sleep or fever or whatever it was started to lift, Roni remembered why he was here, and it wasn't pneumonia.

"Where is Sylvia?" he asked, looking around for his rescue squad.

Had he been too out of it to ask for her?

"She is here, dear, taking a potty break." Mildred patted his hand. "You asked for her and for Barty. The nice security guy who brought you here called Barty, and Barty called Sylvia. She didn't leave your side other than to grab something to eat and bathroom breaks. Such a nice young woman." Mildred leaned closer. "She is a keeper. Don't let her get away." She winked, her kind round face beaming.

Roni decided that he liked Mildred. She was a lot nicer than her dear husband. But Barty was okay too. Had they been here the entire time?

"Why are you guys here?"

Mildred frowned. "Somebody needs to keep an eye on you. Barty tried to reach your parents, but they are not home. He tried several times but no one is picking up."

Yeah, they were probably on one of their cruises, spending the money he'd earned while underage.

"Thank you for staying with me."

Mildred squeezed his hand. "Think nothing of it. I'm glad we could be here for you."

The door opened, and a moment later Sylvia's arms were around him. "Roni. I'm so glad you're awake. I was so worried about you." She planted a kiss on one cheek, then the other.

"Barty, dear, let's give these young people some privacy, shall we?" Mildred tugged on Barty's sleeve jacket.

"Yeah, why not." Barty winked at Roni. "You're only young once. Enjoy it while you can." He wrapped his arm around his wife's rounded shoulders. "How about I invite you for a cup of coffee, Mrs. Gorkin?"

"I'd be much obliged, Mr. Gorkin."

Sylvia smiled. "They are a cute couple. Barty is such an old lecher, I never expected him to love his wife so much."

"You know he is harmless. He just likes to watch you girls."

"I know." Sylvia sat next to him on the hospital bed. "How are you feeling?"

"Horrible. Where is my rescue team?"

Sylvia's smile vanished. "I called them off for the time being. Barty and Mildred wouldn't leave your side. By the way, I don't want you to worry about your parents. They are not answering their phones because we are rerouting the calls, not because something happened to them."

"I'm not worried. Can't you guys take care of Barty and his wife?"

She shook her head. "Too risky. We are waiting for them to go home and the night shift to start. The fewer people who are familiar with you, the easier it will be to thrall them and get you out unnoticed. That way we will have the entire night head start before anyone starts looking for you."

That made sense. "Then we wait."

Sylvia still seemed bothered.

"What's wrong?"

"You have viral pneumonia."

"Or so they think."

"No, you really have pneumonia. The doctor took X-rays."

Roni frowned as an uncomfortable feeling started deep in his gut. "Meaning?"

"Meaning that it might be a false alarm and you're not transitioning. Actually, that's what our doctor thinks. A transition is not accompanied by pneumonia."

"So what do we do? Do we continue with the extraction plan, or abort?"

"You tell me. It's up to you."

The end... for now.

BRUNDAR AND CALYPSO'S STORY

Continues In Book 15
Dark Angel's Seduction

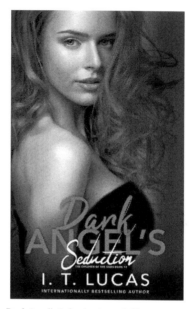

Dark Angel's Seduction is available on Amazon

Dear reader,

Thank you for reading the ***Children of the Gods series.***

As an independent author, I rely on your support to spread the word. So if you enjoyed ***Dark Angel's Obsession***, please share your experience with others, and if it isn't too much trouble, I would greatly appreciate a brief review on Amazon.

Love & happy reading,

Isabell

THE CHILDREN OF THE GODS SERIES

THE CHILDREN OF THE GODS ORIGINS
1: GODDESS'S CHOICE

When gods and immortals still ruled the ancient world, one young goddess risked everything for love.

2: GODDESS'S HOPE

Hungry for power and infatuated with the beautiful Areana, Navuh plots his father's demise. After all, by getting rid of the insane god he would be doing the world a favor. Except, when gods and immortals conspire against each other, humanity pays the price.

But things are not what they seem, and prophecies should not to be trusted...

THE CHILDREN OF THE GODS
1: DARK STRANGER THE DREAM

Syssi's paranormal foresight lands her a job at Dr. Amanda Dokani's neuroscience lab, but it fails to predict the thrilling yet terrifying turn her life will take. Syssi has no clue that her boss is an immortal who'll drag her into a secret, millennia-old battle over humanity's future. Nor does she realize that the professor's imposing brother is the mysterious stranger who's been starring in her dreams.

Since the dawn of human civilization, two warring factions of immortals—the descendants of the gods of old—have been secretly shaping its destiny. Leading the clandestine battle from his luxurious Los Angeles high-rise, Kian is surrounded by his clan, yet alone. Descending from a single goddess, clan members are forbidden to each other. And as the only other immortals are their hated enemies, Kian and his kin have been long resigned to a lonely existence of fleeting trysts with human partners. That is, until his sister makes a game-changing discovery—a mortal seeress who she believes is a dormant carrier of their genes. Ever the realist, Kian is skeptical and refuses Amanda's plea to attempt Syssi's activation. But when his enemies learn of the Dormant's existence, he's forced to rush her to the safety of his keep. Inexorably drawn to Syssi, Kian wrestles with his conscience as he is tempted to explore her budding interest in the darker shades of sensuality.

2: Dark Stranger Revealed

While sheltered in the clan's stronghold, Syssi is unaware that Kian and Amanda are not human, and neither are the supposedly religious fanatics that are after her. She feels a powerful connection to Kian, and as he introduces her to a world of pleasure she never dared imagine, his dominant sexuality is a revelation. Considering that she's completely out of her element, Syssi feels comfortable and safe letting go with him. That is, until she begins to suspect that all is not as it seems. Piecing the puzzle together, she draws a scary, yet wrong conclusion...

3: Dark Stranger Immortal

When Kian confesses his true nature, Syssi is not as much shocked by the revelation as she is wounded by what she perceives as his callous plans for her.

If she doesn't turn, he'll be forced to erase her memories and let her go. His family's safety demands secrecy – no one in the mortal world is allowed to know that immortals exist.

Resigned to the cruel reality that even if she stays on to never again leave the keep, she'll get old while Kian won't, Syssi is determined to enjoy what little time she has with him, one day at a time.

Can Kian let go of the mortal woman he loves? Will Syssi turn? And if she does, will she survive the dangerous transition?

4: Dark Enemy Taken

Dalhu can't believe his luck when he stumbles upon the beautiful immortal professor. Presented with a once in a lifetime opportunity to grab an immortal female for himself, he kidnaps her and runs. If he ever gets caught, either by her people or his, his life is forfeit. But for a chance of a loving mate and a family of his own, Dalhu is prepared to do everything in his power to win Amanda's heart, and that includes leaving the Doom brotherhood and his old life behind.

Amanda soon discovers that there is more to the handsome Doomer than his dark past and a hulking, sexy body. But succumbing to her enemy's seduction, or worse, developing feelings for a ruthless killer is out of the question. No man is worth life on the run, not even the one and only immortal male she could claim as her own…

Her clan and her research must come first…

5: Dark Enemy Captive

When the rescue team returns with Amanda and the chained Dalhu to the keep, Amanda is not as thrilled to be back as she thought she'd be. Between Kian's contempt for her and Dalhu's imprisonment, Amanda's budding relationship with Dalhu seems doomed. Things start to look up when Annani offers her help, and together with Syssi they resolve to find a way for Amanda to be with Dalhu. But will she still want him when she realizes that he is responsible for her nephew's murder? Could she? Will she take the easy way out and choose Andrew instead?

6: Dark Enemy Redeemed

Amanda suspects that something fishy is going on onboard the Anna. But when her investigation of the peculiar all-female Russian crew fails to uncover anything other than more speculation, she decides it's time to stop playing detective and face her real problem—a man she shouldn't want but can't live without.

6.5: My Dark Amazon

When Michael and Kri fight off a gang of humans, Michael gets stabbed. The injury to his immortal body recovers fast, but the one to his ego takes longer, putting a strain on his relationship with Kri.

7: Dark Warrior Mine

When Andrew is forced to retire from active duty, he believes that all he has to look forward to is a boring desk job. His glory days in special ops are over. But as it turns out, his thrill ride has just begun. Andrew discovers not only that immortals exist and have been manipulating global affairs since antiquity, but that he and his sister are rare possessors of the immortal genes.

Problem is, Andrew might be too old to attempt the activation process. His sister, who is fourteen years his junior, barely made it through the transition, so the odds of him coming out of it alive, let alone immortal, are slim.

But fate may force his hand.

Helping a friend find his long-lost daughter, Andrew finds a woman who's worth taking the risk for. Nathalie might be a Dormant, but the only way to find out for sure requires fangs and venom.

8: Dark Warrior's Promise

Andrew and Nathalie's love flourishes, but the secrets they keep from each other taint their relationship with doubts and suspicions. In the meantime, Sebastian and his men are getting bolder, and the storm that's brewing will shift the balance of power in the millennia-old conflict between Annani's clan and its enemies.

9: Dark Warrior's Destiny

The new ghost in Nathalie's head remembers who he was in life, providing Andrew and her with indisputable proof that he is real and not a figment of her imagination.

Convinced that she is a Dormant, Andrew decides to go forward with his transition immediately after the rescue mission at the Doomers' HQ.

Fearing for his life, Nathalie pleads with him to reconsider. She'd rather spend the rest of her mortal days with Andrew than risk what they have for the fickle promise of immortality.

While the clan gets ready for battle, Carol gets help from an unlikely ally. Sebastian's second-in-command can no longer ignore the torment she suffers at the hands of his commander and offers to help her, but only if she agrees to his terms.

10: Dark Warrior's Legacy

Andrew's acclimation to his post-transition body isn't easy. His senses are sharper, he's bigger, stronger, and hungrier. Nathalie fears that the changes in the man she loves are more than physical. Measuring up to this new version of him is going to be a challenge.

Carol and Robert are disillusioned with each other. They are not destined mates, and love is not on the horizon. When Robert's three months are up, he might be left with nothing to show for his sacrifice.

Lana contacts Anandur with disturbing news; the yacht and its human cargo are in Mexico. Kian must find a way to apprehend Alex and rescue the women on board without causing an international incident.

11: Dark Guardian Found

What would you do if you stopped aging?

Eva runs. The ex-DEA agent doesn't know what caused her strange mutation, only that if discovered, she'll be dissected like a lab rat. What Eva doesn't know, though, is that she's a descendant of the gods, and that she is not alone. The man who rocked her world in one life-changing encounter over thirty years ago is an immortal as well.

To keep his people's existence secret, Bhathian was forced to turn his back on the only woman who ever captured his heart, but he's never forgotten and never stopped looking for her.

12: Dark Guardian Craved

Cautious after a lifetime of disappointments, Eva is mistrustful of Bhathian's professed feelings of love. She accepts him as a lover and a confidant but not as a life partner.

Jackson suspects that Tessa is his true love mate, but unless she overcomes her fears, he might never find out.

Carol gets an offer she can't refuse—a chance to prove that there is more to her than meets the eye. Robert believes she's about to commit a deadly mistake, but when he tries to dissuade her, she tells him to leave.

13: Dark Guardian's Mate

Prepare for the heart-warming culmination of Eva and Bhathian's story!

14: Dark Angel's Obsession

The cold and stoic warrior is an enigma even to those closest to him. His secrets are about to unravel...

15: Dark Angel's Seduction

Brundar is fighting a losing battle. Calypso is slowly chipping away his icy armor from the outside, while his need for her is melting it from the inside.

He can't allow it to happen. Calypso is a human with none of the Dormant indicators. There is no way he can keep her for more than a few weeks.

16: Dark Angel's Surrender

Get ready for the heart pounding conclusion to Brundar and Calypso's story.

Callie still couldn't wrap her head around it, nor could she summon even a smidgen of sorrow or regret. After all, she had some memories with him that weren't horrible. She should've felt something. But there was nothing, not even shock. Not even horror at what had transpired over the last couple of hours.

Maybe it was a typical response for survivors--feeling euphoric for the simple reason that they were alive. Especially when that survival was nothing short of miraculous.

Brundar's cold hand closed around hers, reminding her that they weren't out of the woods yet. Her injuries were superficial, and the most she had to worry about was some scarring. But, despite his and Anandur's reassurances, Brundar might never walk again.

If he ended up crippled because of her, she would never forgive herself for getting him involved in her crap.

"Are you okay, sweetling? Are you in pain?" Brundar asked.

Her injuries were nothing compared to his, and yet he was concerned about her. God, she loved this man. The thing was, if she told him that, he would run off, or crawl away as was the case.

Hey, maybe this was the perfect opportunity to spring it on him.

17: Dark Operative: A Shadow of Death

As a brilliant strategist and the only human entrusted with the secret of immortals' existence, Turner is both an asset and a liability to the clan. His request to attempt transition into immortality as an alternative to cancer treatments cannot be denied without risking the clan's exposure. On the other hand, approving it means risking his premature death. In both scenarios, the clan will lose a valuable ally.

When the decision is left to the clan's physician, Turner makes plans to manipulate her by taking advantage of her interest in him.

Will Bridget fall for the cold, calculated operative? Or will Turner fall into his own trap?

18: Dark Operative: A Glimmer of Hope

As Turner and Bridget's relationship deepens, living together seems like the right move, but to make it work both need to make concessions.

Bridget is realistic and keeps her expectations low. Turner could never be the truelove mate she yearns for, but he is as good as she's going to get. Other than his emotional limitations, he's perfect in every way.

Turner's hard shell is starting to show cracks. He wants immortality, he wants to be part of the clan, and he wants Bridget, but he doesn't want to cause her pain.

His options are either abandon his quest for immortality and give Bridget his few remaining decades, or abandon Bridget by going for the transition and most likely dying. His rational mind dictates that he chooses the former, but his gut pulls him toward the latter. Which one is he going to trust?

19: Dark Operative: The Dawn of Love

Get ready for the exciting finale of Bridget and Turner's story!

20: Dark Survivor Awakened

This was a strange new world she had awakened to.

Her memory loss must have been catastrophic because almost nothing was familiar. The language was foreign to her, with only a few words bearing some similarity to the language she thought in. Still, a full moon cycle had passed since her awakening, and little by little she was gaining basic understanding of it--only a few words and phrases, but she was learning more each day.

A week or so ago, a little girl on the street had tugged on her mother's sleeve and pointed at her. "Look, Mama, Wonder Woman!"

The mother smiled apologetically, saying something in the language these people spoke, then scurried away with the child looking behind her shoulder and grinning.

When it happened again with another child on the same day, it was settled.

Wonder Woman must have been the name of someone important in this strange world she had awoken to, and since both times it had been said with a smile it must have been a good one.

Wonder had a nice ring to it.

She just wished she knew what it meant.

21: Dark Survivor Echoes of Love

Wonder's journey continues in *Dark Survivor Echoes of Love*.

22: Dark Survivor Reunited

The exciting finale of Wonder and Anandur's story.

23: Dark Widow's Secret

Vivian and her daughter share a powerful telepathic connection, so when Ella can't be reached by conventional or psychic means, her mother fears the worst.

Help arrives from an unexpected source when Vivian gets a call from the young doctor she met at a psychic convention. Turns out Julian belongs to a private organization specializing in retrieving missing girls.

As Julian's clan mobilizes its considerable resources to rescue the daughter, Magnus is charged with keeping the gorgeous young mother safe.

Worry for Ella and the secrets Vivian and Magnus keep from each other should be enough to prevent the sparks of attraction from kindling a blaze of desire. Except, these pesky sparks have a mind of their own.

24: Dark Widow's Curse

A simple rescue operation turns into mission impossible when the Russian mafia gets involved. Bad things are supposed to come in threes, but in Vivian's case, it seems like there is no limit to bad luck. Her family and everyone who gets close to her is affected by her curse.

Will Magnus and his people prove her wrong?

25: Dark Widow's Blessing

The thrilling finale of the Dark Widow trilogy!

26: Dark Dream's Temptation

Julian has known Ella is the one for him from the moment he saw her picture, but when he finally frees her from captivity, she seems indifferent to him. Could he have been mistaken?

Ella's rescue should've ended that chapter in her life, but it seems like the road back to normalcy has just begun and it's full of obstacles. Between the pitying looks she gets and her mother's attempts to get her into therapy, Ella feels like she's typecast as a victim, when nothing could be further from the truth. She's a tough survivor, and she's going to prove it.

Strangely, the only one who seems to understand is Logan, who keeps popping up in her dreams. But then, he's a figment of her imagination —or is he?

27: Dark Dream's Unraveling

While trying to figure out a way around Logan's silencing compulsion, Ella concocts an ambitious plan. What if instead of trying to keep him out of her dreams, she could pretend to like him and lure him into a trap?

Catching Navuh's son would be a major boon for the clan, as well as for Ella. She will have her revenge, turning the tables on another scumbag out to get her.

28: Dark Dream's Trap

The trap is set, but who is the hunter and who is the prey? Find out in this heart-pounding conclusion to the *Dark Dream* trilogy.

29: Dark Prince's Enigma

As the son of the most dangerous male on the planet, Lokan lives by three rules:

Don't trust a soul.

Don't show emotions.

And don't get attached.

Will one extraordinary woman make him break all three?

30: Dark Prince's Dilemma

Will Kian decide that the benefits of trusting Lokan outweigh the risks?

Will Lokan betray his father and brothers for the greater good of his people?

Are Carol and Lokan true-love mates, or is one of them playing the other?

So many questions, the path ahead is anything but clear.

31: Dark Prince's Agenda

While Turner and Kian work out the details of Areana's rescue plan, Carol and Lokan's tumultuous relationship hits another snag. Is it a sign of things to come?

32 : Dark Queen's Quest

A former beauty queen, a retired undercover agent, and a successful model, Mey is not the typical damsel in distress. But when her sister drops off the radar and then someone starts following her around, she panics.

Following a vague clue that Kalugal might be in New York, Kian sends a team headed by Yamanu to search for him.

As Mey and Yamanu's paths cross, he offers her his help and protection, but will that be all?

33: Dark Queen's Knight

As the only member of his clan with a godlike power over human minds, Yamanu has been shielding his people for centuries, but that power comes at a steep price. When Mey enters his life, he's faced with the most difficult choice.

The safety of his clan or a future with his fated mate.

34: Dark Queen's Army

As Mey anxiously waits for her transition to begin and for Yamanu to test whether his godlike powers are gone, the clan sets out to solve two mysteries:

Where is Jin, and is she there voluntarily?

Where is Kalugal, and what is he up to?

35: Dark Spy Conscripted

Jin possesses a unique paranormal ability. Just by touching someone, she can insert a mental hook into their psyche and tie a string of her consciousness to it, creating a tether. That doesn't make her a spy, though, not unless her talent is discovered by those seeking to exploit it.

36: Dark Spy's Mission

Jin's first spying mission is supposed to be easy. Walk into the club, touch Kalugal to tether her consciousness to him, and walk out.

Except, they should have known better.

37: Dark Spy's Resolution

The best-laid plans often go awry...

38: Dark Overlord New Horizon

Jacki has two talents that set her apart from the rest of the human race.

She has unpredictable glimpses of other people's futures, and she is immune to mind manipulation.

Unfortunately, both talents are pretty useless for finding a job other than the one she had in the government's paranormal division.

It seemed like a sweet deal, until she found out that the director planned on producing super babies by compelling the recruits into pairing up. When an opportunity to escape the program presented itself, she took it, only to find out that humans are not at the top of the food chain.

Immortals are real, and at the very top of the hierarchy is Kalugal, the most powerful, arrogant, and sexiest male she has ever met.

With one look, he sets her blood on fire, but Jacki is not a fool. A man like him will never think of her as anything more than a tasty snack, while she will never settle for anything less than his heart.

39: Dark Overlord's Wife

Jacki is still clinging to her all-or-nothing policy, but Kalugal is chipping away at her resistance. Perhaps it's time to ease up on her convictions. A little less than all is still much better than nothing, and a couple of decades with a demigod is probably worth more than a lifetime with a mere mortal.

40: DARK OVERLORD'S CLAN

As Jacki and Kalugal prepare to celebrate their union, Kian takes every precaution to safeguard his people. Except, Kalugal and his men are not his only potential adversaries, and compulsion is not the only power he should fear.

41: DARK CHOICES THE QUANDARY

When Rufsur and Edna meet, the attraction is as unexpected as it is undeniable. Except, she's the clan's judge and councilwoman, and he's Kalugal's second-in-command. Will loyalty and duty to their people keep them apart?

42: DARK CHOICES PARADIGM SHIFT

Edna and Rufsur are miserable without each other, and their two-week separation seems like an eternity. Long-distance relationships are difficult, but for immortal couples they are impossible. Unless one of them is willing to leave everything behind for the other, things are just going to get worse. Except, the cost of compromise is far greater than giving up their comfortable lives and hard-earned positions. The future of their people is on the line.

For a **FREE** AUDIOBOOK, PREVIEW CHAPTERS, AND OTHER GOODIES OFFERED ONLY TO MY **VIPs**,

JOIN THE VIP CLUB AT ITLUCAS.COM

TRY THE SERIES ON

AUDIBLE

2 FREE audiobooks with your new Audible subscription!

THE PERFECT MATCH SERIES

PERFECT MATCH 1: VAMPIRE'S CONSORT

When Gabriel's company is ready to start beta testing, he invites his old crush to inspect its medical safety protocol.

Curious about the revolutionary technology of the *Perfect Match Virtual Fantasy-Fulfillment studios*, Brenna agrees.

Neither expects to end up partnering for its first fully immersive test run.

PERFECT MATCH 2: KING'S CHOSEN

When Lisa's nutty friends get her a gift certificate to *Perfect Match Virtual Fantasy Studios*, she has no intentions of using it. But since the only way to get a refund is if no partner can be found for her, she makes sure to request a fantasy so girly and over the top that no sane guy will pick it up.

Except, someone does.

Warning: This fantasy contains a hot, domineering crown prince, sweet insta-love, steamy love scenes painted with light shades of gray, a wedding, and a HEA in both the virtual and real worlds.

Intended for mature audience.

PERFECT MATCH 3: CAPTAIN'S CONQUEST

Working as a Starbucks barista, Alicia fends off flirting all day long, but none of the guys are as charming and sexy as Gregg. His frequent visits are the highlight of her day, but since he's never asked her out, she assumes he's taken. Besides, between a day job and a budding music career, she has no time to start a new relationship.

That is until Gregg makes her an offer she can't refuse—a gift certificate to the virtual fantasy fulfillment service everyone is talking about. As a huge Star Trek fan, Alicia has a perfect match in mind—the captain of the Starship Enterprise.

FOR EXCLUSIVE PEEKS AT UPCOMING RELEASES & A FREE COMPANION BOOK

Join my *VIP Club* and gain access to the VIP portal at ITLUCAS.COM

<u>CLICK HERE TO JOIN</u>

(or go to: http://eepurl.com/blMTpD)

Included in your free membership:

- <u>FREE Children of the Gods companion book 1</u>
- FREE narration of Goddess's Choice—Book 1 in The Children of the Gods Origins series.
- Preview chapters of upcoming releases.
- And other exclusive content offered only to my VIPs.

Printed in Great Britain
by Amazon